About the Author

Having served in the Fleet Air Arm of the Royal Navy and with the 845 Naval Air Squadron for a period of that time, Trevor Brian left the service after fourteen years to pursue a career in the finance industry as a computer consultant. Now in early retirement, he has taken the plunge into a lifelong desire to write. It is hoped you as a reader will enjoy this book as much as Trevor enjoyed writing it.

The FOB Incident

Trevor Brian

The FOB Incident

Olympia Publishers
London

www.olympiapublishers.com
OLYMPIA PAPERBACK EDITION

A CIP catalogue record for this title is
available from the British Library.

ISBN: 978-1-83543-469-7

This is a work of fiction.
Names, characters, places and incidents originate from the writer's
imagination. Any resemblance to actual persons, living or dead, is
purely coincidental.

First Published in 2024

Olympia Publishers
Tallis House
2 Tallis Street
London
EC4Y 0AB

Printed in Great Britain

Dedication

I would like to dedicate this book to all the members past and present of the 845 Naval Air Squadron and to all members of the military who strive to keep us safe in uncertain times.

Acknowledgements

I would like to thank my longtime friend Andrew Garside, who has been my muse in the writing of this book. I would also like to thank a very patient friend, Lucie Walker, who helped me by reading and correcting my mistakes. A special thank you to my wife Nuala, whom I love dearly. She kept me fed and watered and supported me throughout the long process of writing this book.

Chapter 1

Dave Waters, (aka) Muddy, had driven the bowser (fuel tanker) as fast as he dared across the uneven dirt track leading away from the FOB (Forward Operating Base) towards the nearest tarred road and the closest village to the exercise area, approximately fifteen miles away.

Muddy was a twenty-four-year-old West Country lad from Shepton Mallet in Somerset. He was six feet two inches tall with blond close-cropped hair and built like the proverbial brick shit house. Normally rock solid in his abilities, he had been shaken to the core with the events at the FOB this morning.

"What the fuck just happened back there, Muddy?" asked Pete Hamilton, aka Hammy. Hammy, twenty-three years old, was the opposite in stature to Muddy, at only five feet five inches tall with short brown hair and skinny as a rake. Shocked and shaken up from the unexpected events this morning, it showed in his voice.

"I have no idea, mate, but I do know this. If Tetley had not been with us and went all Rambo, we would be lying dead back there along with the other lads. Tetley is one mad bastard, and I for one am glad he is on our side," replied Muddy.

Andrew Garside, aka Tetley, was another member of the aircraft engineering team at the FOB. Thirty years old and five feet ten inches tall with short military cut brown hair, trim and fit as a fiddle, he had sent Muddy and Hammy on this important errand to call for help after the events at the FOB.

After about five miles, they hit a tarred road and Hammy, who was in the passenger seat beside him, directed him to turn left towards the village.

When they finally arrived in the tiny village, they looked for a phone box only to discover it vandalized, so they headed for the village pub, where they knew there would be a working phone.

The pub was still closed at this hour, but having drank there on many occasions, the lads knew that the landlord lived above the bar in a small apartment, so Muddy banged on the door until he appeared.

"What is all the banging about, we're closed and not open until 11am?" said the landlord who answered the door.

"We need to use your phone, mate; it's an emergency and the phone box in the village has been vandalized," replied Muddy.

"The phone is at the far end of the bar in the hallway leading to the toilets," replied the landlord.

Muddy and Hammy rushed past him and through the bar to the telephone. Muddy lifted the receiver and dialled the number for the telephone exchange at Royal Naval Air Station Yeovilton. When the operator answered, he put coins in the slot and then he asked to be put through to the 845 Squadron's flight line office, saying that this was an emergency.

The phone rang in 845 Naval Air Commando Squadron's flight line office and duty NCO Chief Petty Officer Sandy Saunders picked it up.

"845 Squadron flight line office, CPO Saunders speaking," he answered.

He listened to Muddy for several minutes, then asked, "Are you serious, Waters?" He listened as a frantic Muddy explained again what had happened, and after Chief Saunders assured them help was on the way, he hung up.

Chief Saunders ran upstairs to the senior pilots office, where Lt Commander Smythe, who was in temporary command of the squadron, was busy with paperwork.

The Commanding Officer Lt Commander Benson was on the military exercise on Dartmoor, where Muddy had just called from.

Chief Saunders knocked on the door and waited for Smythe to shout 'Enter' before rushing in to explain the phone call he had just received from AEM (Air Engineering Mechanic) Waters (aka Muddy).

"Sir, I have just received an emergency call from AEM Waters, who is with the exercise detachment on Dartmoor. He was calling from a payphone in a pub in the nearest village. He was saying the exercise area has been attacked and there are multiple dead and injured and they require urgent assistance ASAP."

"Are you sure this is not some kind of joke, Chief?" asked Smythe.

"It's no joke, sir. I was dubious myself, sir, but Waters was in a right state when he called this in and insisted they needed urgent help, both medical and armed support," replied Chief Saunders.

"Very well, Chief, get four Merlins ready to go ASAP and configure two as gunships. I will run this up the chain of command and get authorisation," ordered Smythe.

"Yes, sir," replied Chief Saunders, then turned and raced to the crew rooms to get the engineers to ready the aircraft at the double.

Lt Commander Smythe called the captain of RNAS Yeovilton's office, relayed the information received from AEM

13

Waters to the skipper and asked for emergency authorisation for arming the Merlins with live ammo.

The skipper, Captain Roger Standen, was in a state of shock at the news, and after it sank in, he suggested alerting the Royal Marine Quick Reaction Force based at Yeovilton under the command of Major Barnes.

They would go in with the aircraft to provide an armed ground force to secure the area around the FOB. He also ordered Smythe to contact the sick bay and take whatever personnel they had available with them to tend to the wounded. The skipper explained he would also inform his boss, FONAC (Flag Officer Naval Air Command), who no doubt would push it further up the chain of command in London.

Lt Commander Smythe called Major Barnes, who said his men would be ready and at the squadron within fifteen minutes. He then called the sick bay, explained the situation to the senior Doctor, Commander Forbes and told him that all available medics were to pack whatever trauma kits they would need and be at the flight line in fifteen minutes. His last call was to all his flight crews to muster in the ready room so he could brief them on whatever little information he had regarding the attack and their flight plans.

Twenty minutes later, four Merlin helicopters were sitting on the flight line with engines running and rotors turning, with the Marines and medics on board, ready to take off. The engineers standing in front of the Merlins gave the signal for the chocks to be removed from the wheels and then gave the OK for the aircraft to take off immediately instead of the normal practice of taxiing to a runway.

The Merlins lifted into the air, then turned left, before

dipping their noses and flying off to the site of the FOB at top speed.

Lt Commander Smythe and the remaining officers and men watched as they headed off into the distance to God knows what.

The four Merlins arrived at the FOB (Forward Operating Base) site about forty-five minutes later.

As they overflew the exercise area, there were still plumes of thick black smoke rising from the ground around the FOB, and no one seemed to be visibly moving around the site. There were many bodies visibly littered around the area.

"Land over there away from the area, Lieutenant; my men and the medical teams will disembark and walk our way in and secure the area," ordered Major Barnes over the aircraft's comms system.

"Yes, sir," replied the pilot, who got on his radio to inform the other aircraft where to land.

The Merlins landed and disembarked their passengers, and then the two Merlins, configured as gunships, took off again to act as sentries in case any hostile forces were still around.

Major Barnes ordered his men to spread out and move to the FOB area from all directions. He instructed the medical teams to stay with him.

AEM Garside (Tetley) had heard the Merlins arrive and land. He climbed out of a severely damaged Merlin in the FOB area and ran to meet the arriving men.

He approached Commander Forbes (the doctor) first and reported that the only survivors other than his team were in the damaged Merlin, being cared for as best they could, given the meagre medical supplies they had available. The commander thanked him and ran with his medical team to the badly damaged

Merlin to assess the situation with the wounded.

Tetley then reported to Major Barnes and gave him a detailed sitrep (situation report).

Major Barnes listened and thanked him, then asked, "Who is in charge here, Garside?"

"At present, I am, sir, although Petty Officer White is the ranking NCO. I have sent him and three others to form a defensive ring as best they can around the FOB area. I have also sent two lads to the nearest village in the undamaged bowser to raise the alarm. They should be back shortly," replied Garside.

Just then, AEM Tommy Baker (Ginger) came running up the track, and after saluting Major Barnes, he reported to Garside that the bowser was returning.

"Thanks, Ginger, go round up the others and get back here, pronto, mate," ordered Garside. Ginger ran off to round up the others who had survived the attack on the FOB.

"You should go and get on one of the Merlins, Garside," ordered Major Barnes.

"Not until all the lads have returned and the wounded have been evacuated, sir," replied Garside.

"Very well. As soon as the others return, you are all flying back to Yeovilton with the wounded," ordered Major Barnes.

Soon all the lads returned from their various positions and stood with Garside as the medics stretchered the wounded to the waiting Merlins. Garside told them Major Barnes had ordered them back to Yeovilton, and they all walked to the nearest Merlin, unloaded their weapons to make them safe, then boarded.

The two Merlins lifted off the ground slowly, turned and headed back in the direction of RNAS Yeovilton. The two gunships remained as sentries orbiting the FOB area, and the Marines of the QRF secured the site.

The medics on board continued to tend to the wounded men, getting saline drips set up and hanging them from the fuselage. They also administered morphine shots to the more seriously wounded and made sure they were comfortable during the flight.

Muddy and the other lads stayed out of the way and just sat on the cabin floor in silence and watched the medics tend the wounded.

Unable to communicate, as they had no headsets, they were left to their own thoughts.

Chapter 2

When the Merlins landed and taxied to their spots on the apron in front of the squadron HQ building, and after the wounded were carried off to waiting ambulances, the survivors were met by a group of officers and security personnel.

Each of the survivors was relieved of their weapons and ammunition, then escorted by a navy lieutenant and two security personnel and taken into the squadron building. There, they were split up and taken into separate offices. Tetley asked what was going on, and his escort, Lt Pete Chalmers, a squadron pilot, explained that they had been isolated so that each man could tell his story of the FOB attack. Chalmers went on to explain that there would probably be a full military inquiry and the government wanted answers, as the media had already gotten wind of the incident. They had been instructed to await the arrival of naval legal personnel from Whitehall and were to remain in isolation until they had been interviewed.

Lt Chalmers explained the lawyers were en route to RNAS Yeovilton from RAF Northolt in London and would arrive in the next half hour.

"Any chance I can get some scran and a cup of tea? I'm starving," said Tetley.

"I'll see what we can do; I could murder a brew myself," replied Lt Chalmers.

He sent one of the security team standing guard at the door off to see if he could rustle up some food and drink. What Tetley really needed was sleep as he was knackered, having been up since 03:45 when he was woken up for the sentry change over that morning. The adrenaline that had kept him going during the battle had seeped away, leaving him extremely exhausted. He stretched out on the pusser's chairs in the office and closed his eyes, hoping to get forty winks, but just as he was about to nod off, the door crashed open and the security guard returned with a tray stacked with bacon butties and mugs of hot steaming tea. Tetley and Lt Chalmers sat around a desk, scoffing the scran and drinking the tea, which tasted better than any pusser's grub he had ever eaten before for some reason. After a glug or three of tea, Tetley said, "If I'm in the shit and get sent to Colchester (military prison in the UK), can I take the chef with me? This scran is excellent."

"I doubt it will come to that, Garside, so stop worrying so much! You know what the navy is like; they love to tick all the boxes, and there is always someone wanting to cover their arse just in case. We can't discuss the incident until the legal eagles arrive, so chill out until then," replied Lt Chalmers.

He was right, of course, no point fretting over spilt milk as his mother would have said. Look on the bright side – you're still in one piece, matey, thought Tetley.

The sound of a taxing aircraft reverberated through the windows from the flight line as a fixed-wing Heron taxied to a vacant spot out on the apron. When it had shut down and the doors opened, a group of naval officers disembarked and headed for the HQ.

"Looks like they have finally arrived," said Chalmers. "This will be sorted soon, Garside, and then you can relax," replied Lt Chalmers. Sure enough, ten minutes later, a commander and a sub-lieutenant came into the room and asked the security lads and

Lt Chalmers to leave.

Tetley spoke up before they were out of the room, "I would like Lt Chalmers to stay, please, as he is my DO (Divisional Officer), and I want someone I know and trust to witness what is being said."

The commander explained, "I will need to get permission from a higher authority before anyone else can attend the interview."

"Higher authority sounds like I'm in the shit," said Tetley, "I want him here, or I'm not talking to anyone."

The Commander was not happy and certainly not used to ratings like Tetley demanding things, "You are a Royal Navy rating, and you will do what you are ordered. However, I will seek clarification on the process from a higher authority before we continue. It will not reflect on you very well, Garside, if you do not co-operate fully with the investigation."

"No disrespect, commander, but I've been in the navy for almost fourteen years now, and yes! I'm still an AEM, by my own choice. I have seen a lot of crap in this mob over the years, and everyone is always looking to cover their own arses and shit on someone below them, where possible. My DO stays, or my mouth stays shut, so you can get back on the Heron, and with all due respect, sir, Fuck Off."

The room was silent for a minute or two before the commander and his sub-lieutenant left the room, leaving Tetley and Lt Chalmers still standing and looking at each other.

"You were out of line, Garside! You should not address senior officers like that, even if I do agree with some of your sentiments."

"Sorry sir, but I'm knackered! I've been through a firefight that I didn't expect on a so-called training exercise with the

Bootnecks here in the UK, and that commander is only here to apportion blame to someone for all the dead bodies up on that moor. I can tell you this much; they aren't making a scapegoat out of me just because I survived. I just hope the others are doing the same and watching their own backs."

An hour passed before the door opened and Captain Standen walked into the room, followed by the commander and his underling.

Tetley and Lt Chalmers stood to attention before the skipper said, "At ease, gentlemen!"

The skipper sat down at the desk and instructed Lt Chalmers and Tetley to sit in the chairs opposite.

"Now listen, Garside, and listen, good! It has been agreed by the Attorney General in London that all the survivors should have their divisional officer present when they are being questioned by legal counsel. This is not because you threw a schoolboy tantrum in front of Commander Evans, but because it was deemed by the AG that someone the survivors trusted should be in attendance. This will undoubtedly reach the papers before too long, and if it was reported that you had no support after such a traumatic incident, the navy would be held accountable at some point in the future. Now, I am not legally allowed to instruct you on what to say or what not to say, but you can choose to confer with your DO at any point. However, I will ask you, as a naval airman, to co-operate with this investigation so that we can discover what has happened and how we can better prevent it in the future. I will leave you now, Garside, so you can have an hour to discuss any points you may need to share with your DO.

"Commander Evans and Sub. Lt. Hayward will return to commence the interview. Can I get you anything while you confer?"

21

"Please, sir, some notepads and pens for note-taking," requested Lt Chalmers.

"And some more hot tea, please, sir," said Tetley. With that, Capt. Standen left Chalmers and Tetley alone in the office once again.

"Fuck me! The attorney general is involved. That means the prime minister is pulling the strings here, sir; we really are deep in the shit," blurted Tetley.

"Calm down, Garside! It is protocol that any attack in the UK is reported to the PM and the AG. This is all standard procedure. As you pointed out earlier, a lot of arse covering is going on."

Ten minutes later, a security guy came in with a huge pot of tea, some ham and cheese toasties and the notepads and pens. Tetley knew the guy, Duggie Allison.

"Hey, Duggie, what's the score?" said Tetley.

"Hey, Tetley… sir, just doing what I'm told, mate, lots of brass around, and everyone is in a right tizz. We are escorting the officers from the smoke everywhere around the base. The base is on full lockdown, with armed patrols and aircraft covering every inch of the place."

Tetley asked Duggie, "Have you seen any of the other lads from the exercise, Duggie?"

"Yeah, mate! They are in various rooms around the building, and like you, no one wanted to talk without their DO with them. That commander threw a wobbly when he came downstairs after speaking with you, mate. He was not happy, whingeing to the skipper about you telling him to 'Fuck off' and demanding you be court martialled. The skipper asked him if he had been shot at this morning, and of course he said, 'No sir,' at which point the skipper told him to wind his neck in and give you lads some respect. Fair dues to the skipper. I better get back, mate, before they start asking questions. Good luck, Tetley!" said Duggie.

An hour to the minute after the skipper left, Commander Evans and Sub-Lt Hayward returned. With legal pads in hand, they sat down opposite them at the desk. The commander removed a recording device from his briefcase and set it on the desk in front of them. Sub-Lt Hayward unboxed a video camera and set it up at an angle that covered the whole desk and the four attendees.

"OK, Garside, before we begin, I'll explain the process for the debriefing. We will record and film everything that is said in the debrief. We'll make copies afterwards, they'll be signed and attested as such, with a copy given to your divisional officer, Lt Chalmers.

"If we need to revisit anything after the debriefing has been completed, we will convene again under the same conditions and with your DO present as requested. Are you happy with these stipulations?" asked Commander Evans.

"Yes, I am happy with these conditions, sir," said Tetley. Commander Evans then turned on the recording device on the table, and Sub-Lt Hayward switched on the video camera before returning to sit beside Commander Evans at the desk.

"For the sake of the tape and video recording, I am Commander Evans of the Naval Legal Services, and I'm here today with Sub-Lt Hayward, also from Naval Legal Services, to debrief AEM (M) Andrew Garside in the presence of his Divisional Officer, Lt Peter Chalmers. The date is Friday, 18th October 1998 and the time is 14:00 hours. This morning there was an incident during a military exercise on Dartmoor that consisted of three Merlin Mk.4 Commando helicopters from 845 Naval Air Commando Squadron led by Lt Commander Benson with five NCOs, nine air crew, seventeen Naval ratings, one Royal Marine colour sergeant and twenty-four Royal Marine cadets. In your own words, AEM Garside, can you please tell us what happened this morning?"

"Before I begin, sir," said Tetley. "Can you please tell me if the casualties I returned with are OK?"

"The latest news I have from the hospital is that two seriously injured airmen are in the operating theatre and two are in intensive care.

"Lt Commander Benson is being treated for his wounds and should make a full recovery given time," answered the commander.

"OK, sir, thank you for that. To begin, I must explain the strange layout of the FOB.

"As you may not be aware, these exercises happen on a regular basis, and the purpose of the exercise is to give the squadron personnel experience of operating from an FOB, teaching aircraft maintenance in the field along with teaching defensive tactics and field craft. On the flip side, it is used to give tactical field training to the Royal Marine Cadets, culminating in the Friday War, which, as always, is scheduled to begin at 07:00 hours on Friday morning. This entails the Marines attacking the FOB from their raised positions in the field and a follow-up attack through our defensive positions. We in turn have to defend ourselves long enough for the pilots to take off in the aircraft, which in turn will help us defend our positions. Now the Bootnecks have all week to devise their attack plan, and because they always have the high ground on these exercises, they are able to watch our every move. They observe our daily routines and watch us dig our defensive positions and put out our trip flare traps. That is the normal plan; however, we were getting fed up with always losing to the Bootnecks, so we devised a cunning scheme that the boss, Lt Commander Benson, agreed with.

"The idea was to turn the tables on the Marines and lead them into a trap. During the week, as normal, we dug in and did our normal thing, but unbeknownst to the Marines, during the night when the lads were on sentry duty, they were digging three extra slit trenches away at right angles to the main defensive trenches and camouflaged them during the day so that the Marines would not see them. Come the stand-to for the Friday War, the trenches would be manned by Petty Officer White, myself and five other ratings. The plan was that when the Marines attacked the FOB, they would charge past our positions in the secret trenches on open ground to attack the main defensive positions. When they had passed us, we would open fire, initiating a surprise ambush and defeating the Marines on the open ground. At least that was the plan.

"What actually happened was this; during the early hours of Friday morning around 02:00, shots were heard from the area where the Marines had their camp and the sentries in the trenches, called a stand-to just in case the Marines had decided to start the war early. We all went to our assigned positions in our trenches, but after thirty minutes, nothing happened. The boss gave it another thirty minutes before standing everyone, except the sentries, down. Those of us who could went back to our tents and got our heads down, and at 03:45 this morning, I got called for my turn on 'stag in the trench. I relieved AEM Waters in our trench at 04:00 and he went back to the tent to sleep. It was cold and very wet as it had been raining most of the week off and on, and the trenches had about three inches of water in them, so I spent most of my time bailing out on and off, taking breaks to warm my hands in my jacket pockets. The place was very quiet, and I was a bit on edge after the earlier shooting, but nothing more happened.

As planned at 06:30, I got on the field telephone to call the stand-to, ready for the war to commence at 07:00. Myself and the other assigned men moved to the secret camouflaged positions to get ready for the ambush.

"At 06:45 mortar shells began raining down on the FOB and the main defensive positions. These were live rounds, and they landed in and around the trenches where most of the lads were positioned. The rounds caused a lot of damage and we could see the trenches being battered. They didn't stand a chance; they were slaughtered. Our secret ambush positions were not being fired on, so we just kept our heads down below the surface in case any shrapnel came our way from the blasts. Dave Waters was in my trench, and I told him we are fucked if we don't do something, so I told him I was going to make a run for the trailer that held the emergency live ammo. If we got the live ammo, we could at least return fire if they showed their faces. He wasn't happy. We argued over it, but I decided to go anyway.

"I slipped out the back of our trench and crawled to a small ridge that bordered the track leading away from the FOB, which was used to bring in the fuel bowser. From there, I legged it to the nearest aircraft. I caught my breath there and had a look around the area but could see no one; I just hoped they were hugging the bottom of the trenches, staying below the ledges away from flying shrapnel. The FOB was blanketed by thick cordite smoke from the exploding mortars, and it afforded me some protection, so I ran towards the back of the fuel bowser, but about halfway there, a shell exploded close by and I was thrown about fifteen feet away. When I realised I was uninjured except for a few bruises, I got up and sprinted to the trailer. It was positioned close to the HQ tent, which had already been destroyed, and I used my weapon to smash off the lock. I took off the blank firing attachment, unloaded my own weapon of blank rounds and re-loaded it with live ones. I then grabbed some boxes of ammo and grenades and headed back the way I came.

"When I got to the last aircraft, one of the others close to me took a direct hit. I threw myself under the Merlin I was beside and tried to dig in with my hands to protect myself. The cab above me was being hit by shrapnel from the explosion and I could hear the airframe getting ripped apart. I just buried my face as deep as I could in the mud and grass. After a while, I got out and made my way back to the trench where Muddy was, and crawled in on top of him. I told Muddy to remove the blank firing attachment from his weapon, and then he unloaded the blank ammo and opened the boxes of live rounds to load his rifle and an extra mag. I gave him the ammo boxes and told him to crawl out to the next two trenches and get the lads to follow suit. I asked him to explain that if the Bootnecks or whoever was doing the shooting came down that hill to finish everyone off in the main positions, I was going to mow them down no matter what happened. I told him to tell the others that when I yelled 'NOW!' I was going to open fire on the Bootnecks and they should do the same. PO White was worried about the repercussions, but he did not have any other suggestions.

"Muddy returned to our trench, and we waited for a lull in the mortar barrage when hopefully whoever they were would come down the hill to finish the job and we could spring our ambush. After a while, Muddy spotted figures coming down the hill, and as the smoke cleared, we noticed they were all wearing civvies, which was bloody odd indeed. So as soon as they had passed our positions, which they hadn't spotted, I shouted 'NOW!' and started firing into them.

"The strange thing was they were all fairly close together, not as you would imagine moving in a combat tactical formation. This made it easier for us, as they were caught in the open so close to our fire that we easily mowed them down. I jumped out of the trench and shouted for the lads to follow. We threw some grenades and continued to fire until we finished them off. We then ran to check on the lads in the main trenches, but it was utter carnage; bits of bodies everywhere, and in some cases, just blobs of mush. We found the boss and three others still alive and bandaged them up as best we could, considering all we had were field dressings. We moved them to the back of the least damaged aircraft to keep them out of the weather. I sent two lads to raise the alarm and get help in the bowser because the comms gear was trashed. I also sent two lads to check the Bootnecks' camp, then set up defensive positions and waited for help to arrive.

"When Commander Forbes arrived with the medics, I led him to the injured. I then reported to Major Barnes and gave him a sitrep. He wanted me to leave on the first aircraft, but I refused until all the casualties had been loaded into the Merlins and the lads who survived with me had all returned to the FOB after being relieved by the Marines. Only then did we all fly back here to Yeovilton. That's my story, sir, now can I please go and get my head down? I'm shattered."

"I'm afraid not just yet, Garside. We have to coordinate statements with the other survivors and discuss what steps have to be taken next before we can let you back into circulation on the base," explained Commander Evans. "This is some story you have related here today. I am sure there will be others who would want answers to more questions once they have seen your

28

debriefing.

"Sit tight here for the moment and try to get some sleep in these chairs if you can, and we'll get back to you as soon as possible. That must apply to you too, Lt Chalmers, I'm sorry to say. I'll arrange for fresh food and tea to be delivered to this room as soon as I leave here. Thank you both for your cooperation so far, and can I just say, Garside, based on the story you have just relayed to us, congratulations on getting yourself and the other survivors out of that mess alive! Now, if you will, please excuse Sub-Lt Hayward and me for a while."

"Thank you, Sir," said Tetley.

The commander and Sub-Lt Hayward left the room, and for a while there was complete silence, with the only noise coming from the flight line at the front of the building as aircraft were moved or being worked on by the line crews.

After what seemed like ages to Tetley, Lt Chalmers said, "Fuck me, Garside! That was some story you related to the commander. Was that all true? Did that really happen this morning?"

"I'm sorry to say, but yes! It did, sir; a lot of lads died this morning and not in an easy way. I'm a lucky bastard just to be sitting here in this office with barely a scratch on me, yet many families will be getting visits from the welfare staff informing them of the deaths of their loved ones, and all I can think of is how tired I am and just how old I feel at this moment in time," said Tetley in a slow, sad tone.

"Can I ask you, Garside?" started Lt Chalmers before Tetley interrupted him.

"Please, call me Tetley, like everyone else, sir. No need to be all formal with the Commander and that gone."

"Fair enough, Tetley, you can call me Pete, but only when

29

we are on our own OK?" answered Lt Chalmers.

"Thanks, Pete! That would be great! Now what were you just about to ask me?" replied Tetley.

"Well," he began, "In my understanding, it was your idea that the secret trenches should be dug to surprise the Marines when they attacked this morning, just to get one over on them for a change and the boss was OK with that?"

"He was Pete! The boss thought it was about time that we got some payback for a change instead of giving the Marines free rein as usual. He thought it would shake things up a bit when planning for future training. He felt, like I do, that the training should not just be about the navy training the lads to operate from an FOB, but also about successfully defending the same FOB from any and all attacks," explained Tetley.

"I can see that," said Pete, "having been on a few of these exercises before myself. But what I cannot understand and I am sure the commander will be back and put this question to you, is this; why did you take charge when the rounds started landing in the FOB area? Why did your petty officer not organise things as was his duty?"

Tetley stood up and walked over to the windows, looking out over the apron where the aircraft were lined up. He didn't speak for a minute or two, then he suddenly turned and replied, "Well, Pete, I look at things like this. Sometimes people are put into situations not of their own making, and some people react one way and others react another way. Some people fail to react at all and just freeze. I just reacted automatically. I saw the only possible way out for myself and maybe the others. There was no point sitting on my arse in the water at the bottom of that trench with Muddy and waiting it out. These were live mortar rounds raining down on the area; they meant to kill us all. We were caught cold with only blank rounds in our weapons, which were about as much use as a chocolate fireguard.

"I knew we needed live ammo if we were to have some chance of survival. We still might die, but we might be able to take a few with us. Knocker White was too far away from me to call out to, and the cables to the field telephones had been cut by the mortar explosions, so I made my own call to try and get the ammo, and luckily it paid off. I could have gotten blown to kingdom come at any point along the way, but if I did, I would at least die trying. When I got the ammo and got Muddy to distribute it among the lads, including Knocker White, they all joined in the attack plan with Gusto. As I said, I just reacted first, that's all."

Just then someone knocked on the door and Duggie Allison came in with another huge pot of tea and some sandwiches. "Compliments of Commander Evans, Tetley," he said cheerfully. "I think he likes you, mate; did you kiss and make up after telling him to fuck off?" he asked, laughing so much that he nearly dropped the sandwiches.

"Fuck off, Duggie." laughed Tetley. "Put those sandwiches down before you chuck them on the floor. Have you got any news on the others, mate?"

Duggie set the tea and sandwiches on the table, then turned and said,

"All the debriefs have finished and the legal eagles have decamped over to FONAC for some highbrow conference. I don't know when they are due to return. If I hear anything, I will let you know, mate."

"Cheers, matey!" said Tetley. FONAC was Flag Officer Naval Air Command. He was a rear admiral in charge of the whole Royal Navy Fleet Air Arm, and his office space was over

31

the other side of the sports pitches next to the base.

"I assume they have gone to conference with the admiralty and the politicians in London using the admirals secure line," said Pete. "All the decisions will be made by them based on the testimonies you have all given, Tetley. Whatever comes back, you can guarantee that the PM and the cabinet will be the ones to make the final call based on the recommendations of the AG and the admiralty."

Tetley poured himself a brew and picked up one of the sandwiches, inspecting it before taking a bite and washing it down with the tea. He sat down on a pusser's chair and just stared into space for a while before finishing his sandwich and setting his tea on the floor beside himself. He then just closed his eyes and went straight to sleep. Pete just poured himself a cup of tea and ate a couple of sandwiches whilst he browsed through a flight safety mag that was sitting on a bookshelf.

At around 19:00 hours, Duggie came back into the room, which startled Tetley awake.

"Sorry, mate, I just made the excuse to take the teapot and plate back and refresh them to let you know the legal eagles are on their way back."

"Cheers, Duggie, mate! Much appreciated! You're a good mate," said Tetley. About twenty minutes later, Commander Evans and Sub-Lt Hayward entered the office and sat down in their seats at the table.

Tetley spoke first, "Are we free to go now, sir?"

"Not just yet, Garside. We have a couple more questions to ask you to clarify some queries. If you would be seated at the desk as before, we'll start the recording devices and get going. I can't assure you this will be the last of the questions, but I can confirm you will be free to go back to your quarters afterwards."

Tetley and Lt Chalmers sat in the assigned chairs while Sub-Lt Hayward got the techie stuff running again. Once he was seated, Commander Evans went through his preamble introduction again, stating for the camera those present:

"AEM Garside," he started, "can you explain why you took control of the situation and not your direct superior, Petty Officer White?" Tetley looked over to Lt Chalmers, and they shared a smile before he explained his decisions, as he had done earlier, to the lieutenant.

"The next question may seem strange, given the circumstances, but could you explain why you took no prisoners?" asked Commander Evans with a slight grimace.

"Simple, sir," said Tetley. "They gave no quarter when they blasted the FOB and the lads to bits, and I was somewhat pissed off, to say the least, so when they had the neck to follow up the bombing and came down that hill with the full intention to finish off anyone still alive, I think the least we could do was return the gesture. They had it coming; I won't apologise to anyone for that, and I would willingly do the same if I found myself in the same position again, God forbid."

"Thank you, Garside. That now concludes this debrief. You are required to stay on base until otherwise informed. You may go about your duties as normal with the squadron. We may need you to answer further questions in the near future, depending on how this investigation evolves. Just to update you, Lt Commander Benson is out of critical care in the hospital. Thank you for your patience with us today, Garside. Lt Chalmers, you're free to return to your duties." With the debrief completed, Commander Evans and Sub-Lt Hayward started to pack up.

"Just before you go Sir, I have a final question that you may or may not be able to answer," said Tetley.

"What question is that, Garside?" The commander asked.

"Well, sir, does anyone know who the hell attacked us today?"

"At this moment in time, we don't have any answer to that. Investigators from the MOD and civilian authorities are at the scene now. It may be some time before that question is answered." With their packing completed, they left the room.

Lt Chalmers spoke first, "that was some after-action report, Tetley. If all you said is true, you deserve a bloody knighthood for your actions, never mind a medal. Lots of lads have died today, and we both knew all of them. It's going to take some time to process it all, and I dare say the media are already all over this.

"This will be headline news for some weeks to come, and if I were you, I would stay on the base for as long as possible to avoid being chased around the place by those sewer rats. What are you going to do next, Tetley?"

Tetley sat quiet for a moment then replied, "I never thought about how this would pan out, Pete, and you're right, staying on base for the foreseeable is the best policy. I think, first things first, I'm going downstairs to the crew space to see if the other lads are there, and then see if we can find somewhere to have a drink or seven. You're welcome to join us, sir."

Pete laughed, then said, "I might just take you up on that, Tetley. Officers aren't allowed in the NAAFI, so how about the Rugby Club, say, in an hour?"

"See you there, Pete," said Tetley.

Tetley and Lt Chalmers left the room for the first time since early that morning.

Chapter 3

The upper corridors of the squadron building were very quiet.

The building had two floors and was spread out facing the apron where the aircraft were spotted and operated from; it was split in two between 845 and 846 Naval Air Commando Squadrons, who shared the complex but had different hangars for their aircraft. Most of the lads on the squadrons knew each other and had spent time on 707 training squadron together at some point. There was great rivalry between the two squadrons and there were frequent sporting competitions between them when they were on base in Yeovilton and not on missions around the world or at sea on one of the carriers or Royal Fleet Auxiliary ships (RFAS).

Lt Chalmers headed for the officer's ready room and Tetley headed downstairs to the ratings crew room. Tetley opened the door to the crew room and walked in, hoping to find Muddy and the other lads to catch up from this morning. As he entered, there was huge cheering and whistling. The crew room was packed with lads standing in just about every space available. Tetley just stood there with his mouth gaping, looking round the room. Muddy came over and gave him a huge bear hug and shouted in his ear,

"Thanks, mate! If it wasn't for you, Tetley, I would be pushing up daisies; same goes for the other lads in our trenches."

Ginger Baker pushed through the rowdy crowd and handed Tetley and Muddy a brew, then shouted, "silence, lads!

SILENCE!" He then stood on a chair between a couple of lads and spoke, "Welcome home, Tetley. I can honestly say for me and the others who flew back with you this morning, thanks for saving our arses. If you hadn't gone all Rambo this morning, I doubt any of the eleven survivors from the FOB would be around to see tomorrow."

Looking around the packed room at all the crews assembled, he raised the brew he was holding and said, "I would like to propose a toast. To the craziest bastard in 845 Squadron, thank fuck he is on our side." Raising the mug in his hand, he shouted, "Tetley!"

The room went into hysteria with the lads shouting, "Tetley, Tetley!" and pushing through to shake Tetley's hand and slap him on the back. Tetley took a long drink of his brew. Then someone shouted, "Speech!" which then erupted in a loud chorus round the room. After some cajoling, Tetley was pushed on top of one of the chairs to loud cheers from the crowd and raised his hand in the air to silence them. It took a while, but eventually the room hushed and waited for Tetley to speak.

"Thanks, lads, for this reception. I'm not sure about the whole Rambo thing. I just did what I had to do to survive, and I had a lot of help from some of you standing in front of me. I'm not going to say much more than this. It's great to be a member of this squadron and to serve with some great lads. Some wankers, to mind you," he said, laughing.

"We lost some great mates today and their families will take a long time to recover, so we must think of them at this sad time. Last but not least, I'm heading down to the Rugby Club for a few beers, and anyone who wants is welcome to join me."

Just then, someone shouted, "Officer on deck!" The room stood to attention as the senior pilot, Lt Commander Smythe, along with the other squadron officers entered the room. Tetley stepped off the chair and stood to attention along with the other lads.

Lt Commander Smythe stood on the chair Tetley had just vacated and looked round the room at all the men in attendance, then said, "Good evening, gentlemen."

Everyone replied in unison, "Good evening, sir."

Commander Smythe continued, "Gentlemen, this has been a bad day in the history of our squadron. Never in the squadron's history have we lost so many men, and yet at the same time proved that we are a mighty squadron with brave and courageous men serving in her. I heard from Lt Chalmers that a few men were planning to meet for drinks at the Rugby Club, and I thought this was a fine idea to toast our fallen comrades and to congratulate the victorious. With that thought in mind, I would like to ORDER all squadron members to gather at the Rugby Club where the squadron will pay for the beverages." A huge cheer erupted from all the men gathered in the room and from those outside the room who could not squeeze in.

"Thank you, gentlemen," finished Lt Commander Smythe. He then stood down and left the room with the other officers.

"You'll have to save the world again if this is what happens every time, mate." laughed Muddy. "Let's get over to the Rugby Club before anyone else and get some beers in before the crowd."

They both pushed their way out of the crew room, stuck on their berets and headed out of the building. It was a good walk from the squadron building to the other side of the base, where the accommodation blocks, galleys, NAAFI and Rugby Club were situated, and all along their route, people either stared as they passed by or came over and shook Tetley's and Muddy's hands. The air was cool, and although he had been up for many hours, Tetley no longer felt tired and he looked forward to having a few pints with the lads.

When they got to the Rugby Club, only a few people were inside, and each one came over to Tetley and Muddy and shook their hands.

Tetley and Muddy went up to the bar and the barman asked them for their order.

"Two pints of Guinness, please, mate, and two shots of pusser's rum while we are waiting for the Guinness," said Muddy. When the rum arrived, they picked up their glasses and toasted each other, then threw it straight down their necks in one.

"Same again, please, mate," shouted Tetley, just as the barman set the Guinness down on the counter.

He was just about to hand over the money for the drinks when Lt Commander Smythe and a gaggle of officers, including Lt Chalmers, entered the bar, saw what was happening and shouted, "Put your money away, Garside; the drinks are on the squadron tonight."

Lifting his cash and his rum off the bar, he turned to Lt Commander Smythe and, raising his glass, said, "Cheers!" and threw the rum back in one.

The commander nodded and ordered himself a gin and tonic, then turned to Tetley and Muddy and said, "The squadron and the men whom you brought back this morning, including the boss, owe you a great debt of gratitude, Garside. You too, Waters. When I heard the lawyers recounting the events on the video conference to their colleagues in London, I was completely taken aback. If someone had gone to a movie mogul in Hollywood with the account I heard this morning, I doubt they would have taken it on. Too fanciful, they would say. I am sure that given the events of today, there will be many repercussions and I doubt we have heard the end of it yet. I would imagine you will be in high demand, Garside. People will want to hear your story."

"Well, sir," began Tetley, "they can ask all they want. My story stays with me and the navy. Too much grief, if you ask me, and some dickhead will figure a way to turn everything around and blame us for what happened. No, sir! What happens in the mob stays in the mob."

"Fine sentiments, Garside. However, not just the civilian media will want their hands on this story. I would think there will be ripples throughout the MOD and Whitehall after today's events, and your presence will be required at many a briefing before all this settles down. All I'm saying is prepare yourself for what is coming," said Smythe before taking a long drink of his gin. "In the meantime, let's all get deservedly pissed."

"Now that's my kind of order, sir," said Muddy, knocking back the remains of his Guinness and holding up his empty glass for the barman to see. Soon, the bar was packed with personnel from the squadron and from all over the base, many squeezing past to come over and congratulate Tetley and the other seven secret trench survivors who were now congregating in a group round a large, tall table, drinking heavily after their ordeal that morning.

Knocker White asked Tetley, "I was questioned severely this afternoon by the Head Shed as to why I did not act quicker and take control of the situation."

"What did you tell them?" asked Tetley.

"Well, I told them I was too busy keeping my head down as low as possible, trying to keep from getting blown up along with the other lads. Then they asked me why did you manage to keep it together and run for the live ammo then attack the enemy or whoever they were? I just said, have you met Tetley? He is one crazy bastard! There was no way in hell me or any of the other lads were going to stick our heads above the edge of the trenches to get blown apart by those mortar rounds. The fact that you had made it to the ammo trailer and back was a miracle in itself. Then you sent Muddy to share the ammo and tell us the plan. The easier path then was to follow your lead, as you had done so much at that point, even if I had my doubts, which I had voiced to you. You would have gone ahead, anyway. Looking back at events this morning, you are one lucky bastard, Tetley."

"I'll drink to that," he replied, raising his Guinness and then taking a long sup. The evening continued into the small hours of the following morning, and bit by bit, people started to head back to their accommodation blocks. Tomorrow was a school day, after all, and some lads might even be heading straight back to work. Tetley just had a thought; he had no idea what time to muster at the squadron that morning, as he would normally be off for a couple of days after the exercise. He looked around the bar and saw all the Ruperts (officers) gathered together in one corner, so he made his way over to chat with Lt Commander Smythe.

He saw that he was chatting away with the others and had spotted Tetley coming over.

"Ah, Garside, I thought you might have slunk back to your mess by now; what can I do for you?" he asked.

"Well, sir, I was just wondering what time I need to be back at the squadron this morning," Tetley replied.

"Good point," said Smythe. "I think come in after lunch, say 14:00 hours. It should be quiet, but after the FOB incident, I doubt we'll get much rest for some time. If you are needed urgently, I'll send someone to fetch you. Tell the other lads from the FOB that the same applies to them."

"Thank you, sir, I will pass on the message to the others."

Tetley made his way back to his mates, where he filled them in on the late start. They were delighted by Tetley's news and were all for getting more drinks in, but Tetley decided he'd had enough for one night and was heading off to his pit. Ginger and Hammy were in the same room as Tetley, so they decided they would go with him back to the mess, so was Muddy but he was staying for a few more beers with Stinker, Nobby and Knocker.

"Be it on your own heads tomorrow, lads. I have a feeling it's not going to be as quiet as Smythe thinks. There'll be a lot of fallout from the exercise and the worst is yet to come. I, for one, want a good night's kip and a fairly clear head tomorrow."

It took the three of them some time to get through the drunken mob that stopped them every few feet to talk and try to ply them with more booze, but eventually, they made their way out into the cold morning air. The base was very quiet except for the noise coming from inside the bar as the lads walked the eight hundred yards or so back to their accommodation block. The only other people they met were three security patrols doing the rounds of the living quarter's side of the base.

Their room was on the middle floor of Yeovil Block. It had three floors with four beds per room, and the squadron had the bottom and middle floors. The top floor was reserved for junior airmen, which are airmen under the age of eighteen and their guardian, a duty leading airman.

Back in their room once the door was closed, Hammy said, "We bloody stink of smoke, earth and stale beer. I'm off for a shower before turning in."

Tetley and Ginger agreed and decided a shower was desperately needed before hitting the sack. So off they trooped to the shower room. They eventually hit the hay and soon went off to a deep sleep.

Chapter 4

They were suddenly woken at 10:00 hours by one of the squadron lads sent by Smythe, who was now acting CO while Lt Commander Benson was recovering in hospital from the wounds he received in the attack on the FOB the day before. The lad's name was Harry Maguire, and Muddy shouted, "What the fuck, Harry, who's on fire?"

Harry replied, "Smythe wants you lads to get dressed and down to his office ASAP."

"What's going on, Harry?" asked Tetley. "He said we didn't have to muster until this afternoon unless it was urgent."

Harry replied, "Some bigwig from London arrived on a flight an hour ago, and all the Ruperts have been in a meeting in the boss's office ever since. Smythe called the crew room and told the duty PO to get one of the lads to rouse you guys and get you down there, pronto."

"Fine, Harry, thanks for the heads up, mate. You'd better wait for us, or you'll be asked a million questions about where we are if you get back before us. Give us ten minutes to get dressed," said Tetley.

The four of them were still very tired and, in one case still worse for wear after the previous night's drinking at the Rugby Club bar. Tetley urged, "Come on, you fuckers, get out of your pits and get sorted sharpish. I have a feeling this is not going to be a good day for us. Fuck's sake, Muddy! Look at the state of you; you look like death warmed up. What time did you call it a night?"

"Got in around half five, mate, at least I think it was then; I'm not completely sure. They were still drinking hard when I left, including Smythe and most of the Ruperts. I feel like shit, so God knows what they are like this morning. The poor bastards have been at work since 08:00 hours. They'll be like the walking dead, mate. The whole squadron will be suffering after last night. The brass from London will think they have walked into a movie set of *Zombies*," Muddy said, laughing so much he nearly puked, which sent him running for the heads (bathrooms).

The three other lads ran for the heads to wash and shave before dressing in their number eight work clothes, which were a blue shirt, navy-blue trousers and steel-toe-capped anti-static work boots, commonly known as 'steaming bats'.

Outside, Harry had a short-wheel-base Land Rover to get them back to the squadron building as fast as possible. Once dressed, Tetley climbed in the front beside Harry, and the others jumped in the back over the tailgate. Then, Harry set off for the working side of the airfield. Harry had them there in four minutes and pulled up right in front of the main entrance. Tetley and the lads thanked him and headed inside the building, going up to the first floor, where the CO's office was located next to the ready room. Tetley knocked on the door and waited. When the door was opened by one of the junior pilots, Tetley announced, "Reporting as ordered, sir."

"Wait here, Garside," said the pilot before going back into the room and closing the door. A few moments later, the door was opened again, and Tetley, Muddy, Ginger and Hammy were ushered in, and the door closed behind them. They looked around the office and noticed Nobby Clarke was there, along with Stinker Rankin and Petty Officer Knocker White.

"Over here, lads," shouted the acting CO. The lads moved over to where the others were gathered round a briefing table covered in aviation charts of the UK airspace.

When he got next to PO White, he whispered, "How long have you been here, Knocker?"

He whispered back, "About ten minutes before you."

He was about to ask what this was all about when Smythe said, "Gentlemen, I would like to thank you for your promptness in getting here ASAP. I know I promised you this morning to recover from your escapades yesterday. However, I summoned you because this gentleman beside me requested your presence and he would like to address you all. I will let him introduce himself, then he can explain everything."

"Thank you, Lt Commander Smythe," the stranger said, before continuing, "My name is John Henderson and I'm from the Home Office anti-terrorist investigation team. I've been sent here to ask all the survivors from yesterday's incident to accompany me back to the MOD offices in Whitehall, where some very senior officers and politicians would like to speak with you all. I know it's a weekend. However, there is some urgency to discover who attacked the exercise area yesterday and how they had the information as to when the exercise was to take place. We think you may help us discover the answers to these and other questions. I arrived on a private jet, and it's being refuelled for the journey back to RAF Northolt and from there, transport is being arranged to take us all into Central London. I would like us to leave ASAP. Your acting CO has informed me that you will be required to wear your number one dress uniform for the trip to Whitehall. How long will it take you all to get ready, gentlemen?"

They all stood and looked at each other in disbelief at what

44

was happening before PO White said, "Well, sir, none of the lads have eaten this morning as yet, but if you give us an hour, we will be back here ready to go."

"That is acceptable, PO White. Don't worry about eating as food will be provided on arrival in London," replied John Henderson.

With that, the lads were dismissed and went to find Maguire to drive them all back to the accommodation block to get changed. Maguire was in the crew room, as he had been told on arrival to wait for the lads. He heard them all coming down the stairs talking loudly to each other, asking what the hell was going on, who was this Henderson bloke and why were they being whisked off to London for some interview after they had already given all the information to the legal guys the day before.

PO White saw Maguire and shouted to him to get the Land Rover started, as they needed to get back to the mess decks to change. Maguire ran out ahead of them to the rover and started the engine. PO White climbed in the front passenger seat as he was the senior rank and the others squashed into the back.

When they were all in, Maguire asked PO White, "What's the score, PO?"

PO White answered, "We've been summoned to the MOD in London to answer further questions by some bloke called John Henderson. Apparently, he has a plane waiting for us, so we have to get back to the squadron buildings ASAP. You can drop me off first at the PO's mess and then take the lads over to their mess decks and then wait for them. Pick me up on the way back and don't be long."

Maguire drove as fast as he could to the PO's mess and dropped off PO White, who leaned in the back of the wagon and shouted, "Quick as you can, lads, I don't want to keep this prick waiting too long." He slapped the side of the rover and Maguire took off like a whippet up a drain pipe heading for Yeovil Block. He screeched to a halt outside and they all bailed out the back.

Tetley shouted, "Keep the engine running, Harry; we won't be long." Inside the mess, the lads all headed for their rooms and stripped off once inside, hanging up their number eight working clothes and sorting out their number one dress uniforms. They sat and gave their dress shoes a quick buff before getting dressed in their uniform. When they were all dressed, they took time to check each other, as was the custom, wrapping a hand in cello tape with the sticky side facing outwards to pat each other down to get rid of any lint. Once completed and cap in hand, they went back out to Maguire and the waiting Land Rover and climbed in, taking care to not disturb any of their dress uniforms or, God forbid, smudge their shoes.

When they were all in, Maguire took off for the PO's mess. "Slow down, you muppet," shouted Muddy. "We have to take care of our number one's."

Maguire apologised and slowed down to a more sedate speed before pulling up outside the PO's mess, where PO White was waiting in his dress uniform. He got into the front of the wagon as before, and they headed back to the squadron building, where there was a minibus sitting outside, an engine running and the driver in his seat. They headed into the building, and PO White told the lads to go to the crew room to wait and he would find out when they were leaving. He headed upstairs, knocked on the CO's office door and waited.

The Acting CO Lt Commander Smythe shouted, "Enter!" and PO White stepped into the office.

What he saw was Henderson, Captain Standen, Smythe and Lt Chalmers standing, talking and drinking tea.

The naval officers were all in dress uniforms like himself, and when they saw him, Henderson said, "Looks like we are all ready for the off, gentlemen." They placed their cups on a tray situated on the desk, then headed out the door. PO White stepped aside to let all the senior officers pass before following them down the stairs.

He stuck his head in the crew room door and shouted, "Right, lads, quick smart," before heading back out the front door of the building. Tetley and the other lads followed closely behind, and only when they were outside did they notice all the brass in the minibus.

PO White pointed them in the direction of the Land Rover and they all climbed back in. The minibus set off across the apron in the direction of the apron in front of the tower, where guest aircraft were parked. PO White told Maguire, "Follow that minibus."

The vehicles pulled up alongside a Bombardier Dash 8 aircraft and everyone climbed out. The officers boarded the aircraft first, followed by PO White and the rest of the lads.

When they boarded the aircraft, they were very surprised to see that FONAC Rear Admiral Fleetwood was already seated in the front row. He was joined by Henderson and the other officers who sat in the seats behind.

PO White and the lads headed to the rear seats and got settled in. Very quickly after getting boarded, the door closed and the aircraft's engines spooled up and before too long; they taxied out of the parking area, heading down the taxiway to the end of the runway. As soon as the aircraft straightened, the engines were pushed to full throttle; the brakes were released and off it set down the runway. The Dash 8 did not need much runway space before lifting off the concrete into the air. Soon, the wheels were up and they turned east and headed for Northolt in London. About ten minutes into the flight, a woman whom they had not seen on boarding appeared at the front of the aircraft. She grabbed the intercom, introduced herself as Veronica, the first officer and co-pilot, and asked everyone to make themselves comfortable for the forty-minute flight. She would be handing out tea and coffee to those who wished. She disappeared again briefly to what must have been the forward galley area, returning with the standard hostess trolley that held a large urn of hot water. Starting with the VIP passengers at the front of the aircraft, she began serving hot tea and coffee and packets of custard cream. When she got to the back of the aircraft, the lads started flirting with her, asking for her phone number and whether she would be available when they were in London for a drink or two. She laughed off all the advances of the lads, stating she was a married woman, even flashing her wedding ring in front of Muddy's face, much to everyone's joy.

Tetley was sat beside PO White and he said to him, "Some turnout we have here, Knocker, all the FAA head shed on one flight. This must be some gig we are heading to at the MOD. There's more to this than meets the eye, mate."

PO White was quiet for a minute before looking at Tetley and answering him, "I can tell you, Tetley, I am bloody worried myself. When I saw FONAC on this flight, I thought we are heading into a shitstorm at the MOD. The head shed are along to cover their own arses and we are being offered up as sacrificial lambs. They are just buttering us up with the tea, coffee, biscuits and the good-looking pilot, mate. How many times have you seen FONAC?"

"Only once every four years, mate, on Admiral's inspection," answered Tetley.

"And yet here he is on this aircraft with us and the skipper. It doesn't bode well, Tetley."

"Fuck it, mate! The worst that can happen is that they chuck us out of the navy. If that happens, I'll go to the press and create an even bigger shitstorm." laughed Tetley before taking another slug of his tea. The rest of the flight was uneventful and soon the pilot was announcing they were on the approach to Joint Headquarters Northolt and would be landing in five minutes. Everyone buckled up, and those who could, looked at the view of London below them.

Chapter 5

When they landed and taxied to the aircraft parking stand, the doors were opened, and they were all asked to disembark and get in the waiting coach at the bottom of the steps.

The coach would take them all into Central London to the MOD buildings in Whitehall. The officers disembarked first and took up the seats in the front of the coach.

The others made their way to the rear, keeping their distance from the officers. Henderson sat on the jump seat opposite the driver in the position a tour guide would take if this were a guided tour of Olde London town. Once all were on board, the driver was instructed to drive on.

As if on cue, Henderson grabbed the microphone from a holder next to his seat and spoke to them all.

"We are now going directly to the admiralty office spaces in the MOD building, where there will be brunch laid on in one of the briefing rooms. This will also be attended by the First Sea Lord and the joint chiefs of staff of the British armed forces. This will be more of an informal meet and greet session. This afternoon's itinerary will begin at 14:00 sharp with interviews with the joint chiefs followed by an individual meeting with the First Sea Lord.

"Squadron senior officers will have a separate meeting with the First Sea Lord and the joint chiefs during the lunchtime break and this will be held in the admiralty boardroom on the top floor of the building.

"Junior ratings will have their divisional officer present for their interviews. However, the joint chiefs may ask him to leave should they feel it necessary on security grounds. You will also be staying in London for the next three days, as further meetings may need to be scheduled. You will all be staying at the Radisson Blu Hotel close by, and you need to pick a roommate to share with. The MOD has secured the third floor of the hotel specifically for your visit, purely on security grounds, you understand. The floor will be patrolled by armed security teams and each room will have a guard on the door. This guard will accompany you throughout your stay at the hotel. All expenses at the hotel will be paid by the MOD. Dining at the hotel will be in a conference room situated on the third floor, and while at the hotel, you are not permitted to speak to anyone outside the people on this coach, and leaving the hotel is not permitted unless directed by me. I hope I have made myself clear, gentlemen."

"Fuck me," said Stinker before continuing, "looks like we are being banged up in a posh jail, lads. If all expenses are paid for, the minibar is getting demolished tonight."

The lads all laughed and joked about drinking the hotel dry, when PO White said, "Look, lads, this is no jolly; this is serious shit here and we are up to our necks in it. We can't be getting pissed.

"We might say something that will sink us for sure. Can you imagine us getting hammered tonight at the hotel then first thing in the morning, having to face the First Sea Lord stinking of booze and wanting to race to the heads to chuck up? I think we should all be very careful here, lads. This is the big leagues and we don't want to make arses of ourselves or let the squadron down. Drink, yes, but in moderation. No kicking the arse out of it. The fact we are here means one of two things:

51

"One, they're going to wine and dine us in intimidating surroundings, hoping we may drop our guard and we slip up and drop each other in the shit, then hang us out to dry.

"Two, they will wine and dine us, give us a big pat on the back, pin a medal on our chest, then ship us out on a long sea deployment away from prying eyes and ears.

"The fact they have us stashed in a hotel guarded like the crown jewels tells me they are shit scared of us talking to anyone, whether it be spinning dits after a skinful at the bar or talking to some reporter out to get a big story."

"Knocker is right, lads," said Tetley. "We need to be on our guard the whole time we are up here in the smoke. Trust no one and look out for each other. Don't hit the booze too heavy. Pick a buddy for a roommate for our stay. You up for it, Muddy?"

"Sure, Tetley, I'll bunk with you," Muddy answered. The others buddied up with PO White having a room on his own.

They soon arrived in Central London and the traffic there was a lot slower as the coach made its way to the MOD building in Whitehall. When the coach arrived, security personnel stepped on board for an ID check before everyone was allowed to proceed into the inner courtyard. Once the coach stopped, Henderson stood up and spoke using the microphone again.

"We have arrived, gentlemen. Please disembark the coach and wait outside until everyone is together, then please follow me into the building, where you will each receive a visitor's badge, which you must wear at all times when in the building. When we leave this evening, you will be asked to sign out and surrender your visitor's badge to security. Thank you, gentlemen."

Everyone slowly disembarked from the coach, starting at the

front. Then everyone waited outside, as instructed by Henderson. Henderson had disappeared inside the building, so they waited until he returned carrying a box full of visitor badges.

"When I call your name, please come and collect your visitor's badge and pin it on your uniform," he shouted to everyone. It took a little while to get everyone sorted and then they were led inside the building to a bank of lifts. The officers were asked by Henderson to step inside and the others to await his return. The lads watched the floor numbers on the lift exterior display climb until it got to the eighth floor – the top floor – where all the admirals and generals worked. Soon the lift descended and the door parted to reveal Henderson standing there.

"Right, gentlemen, get in the lift," he said, and they all stepped into the large lift. Henderson pressed the button for the eighth floor and up it went. When they arrived on the eighth floor and the doors opened, Henderson stepped outside into a carpeted hallway and beckoned for the others to follow him.

"Posh carpet this, lads," said Stinker. "I wouldn't mind this on the floor of our mess deck."

They all laughed and followed Henderson to a double door halfway down the long corridor. He opened the doors and stepped into a large meeting room that had a large single table set for dining. He ushered the lads in and told them to sit where they wished.

Tetley made for the seat furthest from the officers who sat at the far end of the table. Muddy and PO White followed, sitting next to Tetley while the lads filled the other empty seats. Tetley watched as Stinker and Ginger ended up sat next to the Ruperts and he smiled. Ginger gave him the finger and Stinker joined in the sentiment by giving him two. A few minutes later, the doors opened and in walked more gold braid than Tetley or any of the others had ever seen in one place. Leading the pack was the First Sea Lord, the most senior rank in the Royal Navy, the commandant of the Royal Marines, three generals of the Army, an Air Chief Marshal and Marshal of the Royal Air Force, followed by a gaggle of other senior officers who Tetley took to be aides.

Everyone stood up to attention, and the First Sea Lord Admiral Sir Robert Beaufort, said, "As you were, gentlemen," and they all sat down again and waited.

Sir Robert introduced himself and the other flag officers that made up the general staff of the British armed forces and then turned to one of his aides and said, "Ask the stewards to start serving brunch, please, Coleman." Captain Coleman turned and left the room to organise the scran. All the lads were starving, having been rudely woken to get ordered up here to London, for God knows what. The flag officers sat at the end of the table where the squadron officers had seated themselves. Their places were marked by name cards showing just their rank; hence, these seats had been left empty by squadron personnel. The aides all sat around the edges of the briefing room on individual chairs, awaiting the call from their bosses to leap into action.

Sir Robert spoke first, welcoming the squadron personnel to the MOD building and telling them to relax, enjoy their food and feel free to talk. A moment later, the double doors opened and several stewards walked in, pushing what looked like hostess trolleys, the type that kept the food warm when being transported. They took up positions at various points behind the seated personnel, and with a nod from Sir Robert; they began serving a full English breakfast along with piping hot tea served on the best bone china that surely any of the lads had ever seen. The lads were delighted and looked up the table, awaiting the approval from Sir Robert before they got stuck in. Sir Robert was served first, of course, followed by the other flag officers, then the squadron officers and finally PO White and the rest of the lads.

As soon as the last plate hit the table, Sir Robert said, "Please start, gentlemen! Don't stand on ceremony. We wouldn't want the food to go cold. If you require anything else, please feel free to ask the steward closest to you."

When the lads got stuck into the scran, Muddy turned to Tetley and PO White and said, "I bet whoever cooked this wasn't a navy chef, this is outstanding."

"Maybe because it's your final meal, Muddy," said Tetley, "And they don't want to hang you hungry."

PO White burst out laughing, nearly choking on his food. The stewards asked each individual if they would like tea or coffee before pouring the brew into the correct cup on the table. Tetley chanced his arm and asked if they had Earl Grey tea. "No problem," the steward replied. "I'll fetch a fresh pot for you."

The lads all looked at Tetley in amazement, and Muddy piped up, "Maybe you should be sat at the other end of the table, Tetley, you and your ponsey posh tea. Maybe you're really an undercover Rupert."

All the lads around Tetley roared with laughter so much the officers at the other end looked up to see what was going on. The lads spotting this quieted down to a more formal level. Once brunch was over, the table was cleared and the stewards left the room.

Sir Robert nodded to his aide, and he stood and locked the doors, flicking a switch on the wall that lit a red light outside the room, showing it was occupied with a 'Do not disturb' sign.

Sir Robert stood up and addressed the personnel around the

table, "Gentlemen, I will start by offering apologies on behalf of myself and the other flag officers here present for dragging you up to London at such short notice. I doubt any of you have ever set foot in this building, and I dare say you never wanted to. I am also aware how much horror the appearance of a flag officer causes when he visits a base or ship and the preparation and work involved for those visits. Yet, here you all are in the hallowed halls, seated around a table with the whole joint chiefs of staff of the British military. If I were in your shoes, I would be quaking too. However, I am at pains to assure you none of you are in any trouble; in fact, quite the opposite. We have all listened to the debriefings that were conducted yesterday by the legal department, and we wanted to meet the personalities involved. I myself have a few questions I would like answered, as I'm sure the other flag officers here have too, hence the purpose of this visit.

"I would also like to inform you that your commanding officer, Lt Commander Benson, is recovering well in hospital. He has been debriefed by the legal team and has, in fact, recommended commendations for many of you here present. Commendations I will be happy to approve in due course. I have some further news for you all. I received a call this morning before I came into this room and it seems your presence has been requested by the prime minister at a small gathering tomorrow evening at Number 10.

"I am sorry this is all a bit of a whirlwind and somewhat confusing for you; however, that is not our intention. We are going to commence by speaking to all of the survivors from the incident on the exercise area on Dartmoor right away. We will be talking with you individually so we can get a clearer picture of events and so that interruptions from others do not confuse matters. These chats will take place in the room next door, starting in fifteen minutes. If any of you gentlemen need to use the heads, please do so now. The heads are three doors down on the right from this room.

"Thank you, gentlemen."

The flag officers, Captain Standen and their aides trooped out of the room, leaving the squadron personnel alone in the room with Henderson.

"OK, lads, you heard Sir Robert. If you need the heads, sort it out now," said Lt Commander Smythe.

Most of the lads got up, left the room and headed for the heads to relieve themselves. When they returned, Tetley said to PO White, "The heads are like five-star hotel-quality facilities; they even have small hand towels to dry your hands instead of paper and the bog roll is soft, not like the grease-proof paper they supply us with. Now I know why you keep pushing for promotion."

PO White laughed at him and said, "Our heads are no different to yours, mate; we don't get soft bog roll either, not unless we buy it ourselves."

Fifteen minutes later, the admiral's aide returned and asked PO White and Lt Commander Smythe, who was Knocker's DO, to accompany him to the next room. He was gone for about twenty minutes when they returned, accompanied by the aide, who then asked Muddy and Lt Chalmers to follow him. This time, thirty minutes passed before Muddy returned alone when Hammy was requested to follow the aide. This pattern continued until everyone had been interviewed except Tetley. No one spoke of what was said next door on the orders of Henderson, who was still in the room with them all. So, they chatted about the trip to London and the impending visit to Downing Street the following evening. Finally, Tetley's turn came and he was asked to follow the aide next door. The aide opened the door, went in and announced, "AEM(M) Garside, sir," and ushered Tetley into the room to a chair next to Lt Chalmers, his DO, facing the General Staff members, then turned and left the room.

"Good afternoon, Garside," began Sir Robert. "This little question-and-answer session is being filmed and recorded just for the record, you understand. I'm afraid neither you nor your divisional officer will be permitted to have any copies of these recordings, as we have classified them as sensitive to national security. I also wish to reiterate that no action will be taken against you and you are not in trouble in any way. Do you understand what I have said, Garside?"

"Yes, sir," Tetley replied.

"Jolly good, then let us begin," said Sir Robert before asking, "We have listened and watched your debrief with Commander Evans in Yeovilton yesterday, but we would like to hear the events recounted by you in person, just so we are clear on the timeline and the actions taken. Could you start at the beginning, please, Garside?"

Tetley took a deep breath and started recounting his story. When he got to the part where he left his slit trench, the Commandant of the Royal Marines Brigadier Watson interrupted him and asked,

"Were you sure it was Royal Marines launching those mortars at the FOB, Garside?"

Garside replied, "Who else could it have been, sir? The Marines were positioned on that ridge since the start of the week, and we had not been informed of any other units joining the exercise."

"I see," was all the Brigadier could manage in reply. Tetley carried on recounting his story just as he had done with Lt Commander Evans until he got to the part when they arrived back at RNAS Yeovilton.

There was silence in the room for about five minutes, and Tetley looked at his DO Lt Chalmers, who just shrugged his shoulders, then looked forwards at the joint chiefs again. Finally, Sir Robert poured himself a glass of water before speaking to Tetley.

"Garside, I must say, in all my thirty-eight years in the Royal Navy, never have I heard of such a heroic action performed by any member of the armed forces. Such acts of extreme heroism are rarely seen. Do you realise you are responsible for the survival of ten men, not including yourself of course, and also the destruction of a sizeable enemy force that was better armed?"

Tetley reddened before he said, "Well, sir, I did have help from very well-trained sailors in my squadron. I did not do this by myself, nor probably could I have. Yes, it may have been my plan, and I just happened to be best placed to carry it out, but that is what we are trained for. That's why we have these training exercises.

"There was also a large element of luck in that we had laid a trap for the Marines by digging extra slit trenches, and luck also in that I was able to make to the ammo trailer and back. Once we had the capability, all the lads in those trenches were up for taking the fight to the enemy and for getting medical help and assistance once the battle was over. The Navy Commando Squadrons are very proud of their history and their capabilities; rarely do we have to face the enemy, but when we do, we are all capable, well-trained sailors, sir."

Sir Robert smiled and said, "May I ask you, Garside, why are you still just a naval airman? Why have you not progressed up the ranks? You clearly have the ability to lead men; you have proven that skill very adroitly."

"Sir, when I joined the navy as an airman and stepped out on the flight deck on my first carrier posting with the squadron, it was the culmination of a boyhood dream. I had not thought anything about being an NCO or even an officer. The men I served with were mostly good lads, and for me, life was great. Contentment is a much-underrated emotion, sir. I am happy being an airman, getting my hands dirty working on aircraft and even digging trenches. That is my sole being, sir. I have experience of years that I can pass on to other junior airmen and they mostly listen to what I have to say. Some learn and some don't, but those that do go on to bigger things, and some of them have returned and have been my seniors and it is an honour to serve alongside them," answered Tetley.

"I feel things are about to change for you, Garside, and you may no longer be able to hide in the shadows. You had better prepare yourself for what is about to happen to you and your career," replied Sir Robert.

Sir Robert looked around at the other flag officers and asked, "Has anyone any further questions to put to Garside?" They all nodded 'no', and then Sir Robert stood and approached Tetley, who stood up to attention along with his DO Lt Chalmers.

Sir Robert thrust out his hand and said, "I want to shake your hand, Garside, and thank you for being an outstanding member of the Royal Navy. We are very thankful to have men like you in our ranks."

Tetley shook his hand and then the other flag officers, in turn, did the same before Sir Robert said, "You may both return to your shipmates. I will catch up with you all tomorrow at some point."

"Thank you, sir," said Tetley, then he turned and followed

his DO out of the room and closed the door behind him.

Outside in the corridor, Chalmers turned to him and said, "Garside, you are the golden boy now and a lot of shit is going to come your way. Every man and his dog in the military are going to want to shake your hand, and the press is going to hound you for years. It sounded to me like the general staff are going to make you a hero for the country and a lot of crap is going to come down the pipe in your direction."

"Fuck, sir, that's not what I want; I just want to return to the squadron and continue business as normal. I meant what I said in there, sir. I am happy as a lowly naval airman getting my hands dirty in oil and grease and stinking of hydraulic fluid all the time," said Tetley.

"I'm afraid that your future life is somewhat out of your hands now, Garside. You know what they say," he said, starting to laugh. "If you can't take a joke, you shouldn't have joined up."

With the pair of them laughing, they returned to the room where the other lads and the squadron officers were waiting. When they entered, the acting CO came over and congratulated him, followed by all the other officers and lads. Tetley's face was the colour of beetroot. It looked like he'd been sunbathing in the Caribbean for two weeks, and to top it all, he was lost for words. Thankfully, there was a knock on the door and Lt Chalmers opened it. In walked Sir Robert, FONAC and a steward pushing an oak barrel bounded with heavy brass bands around it and 'HMS Victory' in brass letters across the side and a tap in the bottom. Everyone stood to attention before Sir Robert called, "As you were, gentlemen."

He continued, "The Joint Chiefs, and I think an occasion such as this is worth celebrating in true naval tradition; a few tots are in order, gentlemen. The barrel before us is from Nelson's flagship *HMS Victory* and has been refilled this very morning with a batch of the Royal Navy's finest rum.

"Gentlemen, splice the main brace!"

There was a loud cheer from all in the room, and Sir Robert pointed at PO White and said, "Petty Officer White, as the highest-ranking non-commissioned officer in this room, would you please do the honours and dish out the rum? Can I just point out the dipping cup was used by Nelson himself before the battle of Trafalgar?" PO White went over to the barrel, and the steward handed him the dipping cup, which held one-eighth of a pint of the 95.5% proof rum. He took a long look at the historical cup before filling it from the tap. The steward handed him a silver tankard and he filled it with the rum measure before handing the tankard to Sir Robert. He continued to fill similar silver tankards and passed them round the room until everyone, including himself and Henderson and even the steward, had one.

He turned to Sir Robert, who raised his tankard and said, "A toast, gentlemen, THE QUEEN." Then he downed his rum ration in one hit.

The others raised their tankards and all shouted together, "THE QUEEN," and downed their ration.

Sir Robert looked at PO White and said, "I think another ration is in order, Petty Officer White."

"Yes, sir," replied PO White before filling the dipping cup again and charging everyone's tankards.

Once completed, he turned to Sir Robert, who in turn said to Garside, "Garside, I think the honour of the next toast is yours."

Tetley raised his tankard and toasted, "ABSENT SHIPMATES," and downed his second rum ration.

The others toasted "ABSENT SHIPMATES," then Sir Robert nodded towards PO White and said, "I think one more tot,

Petty Officer White; it's a very special occasion after all."

PO White filled all the tankards again, and this time, Sir Robert turned to the acting squadron CO Lt Commander Smythe and said, "The honour is yours, Lt Commander."

Smythe raised his tankard and said, "A toast TO ALL MEMBERS OF 845 NAVAL AIR COMMANDO SQUADRON." And downed his third rum ration. The others joined in the toast and downed theirs too.

Finally, Sir Robert said, "Thank you all, gentlemen, for upholding the finest traditions of Her Majesty's Royal Navy. I will conclude for this evening by saying you may all keep your tankards as a memento of this fine occasion. Mr Henderson will ensure you are returned safely to your hotel, where dinner will be served to you. I will see you all again tomorrow in this room at 10:00 hours. Good evening, gentlemen."

Sir Robert left the room, and Henderson spoke up, "Transport is waiting in the courtyard to take you to the hotel. If you would follow me down in the lift, sign out and leave your visitor badges with security. Thank you, gentlemen."

The squadron officers all departed with Henderson for the return in the lift. The flag officers and Captain Standen had departed for other offices on the floor. When the lift came back up to the eighth floor empty, PO White and the others stepped in for the short ride to the ground-floor reception area at the back of the building, where they handed in their visitor badges and signed out, noting the time and date. They then climbed on board the waiting coach they had arrived in and were soon on their way to the hotel.

Everyone was in great form, especially after three tots of pusser's rum downed in quick time. Some of the lads were definitely drunk or well on their way there. Muddy started singing on the way back to the hotel, and soon everyone on board was joining in, even the officers. Henderson just sat in his seat at the front of the coach and smiled at the revelry going on around him.

It did not take too long to get to their hotel, and before they all disembarked, Henderson grabbed the microphone and asked for silence from the boisterous crowd of sailors, "Gentlemen, I have a couple of announcements. Firstly, as you were not made aware of this prolonged trip to London and our impending meeting with the PM tomorrow evening, I took the liberty of providing you all with some tracksuits and trainers for you to change into. You will also find suit covers for your uniforms, and if you bring your uniforms in the covers to dinner this evening, I will ensure they are suitably dry cleaned and pressed ready for tomorrow evening. I have also provided a shoe cleaning kit for each of you and the correct polish that I believe is the choice of servicemen and a shaving kit. All this is courtesy of Sir Robert and the Royal Navy quartermasters, and you are welcome to keep all the items provided. Dress code for tomorrow's return visit to the MOD building will be tracksuits and trainers, as we would all wish to look our best for Number 10 tomorrow evening. Lastly, dinner will be served in one hour's time, giving you a chance to shower and change beforehand. Thank you, gentlemen. You may now disembark."

Everyone got off the coach and headed for their rooms to see the 'gisits'(freebies) they had been provided with. Muddy and Tetley went into their room to find everything that Henderson mentioned arrayed on their beds. Muddy picked up a pair of size ten Reebok trainers, took off his dress shoes and tried them on.

"They fit, mate. How did they know my shoe size? And I bet the tracksuit fits as well," he said to Tetley.

"Sure, the navy has all our details from our uniform issue. The data is bound to be on some computer somewhere in that MOD building. This is good kit too, not the normal pusser's kit that falls apart when you first use it. Look at the tracky jacket, Muddy. It has the squadron badge on one side of the chest and our name is embroidered on the other side. They must have been working on these all-day, mate, to get them to us this evening."

He looked at the suit carriers too and they also had been personalised with their names and squadron badges. He picked up the shoe cleaning kit and opened it; it contained two brushes, two-soft lint free cloths, and Kiwi Black shoe polish.

"This is the best kit, mate, and would cost a few bob if we had to pay for it ourselves. We are getting the royal treatment, Muddy, but to what end? Pusser never gives us something for nothing. There is bound to be a catch somewhere along the way; you mark my words, mate," replied Tetley.

"Well, I don't give a shit, Tetley! They fed us some decent grub today and Sir Robert even got us pissed on good pusser's Rum and in a nice silver tankard to boot. Now all this nice kit. I'm going to keep taking it while they're giving it away, mate," said Muddy before heading for the bathroom to shave and shower.

Soon, they all assembled in the makeshift dining room on their floor, which was heavily guarded, and they all sat down around a large rectangular table. They looked like some soccer team on tour in their new navy-blue tracksuits and trainers. Henderson was at the top of the table with the officers seated either side of him and the rest of the lads were seated at the other end. Tetley ended up beside Lt Chalmers in the middle of the group, and he turned to him and whispered, "Do you know who Henderson is, sir? He is sticking to us like glue. No matter where we go, he's there like a bad smell."

"I think he is a civilian liaison officer for the MOD. He seems to be on close speaking terms with all the joint chiefs of staff and even the security personnel at the MOD building entrance call him 'sir'. He certainly carries some authority anyway," answered Lt Chalmers.

Dinner was brought in and served by hotel waiters and consisted of fillet steak, chips, mushrooms, onions and an onion gravy, followed by a choice of crème brûlée or assorted ice cream. There was much talk around the table, and yet no one spoke of the FOB incident. The chat seemed to be based around their new kit and what was the plan for tomorrow at the MOD, seeing as they seemed to be finished with the debriefing. There was also chat about tomorrow night's visit to Number 10 Downing Street to meet the PM. It sounded like no one in the room had ever been through the famous gates, let alone inside Number 10 itself. This was going to be something to tell the grandchildren about in the future. Tetley asked Henderson if it would be possible to get their photo taken on the steps in front of that famous black door, and he seemed to think that would not be a problem, and in fact the PM might join them on the steps for the photo op. That sounded too good to be true, but Tetley thanked him anyway. Once dinner was over and the table cleared, the lads returned to their rooms to relax and watch some TV before hitting the sack.

Chapter 6

Muddy turned on the TV in their room and hit the mini bar and came up with two bottles of Bud. He opened them and passed one to Tetley.

"Turn the channel over to Sky News, mate, and let's see what's going on in the world while we have been wining and dining the night away," said Tetley.

Muddy changed the channel to Sky News and on the screen was a reporter covering the FOB story from Dartmoor. Behind him was a military roadblock manned by armed Royal Marines who stood in front of an armoured Mastiff troop carrier. In addition to the Marines spread out around the vehicle, the driver was in the cab and the gunner manned the GPMG on the roof. The announcer spoke that the area had been sealed off by heavily armed personnel, and survivors had been flown out from the area by helicopter the day before to hospital in Yeovil and to RNAS Yeovilton. The local landlord of a pub in Okehampton reported that two naval personnel had arrived in the village the day before in a fuel tanker and raised the alarm by telephoning RNAS Yeovilton. He continued to state that Merlin helicopters from RNAS Yeovilton arrived soon after into the surrounding area, and armed Royal Marines sealed off the exercise area immediately. He pointed to the Mastiff behind him and explained that further troops had arrived throughout the past twenty-four hours, and there was now a ring of steel surrounding a large area to which no one was being allowed to enter. The reporter went on to explain that Sky News had asked the MOD for further information. However, they had not responded to their requests as yet.

The studio announcer thanked him and continued, "It seems there was some form of gun battle and the locals heard heavy artillery fire. The only thing they knew for certain was an exercise had been in progress. This was normal two or three times a year, but artillery was never used as the area was a protected wildlife zone."

The announcer continued to explain that it seemed as if there had been a major incident and, as yet, they did not have the full details. They would continue to request information from the MOD and would report any new information as soon as it was received.

Tetley and Muddy just looked at each other before Tetley said, "How long do you think the MOD can stay quiet about this? There are too many people involved, and I'm sure reporters are gathered at the hospital trying to get information from the lads there. Family members will also want to know what is happening, too. I bet the phone lines at Yeovilton are red hot at this minute. What if the reporters put two and two together and realise there is a group of servicemen from Yeovilton in London meeting the PM tomorrow night, and those servicemen are members of the squadron who were taking part in the exercise?

"I just had a nasty thought, mate! Are we being buttered up for a big reveal tomorrow night at Number 10? Can you imagine the scene as a load of sailors in dress uniform appear on the steps of Number 10 with the PM for a photo op? It would be like waving a red flag to the journalists who are looking for information, mate. I think we need to have words with Henderson in the morning before we get sold down the Thames."

"You're right, Tetley! Our nuts are on the line here. If the reporters get wind of our visit, we'll never be able to show our faces around town ever again without getting mithered.

"Do you think Henderson will help us, or is he in on the plan?" asked Muddy.

"I'll ask him straight at the breakfast table in the morning in front of everyone. I doubt we are the only ones with these thoughts. He has to give us a straight answer. If he doesn't, I'll ask the joint chiefs when we see them tomorrow. They have to play it straight with us, or I'm getting a train back to Yeovil and the PM can go fuck himself," answered Tetley. They both sat drinking their beer and watched the TV a while longer before calling it a night and getting their heads down for some kip.

The following morning, Tetley awoke with a blinder of a headache. He looked over at Muddy, who was still sound asleep, with a big grin on his face. He grabbed his new shaving kit and staggered into the bathroom, took a look in the mirror and saw the poor hungover bastard that was looking back at him. He went to the shower and turned it on and set the temperature to cold. Maybe a long, cold shower would help ease his hangover and get him back on track for whatever Henderson and Sir Robert had in store for them all today. He stepped into the cold shower and swore so loudly it woke Muddy, who came running into the bathroom.

"Are you all right, Tetley?" shouted Muddy over the noise of the shower running, "What was that loud noise I heard?"

Tetley stuck his head round the shower curtain and laughed as he explained to Muddy, "It was only me, mate.

"I've got such a bad hangover from that pusser's rum we had yesterday that I thought a cold shower would help ease the pain in my head. What you heard was me swearing when I stepped into this fucking cold shower, mate. I am going to stay in here for ten minutes to see if it helps. How are you this morning?"

"Me? I'm fine, mate, and ready for another day at the coal face. You're just a lightweight, Tetley! Your system can't appreciate such fine booze," replied Muddy before leaving Tetley to suffer in the cold shower and returning to the bedroom.

When Tetley came out of the bathroom twenty minutes later, Muddy handed him a brew from a kit provided by the hotel and headed for the shower himself. A couple of minutes later, as Tetley got dressed, he could hear Muddy singing his heart out in the shower. He shook his head and thought to himself that nobody should be allowed to be that cheerful after the session they had yesterday. He opened the door and the guard turned around.

Tetley asked him if he had any headache pills, to which the guard said, "No." But he would go and see if he could scrounge some up for him. Tetley thanked him, closed the door and went back to his brew. When Muddy came out of the bathroom a little while later, Tetley did the honours and handed him a hot brew.

"Cheers, mate," he said and went over to his new clobber to get himself dressed.

There was a knock on the door and Tetley went over and opened it. "Found you a pack of Ibuprofen, mate. Reception sent them up," said the guard.

"Cheers, mate, you're a lifesaver," Tetley replied as he took the pack from the guard and went back into the room. He went over to the minibar and took out a bottle of mineral water, took two tablets out of the pack and washed them down with the water. Muddy watched him, then said, "What do you think the plan is for today, Tetley? I mean, we seem to have finished with the debriefings. What more do they need from us?"

Tetley sat on his bed with his sore head against the

backboard and closed his eyes before replying, "No idea, mate! They must want us for something. Buggered if I can think what.

"I know this much though; they have been the ones asking all the questions, but nobody has given us one clue as to what actually happened at the FOB, mate. I mean, who, for example, were those bastards that attacked us and why? Where did they come from? And how did they know where the exercise would be held and when? I hope at some point today maybe we can start to get some information from someone. The old pals' act is starting to wear a bit thin, Muddy. I think we have the right to get some answers to our questions."

"I don't know, Tetley. I got the impression that since we returned from the exercise, all people want to do is ask us questions. They don't seem too interested in asking us if we have any.

"I mean, what is going to happen to us all now? Do we just head back to Yeovilton and continue on as normal at the squadron? I'm sure they won't let us head into town anytime soon with all the journos hanging around looking for answers from any passing sailor.

"The squadron has also lost a good few men, engineers and aircrew, not to mention the baby Marines. We are also short three Merlins. Are we going to get replacements?" replied Muddy.

"You about ready for some breakfast, mate?" asked Tetley.

"Always ready for scran, mate, follow me," said Muddy as he went to the door, opened it and headed towards the dining room with Tetley and the guard following in his wake. When they got to the dining room, the makings of a full fried breakfast were set out on tables on one side of the room buffet style and there was tea and coffee available from hot urns too. Muddy grabbed a plate and started piling on the food, taking double helpings of

71

everything on offer. Tetley laughed at him and jokingly said, "Are you going to eat that or climb up it and plant a flag?"

Muddy turned around and told him, "This is just a starter, mate, when you get offered grub this good, fill your boots is my motto." Tetley helped himself to some scrambled eggs, three sausages, two rashers of bacon, fried bread and some mushrooms, then headed over to the table and set down his plate. Before he sat down, he went over to the tea urn and filled a mug for himself and added a little milk. He had just sat down when Muddy joined him with his mountain of food and a mug of black coffee. As they ate, Tetley looked around and noted that not all the lads had shown up yet. There were still a few late sleepers, but Henderson was at the head of the table drinking a mug of coffee, chatting with the acting CO Smythe.

Tetley put his knife and fork on his plate, took a drink of his tea, then looked up the table and said, "Excuse me, Mr Henderson, but I have a question that you may be able to answer."

He looked at Muddy, who turned pale, before looking back up the table at Henderson.

"Yes, Garside, please ask your question. If I'm able to answer it, I will, of course," Henderson replied.

Tetley took a deep breath before asking, "This event this evening at Number 10 has me puzzled. Muddy and I were watching the news on Sky TV last night and they were reporting on the incident at the FOB and obviously getting little response from the authorities at the MOD or elsewhere. My question to you is this; Are we getting set up for some big PR reveal by the PM and the MOD at Downing Street tonight? Because if we are, I want out now."

The room fell silent, and everyone first looked at Tetley, and then turned to look at Henderson, awaiting his answer. No one lifted a fork; even Muddy had stopped eating mid-bite. Henderson stood up and looked around the table before looking straight at Tetley, and then he said, "Garside, I can honestly assure you that to my knowledge you all have been requested to go to Downing Street this evening at the behest of the PM.

"This is no PR trap, as you would suggest, but a personal meeting. There will be no journalists or any other media.

"The meeting will not be recorded for any future use, and I can assure you there is no ulterior motive for the invite. I will be accompanying you all as I have done throughout your visit to London, and I can assure you that if journalists were to be involved, I would not be attending either."

"You can understand my concerns, Mr Henderson," said Tetley before continuing, "There are a lot of questions that have yet to be answered, and if the journalists were to put two and two together and realise the PM is hosting a group of RN personnel from Yeovilton, in fact from the very squadron involved two days after the attack, then you can see what I am suggesting." Henderson looked around the room at all the faces of the naval personnel and could see the concern etched over each one of them.

"Garside, I understand your concern and looking around this table, it seems many of you have similar worries. Please let me reassure you all that no journalists will be allowed anywhere near any of you during this visit. I am not privy to the wishes of the joint chiefs. However, I would think it very unwise of them to expose any of you to that sort of scrutiny. You have a meeting this morning at the MOD, the event tonight at Downing Street and tomorrow afternoon you will return to Yeovilton. I hope that gives you all some peace of mind?"

"Thank you for your candid answer, Mr Henderson," replied

Tetley as he picked up his mug of tea and took a slug.

The others in the room decided it was open season on Henderson after Tetley's questioning and the others started to ask him more questions on the same theme.

However, Lt Commander Smythe interrupted them all by stating, "The question has been answered, gentlemen. Please give Mr Henderson some peace to enjoy his breakfast."

The lads then returned to chatting loudly amongst each other and it was clear they were as worried by all the recent events as he was. Conversations were taking place all around the table and top of the conversation list were the FOB and the prying journalists. Between conversations, the lads continued to eat their breakfast. One thing the military had taught them from very early on was to eat and sleep when you can, as you can never be sure when you will be able to next.

"Do you believe him, Tetley?" asked Muddy between large bites of food.

"He seems genuine enough, Muddy, but I don't for a second think he is just a civvy liaison officer. He is further up the food chain than that, mate, and I think he has his own agenda. I feel like a goldfish mate in a small glass bowl; everyone is watching our every move, but to what end?" replied Tetley before standing up to refill his mug at the tea urn. He walked over to where Lt Chalmers was standing talking with Lt Commander Smythe and apologised to the acting CO for speaking out at the breakfast table with Henderson.

Smythe looked at Tetley. He took a drink of his coffee before saying, "Garside, you only asked a question that it seems everyone in this room was mulling over, but did not want to rock the boat by asking. You put the question out there and it opened a can of worms. However, I think more hard questions are going to be asked and answered before this day is out. Like you, I feel this is a bit like a circus and we are being asked to jump through hoops, like performing dogs. I don't like it and the rest of the men seem to feel the same way. Now I was not at the FOB, and from what has been told to me, you performed above and beyond to the point that most of the men in this room would not be alive if it were not for your actions. The flag officers know this, but what game they are playing has yet to be revealed to the rest of us. If they do not reveal their plans soon, emotions are going to boil over, and some of these lads are going to say something that cannot be put back in the box, or they are just going to bolt and run. We think that's the main reason for the guards and why we are confined to this floor of the hotel. They don't want the survivors of the FOB incident talking to all and sundry. Lt Chalmers, who has been acting on all your behalf as divisional officer, has been at pains to point out that none of you have been allowed to contact any family, whom I am sure are very concerned about your wellbeing. He also pointed out that no mention of counselling has arisen in any part of the debriefings, which is against the rules of the military covenant.

"I have spoken myself in private this morning with Henderson and have requested a meeting with the joint chiefs of staff first thing. I need answers before we proceed any further with this road show. Once I have some information that I can share with you all, I promise you I will disseminate that information to all of you as fast as I can."

"Thank you, sir. I really appreciate you going into bat for us all. You can tell Sir Robert that I have a lot of questions too that I would like to be answered, and I, for one, am not going anywhere near Number 10 until they have been answered to my satisfaction. I think that most of the lads here feel the same, sir," replied Tetley before stepping away to chat with Ginger, Muddy, Stinker, Hammy, Nobby and PO White, the other survivors from the FOB, who had gathered in one corner and were watching Tetley talking with Smythe and Chalmers.

When he got to them, PO White said, "What did they have to say, Tetley?"

"Not much, Knocker. I just told them I doubt if any of us will go to this gig tonight at Number 10 unless we start getting some answers from the head shed, mate. Smythe thinks the guards are here to make sure that we do not go wandering and speak with anyone about what happened at the FOB. He has requested through Henderson that they have a meeting with the joint chiefs first thing this morning when they take us into the MOD building," said Tetley.

Just then, Henderson stood up from his chair and asked everyone to finish up, as the coach had arrived to take them to Whitehall. Everyone finished their tea and coffee and followed him out the door and down to the waiting coach.

The coach was the exact same as the day before, with the same unsmiling driver. Henderson took his tour guide seat and the officers sat up the front as is usual. The lads all headed for the rear seats, where they could chat in relative privacy away from the officers. When everyone was on board and seated, Henderson gave the driver the OK to drive on. He then picked up the microphone and started speaking, "Good morning once again, gentlemen. It would seem from conversations I have had with your officers and the questions you put to me at breakfast that trust seems to be in short supply. Seemingly, no matter what I say, will not allay your fears.

"Lt Commander Smythe and Lt Chalmers have requested a private meeting with the joint chiefs first thing before they are willing to let any of you be questioned further. I have not had the chance to speak with Sir Robert as yet but will do so when we get to the MOD building. The same as yesterday, you will all gather in the large meeting room on the eighth floor, where you can wait until I have spoken with Sir Robert. I will, again, give you your visitor badges on arrival and must stress that these must be displayed at all times when in the building.

"Thank you, gentlemen."

The short ride to Whitehall did not take long, and the driver manoeuvred the coach under the arch and parked in the courtyard as before after the obligatory security checks at the entrance gate. The mood on the coach was not great. Few of the lads spoke to each other, preferring to keep their thoughts to themselves. Tetley thought that if things did not go well, the MOD had better call out the guard because things were simmering and that usually meant trouble where sailors were concerned. As before, Henderson passed out the security badges and the lads pinned them on their fancy new tracksuits before he led the officers to the lift and accompanied them to the eighth floor. He soon returned and escorted the lads to the same room as on the previous occasion. The table this time was not set up for eating, but tea and coffee urns were set on trolleys against one of the walls, and mugs, not bone china teacups, were stowed on shelves beneath the urns. The officers were already helping themselves to a brew. Then most of the lads did too. However, Tetley and Muddy refrained.

Hammy and PO White came over to them and PO White said, "Did you notice we are not getting the royal treatment this morning, lads? Just the usual urns and basic mugs. Do you think they have fallen out with us?"

Muddy replied, "Maybe they saw you nicking the crockery

yesterday, Knocker, and they've locked the good stuff away, mate." Everyone laughed, which was good because it eased the tension a little. Tetley noticed that no one had taken a seat at the table and Henderson had left the room, presumably to go and organise the meeting between the squadron officers and the general staff. Everyone milled about the room, and even after thirty minutes, not one of them had pulled a chair out and sat down. Most of them were just standing against the walls chatting with each other about shit as usual, but you could cut the atmosphere with a knife. If the lads did not get some information soon, things were going to get ugly. Forty-five minutes after he left the room, Henderson returned and went straight over to Smythe and Chalmers and asked them both to follow him.

They left the room and Stinker said, "Maybe now we can get some real information instead of being treated like mushrooms." They all knew what he meant by 'mushrooms'. (Kept in the dark and fed shite.)

There was always the 'need to know philosophy' in the military, but that usually pertained to ongoing operations, not like now after the attack on military personnel on exercise in the United Kingdom, for fuck's sake, thought Tetley. Most of these men around the table were survivors from that attack and had stepped up and faced the enemy. Not one man here had stayed in his trench or ran away, for that matter. When the moment came, they all got out and advanced on the enemy, killing them all, despite the overwhelming odds against them. These men were heroes, warriors and men with great character.

Tetley was proud to call them mates.

An hour later, there was still no sign of Henderson, Smythe and Chalmers, and the mood in the room had dropped rapidly and the lads started to get frustrated with the waiting.

"What the fuck is going on? How long does it take for them to tell us the truth?" Shouted Ginger Baker, and all the other lads nodded in agreement.

PO White told them to calm down, but the lads were close to breaking, and Hammy said, "If someone doesn't come in here in the next fifteen minutes with some answers, then I'm fucking off. I'll go to the station and get a train back to Yeovil. I've just about had all I can take of this shit."

PO White went over to him and said, "Look, Hammy, we are all in this together, mate." Looking round the room at the other concerned faces, "I tell you what, if no one comes in here in the next fifteen minutes, we'll all head to Waterloo and get the first train back to Yeovil, OK?"

Everyone shouted their consent. Time was running out fast and there was nothing Tetley could do about it. The lads had enough and wanted back on familiar territory.

If that meant mutiny, then so be it.

The fifteen minutes came and went, and after about twenty-five minutes had passed, Hammy turned to all the lads and said, "That's it. I'm fucking off. Who's with me?"

All the lads agreed, and they headed for the double doors to the room. Hammy flung them open and headed for the lifts.

The lift, luckily, was still on the eighth floor and all the men piled into it, and someone pressed the button for the ground floor.

When they got there, the guy at the security desk protested as all the lads threw their visitor badges at him like they were throwing bricks and headed for the outer doors. Hammy pulled the handles on the outer doors, only to find them locked. He looked back at the security guard and told him to open the doors, but he refused, saying they needed to have permission from Mr Henderson to leave.

Muddy, who was closest to the guard, told him, "Fuck off and open the doors, you twat!" but the guard refused and pressed an alarm button behind his desk, and steel shutters came down around his cubicle and between the interior areas leading away from the entrance and covering the exterior doors to the courtyard.

The men were trapped between the security screens and began banging on them with their fists and feet, making an almighty racket that surely could be heard all round the building, certainly the alarm that the guard had set off could. Before too long, the alarm stopped, but the security shields did not rise.

A voice came over a speaker in the ceiling. It was Henderson. "Gentlemen, please desist with trying to destroy the security shields and I will raise them, and we can return to the meeting room to discuss your displeasures. I'm sure we can answer all your questions fully to your satisfaction."

The men stopped kicking and punching the security shields and then they started to rise slowly.

When the shields went fully up into the ceiling, Henderson stood with two armed guards on each side of him.

"What are you going to do, Henderson? Shoot unarmed men in the back like the lying bastard that you have proven yourself to be? You gave us your word this morning, and now I wouldn't trust you to pour me a cup of tea. Your word is worthless to us now. Just open the exterior doors and let us leave. We've had enough crap to last us three lifetimes," demanded Tetley.

"I'm sorry you feel that way, Garside; I have been entirely honest with you all since we first met. What about your meeting with the PM this evening?" asked Henderson. "I doubt you know what honesty and integrity is, Henderson, if it came and bit you on the arse. I'm glad it was these lads with me at the FOB. I think if you were there, I would have shot you in the back before you did it to us. Now open these fucking doors; we are all going home," replied Tetley.

"I'm sorry, gentlemen. If you will please accompany me back to the meeting room, I'm pretty sure all will be explained in due course," Henderson said smugly.

"Come on, Tetley; we'd better follow him. I doubt they'll shoot us, but they certainly aren't going to let us out, mate," whispered PO White into Tetley's ear.

Begrudgingly, they all headed for the open lift and went in, followed by an armed guard and Henderson. Once the lift opened on the eighth floor, they started heading towards the meeting room where they had all been waiting before, but Henderson kept on walking up the corridor. He motioned for the men to follow him, with the armed guard bringing up the rear to make sure no one deviated from their intended destination. Henderson turned left at the end and continued on until he came to a door that had bio-security locks on it. He bent down slightly, and a light emanated from the circular device on the wall and his iris was scanned.

There was a loud click as the door lock was released, and Henderson pushed open the door and went in. The men followed into what seemed like a large auditorium, similar to a lecture hall at universities that Tetley had only seen on TV. Henderson asked them to take seats along the front row and he disappeared behind a curtain to the left. The armed guard had not come into the auditorium and was presumably situated at the entrance door, just in case he was needed by Henderson. There was a small raised platform at the front and a lectern, just like Tetley had seen at many briefings. There were also two rows of chairs on the platform, comfy chairs with arms and high backs, not the usual plastic or wood and steel chairs they were used to seeing in a briefing setting.

Five minutes passed before Henderson returned and walked onto the platform along with all the joint chiefs, FONAC, Captain Standen and the other squadron officers. They went along the platform until they were all standing in front of one of the chairs. Out of pure habit, all the men stood up to attention when the officers came into the room.

Sir Robert came out last and went straight to the lectern, placed some paperwork on the sloping shelf, and spoke into the microphone, "Gentlemen, quite a fuss you have made this morning. It has been some time since the general alarm in this building was sounded. Do you realise that the whole building was locked down and each person working here was secured in the office they work from and are only being released now? I was not aware of the depth of emotion that was being kept in check by you men, and I suppose it is our fault for not seeing to your wellbeing first and foremost, as is promised in the military covenant that the gentlemen here seated on this platform created. However, I must remind you that you are members of Her Majesty's Royal Navy, gentlemen, and your behaviour here today is tantamount to mutiny.

"We were in a meeting with your squadron officers, trying to answer some of the questions that had arisen this morning at the hotel. It seems we misjudged how important these questions were to you all here. AEM Garside, it would seem, although you do not hold any senior rank, all the people present here from your squadron CO down hold you in great esteem. Would you be willing to be the spokesperson for your shipmates here?"

Tetley swallowed and looked around at all his mates, and each was nodding his head before he turned back to Sir Robert and said, "Yes, sir."

Sir Robert continued, "Very good; please be seated, everyone.

"Before I start asking AEM Garside for the questions that you would all like to put to us, I would like to provide you with a small briefing to catch you up with the most recent developments in the FOB incident. You are all aware of the events of the actual attack and ambush/counterattack that you, gentlemen, successfully carried out under the direction of AEM Garside. To date, there are only eleven survivors from the attack, seven of you sitting here today and four in hospital, of which three are in critical care.

"There were twenty-seven Royal Marines killed in action, twenty-four of whom were cadets in their last two weeks of basic training. The Marines were killed as they slept for the most part, except for the cadet on sentry duty.

"There were twenty-two enemy combatants killed by you men in your fierce counterattack, the identity of whom we are still trying to establish. We do not currently know if they are British citizens or foreigners. Some looked to be of Asian descent, but some were also white westerners, which confuses matters further as to their affiliations.

"An area of sixty square miles around the exercise area has been cordoned off and is patrolled by elements of the Royal Marine Commandos Quick Reaction Force interchanging with elements of regular army regiments.

"A 'no-fly zone' has been put in place within that cordon and is patrolled by helicopters and fixed wing elements from the Royal Navy at Yeovilton and the Royal Navy at Culdrose.

"845 Naval Air Squadron has temporarily been stood down and confined to barracks at RNAS Yeovilton.

"Elements of the squadron currently embarked on carrier operations will remain with the fleet. They are due to return to Yeovilton in one week's time, and should the current restrictions still be in place, they will also be stood down and confined to barracks.

"Maintenance operations of squadron aircraft will continue as normal, and all aircraft will remain on fifteen-minute alert standby in case they may be needed to defend the airfield or supplement the aircraft patrolling the FOB site. The aircraft will be configured half as gunships and half as troop carriers.

"Gentlemen, you have met Mr Henderson, and I know you have already deduced he is not a liaison officer for the MOD. His title, I'm afraid I am not authorised to give you, but I can tell you he has the highest security clearance in the land, matching that of ourselves and the prime minister. I must insist that when you do leave these buildings, you are not to mention his name to anyone outside this room. If you do, you will quickly find yourselves in a cell at Colchester, followed by a swift kick in the arse as you are thrown out of the Royal Navy with a 'disgraceful discharge' notice.

"Do I make myself clear, gentlemen?" he asked.

"Yes, sir," everyone replied. Even the officers sat on the platform.

Sir Robert nodded his head, then continued, "Now I'm afraid that is all the information I can currently share with you at this time. However, I know you all have some questions to ask of us, and, as promised, that time has come.

"If you would stand, AEM Garside, and put your questions to us."

Sir Robert turned and sat on one of the comfy chairs on the platform to await the questions from the men.

Tetley stood and began by saying, "Thank you, Sir Robert, for providing us with some information regarding the FOB attack and the current state of affairs." He turned to the men, and Muddy waved him on, so he turned back to face the joint chiefs before asking his first question, "Gentlemen, as you may, or may not be aware, the men behind me are concerned that we are going to be fed to the wolves. We feel we are being softened up to be thrown in front of the cameras of the mainstream media and newspaper journalists, without our permission, to show the military in a favourable light or to make scapegoats of us as a cover-up to the ineptitude of the MOD to protect its own men in the United Kingdom."

There were a few gasps in the room at the wording Tetley had used, before silence once again descended.

Sir Robert looked at the other joint chiefs and asked, "Would anyone like to reply to that statement, gentlemen?" None of the joint chiefs moved from their chairs, and Tetley thought, *what a bunch of cowardly bastards*.

Sir Robert looked out at the men assembled before him and spoke. "Looks like I'm answering this one, gentlemen." He stood up and approached the lectern again and paused to pour himself a glass of water from the pitcher that was set beside the lectern on a low table.

He took a long drink, then continued, "Gentlemen, I can understand your concern, and yes! You are right! This is a very hot topic in the media at the moment. In fact, our media relations team is inundated with requests for more information.

"The media do not have a clue as to what happened, but we cannot keep a lid on this much longer, as information will leak out at some point. We have yet to remove the dead from the scene, as the coroner and various other authorities wanted them all left in place for forensic examination. The prime minister and various cabinet ministers, including the defence minister, were secretly transported to the site by RN helicopters yesterday so that they could better understand what happened on the ground.

"I can tell you they all came away in a state of shock and found it unbelievable that anyone could have survived the onslaught.

"Your dead comrades will be removed from the site early tomorrow morning and will be flown to RNAS Yeovilton, where they will be held in a makeshift morgue. The coroner and her staff are working very hard to do this as quickly as possible.

"The enemy dead will be transported to a morgue at a different location.

"Once this onerous task has been completed, sometime in the next few weeks there will be a small service in the squadron hangar attended by us all in this room, as well as the PM and cabinet ministers and any family members who wish to attend.

"All the families of the dead have now been informed, and we have respectfully requested that they do not speak to any media for forty-eight hours. To their credit, no one has spoken to the media as yet. The news will get out very soon, unfortunately, and the media will be swarming before too long.

"We plan to make a statement about the attack tomorrow morning at 09:00 hours, at which point the cat will be out of the bag and all hell will break loose.

"They will want details, gentlemen, and we will have to provide them, but only where it does not impact the on-going investigation.

"This will be big news for some time as this is the biggest attack in the UK since world war II. We will provide numbers of dead, wounded and survivors, and I can assure you here and now we will not be giving out names. The problem comes when family members start talking to the press, and it will happen– mark my word!

"We have a short-term plan regarding your immediate future. Initially, you will return to RNAS Yeovilton but be confined to the base, one to protect you from the press and nosey local civilians,; and two to keep you all close at hand should we require further clarification as part of the investigation.

"I hope that meets with your approval."

"Thank you for your candid answer, sir; however, I have two further questions that I think need to be addressed," replied Tetley.

"Now is the time, Garside, so ask your questions," said Sir Robert, who had not returned to his seat but was still standing at the lectern.

"Thank you, sir.

"My next question is about the survivors not being able to contact their families or see their families to let them know we are alive and well. Why are we being stopped from making this contact."

Sir Robert turned to the assembled high-ranking officers on the stage and asked if anyone would like to answer this question?

Captain Standen stood and approached the lectern. "I would just like to say that we understand your concerns and your families' concerns regarding your welfare. Up to this point, we thought it prudent to keep all information regarding the attack on the FOB between ourselves and the investigating team.

"I think that was a mistake on our part, and we should have allowed you to contact your families to stop any unnecessary worry on their part, and as soon as you return to Yeovilton, I will make that happen."

"Thank you, Captain Standen; that is much appreciated by all the men here," replied Tetley.

"My last question is about tonight's meeting with the prime minister at Number 10, sir.

"Do you not think, considering the current heightened awareness of the media surrounding the incident at the FOB of Friday morning and the fact that RNAS Yeovilton personnel were involved, that it would be a bit obvious if a crowd of sailors from Yeovilton arrived for a reception at Number 10? Surely, sir, the media would notice.

"We have been bussed around London in full dress uniform, and now these fancy tracksuits for all to see, sir.

"Do you not think it prudent that we return to Yeovilton immediately before the penny drops and, if the PM needs to meet us, he can do so in the privacy of the base, sir?"

Tetley stood while Sir Robert once again turned to the gathered brass to ask if anyone would like to answer the question. This time, Henderson nodded that he would like to answer the question, and Sir Robert stepped back and sat down as Henderson stood and approached the lectern.

"Thank you for your question, Garside. I can understand how all of you are somewhat reluctant to be seen in public at this moment in time. However, what I can say is the request was made by the PM himself, and as all of us here ultimately report to him, I think we should all turn up as requested. I will make some concessions to this, however, those being that we will all arrive in private cars equipped with window blinds and tinted glass rather than in the coach as previously planned. We will also arrive via the rear entrance rather than through the front door to Number 10, that will take care of prying eyes.

"I'm afraid the trade-off for this is that no photographs will be taken on the front steps, as press and tourists are always in attendance at the gates waiting to get a glimpse of the PM. When the evening has concluded, you will all be taken back to RAF Northolt, where the aircraft you arrived in will transport you back to Yeovilton tonight.

"Does that satisfy everyone's issue on privacy, Garside?"

"Tetley looked at all the men seated around him, and they all nodded their consent. He turned to face Henderson at the lectern and replied, "Yes, it does, Mr Henderson. Thank you for your understanding."

Henderson returned to his seat and Sir Robert stood up and approached the lectern once again. "Well, gentlemen, if that concludes this Q&A session, I think we should all break for lunch. I believe you will all be served in the same meeting room as yesterday, and Mr Henderson will accompany you as usual. Unfortunately, the officers here will not be joining you, as we have other business to attend to. Your squadron officers will re-join you after lunch, after which you will all be returning to your hotel to rest before being collected for tonight's function.

"You're dismissed, gentlemen."

Tetley and the other men returned to the large meeting room with Henderson, and like the previous day, the table was set for lunch, but not with the good crockery. A light lunch of ham and mushroom omelettes with side salad was served by the stewards and the lads all tucked in. PO White sat next to Tetley and they chatted as they ate. "Tetley, they are either going to take you out the back and shoot you, or you're going to get a battlefield commission after that performance. I'm glad they did not ask me to stand up and speak on behalf of us all. I was shitting myself as it was and so was everyone else."

Tetley took a sip of the Earl Grey tea he had requested from one of the stewards and replied, "Knocker, I was just as scared, mate, but we all had questions that needed answering. Unfortunately, they pointed me out, thanks to you lot of chicken shits. We got some answers, mate, but I think this whole mess is still going to blow up in our faces at some point. They seem too laid back about the whole thing, and I am flapping like mad inside, waiting for the grenade to go off. Too many lads are dead, Knocker, and here we are being wined and dined by the head shed. I bet Yeovilton will be in a right mess when we get back tonight. The brass here doesn't seem to have a clue who attacked us and where they got the pile of mortars they hit us with, not to mention the G3's they were all carrying. That's serious kit, mate; you can't go down to B&Q and buy that stuff."

Knocker stopped shovelling eggs into his mouth, took a drink of his coffee, and replied, "You're right, mate, but what the fuck can we do about it? We are just 'Matelots', not superheroes. By the sound of it, half the British armed forces are guarding the FOB site, which takes some serious mobilisation and lot of hardware to be moved at very short notice. A lot of those troops will be trigger-happy, so the journos had better be careful where they wander on Dartmoor, mate."

Muddy sat on the other side of Tetley with Hammy, Ginger, Nobby and Stinker sitting facing them and having an animated discussion. Knocker looked over at Ginger and asked, "What's that all about, Ginger?" Ginger stopped talking to Hammy beside him and said, "We were all thinking that Tetley kicked some serious brass butt in there earlier. We think he should be made the next First Sea Lord; he would get our vote, that's for sure!"

Tetley just shouted, "Fuck off you, tossers!" and continued drinking his tea.

"Look," said Hammy, pointing at Tetley. "He even drinks

that ponsey Earl Grey tea like all the other top brass. We wouldn't be seen dead drinking that shit." They all looked at Tetley, and by this stage most of them were in hysterics, laughing, including Tetley, who saw the funny side of it. Given any chance of a decent brew, he would order it everywhere it was available, including here at the MOD.

He gave everyone two fingers, then lifted his mug of Earl Grey, stuck his little finger out and took a polite sip. Muddy was nearly sick; he was laughing that much and he had to get up and race for the heads. The others were also laughing, and then Stinker threw a bread roll at him, which then prompted everyone else to join in. Knocker shouted to calm them all down despite having thrown one himself, then told them to tidy the place up before they got in anymore shit. The lads begrudgingly started getting the place squared away before the stewards returned to clear everything away.

Shortly after the stewards had cleared up and departed the room, the officers returned and told the men to get ready to depart for the journey back to their hotel. Henderson soon came in, and as was now becoming the norm, he took the officers down first to the ground floor and security. Once they were on the coach waiting outside, he came back up for the rest of the men.

This time when they got to security and were signing out, the security guard in his cubicle shouted after them, "See you lads, I'll miss you all... NOT!"

The lads got on the bus, and as he was heading down the aisle to the back of the coach, Stinker said, "Ungrateful bastard, and after us brightening up his day with a little excitement this morning. There's just no pleasing some people."

The trip back to the hotel was uneventful, and Henderson escorted them all back to their rooms on the third floor. When

Tetley and Muddy entered their room, they saw the suit carriers containing their number one's hanging on the wardrobe doors. They both went over to inspect the contents, taking care of removing the covers and laid out their kit on the bed. Happy with what they saw and the fact that the creases were perfect, they returned the uniforms to the covers and hung them back up on the wardrobe. "We better get our shoes sorted, Muddy," said Tetley as he picked up his dress shoes, inspected them, set them down on the floor and opened the shoe cleaning kit they had been provided. "I think I'll spend an hour on these before getting my head down for a kip."

He opened the polish tin and took the top into the bathroom and filled it with warm water before he sat down with his back against the wall facing the beds and started to buff his shoes to remove any dust. Muddy sat down beside him and started the same process on his own shoes. Tetley then got one of the lint-free cloths in his hand and, covering his index finger with it, dipped it in the polish and began polishing in small circles, covering his toe cap in the polish. He continued to do this, working on one shoe before setting it down and doing the same to the other. When he was happy that the polish he had applied to the first shoe had almost dried, he covered his index finger with a clean portion of the cloth, dipped it in the water this time and began repeating the circling motion until he had a 'bright see your face' shine in the shoe toe cap. They both worked on their shoes until they were satisfied they had the best shine possible, and then they both lay on their beds chatting about this morning's events.

"Tetley, your name is now well known in the halls of power, mate; whether that is a good or bad thing remains to be seen. Maybe you'll start getting regular invites to the joint chiefs' meetings from now on, just to be on hand to offer advice, you understand?" Muddy said in jest as he stretched out on his bed.

"Maybe I will, mate, but more than likely they'll give me the old heave ho, 'persona non grata', mate. Maybe I'm too big a thorn in their backsides, mate. With everyone there today from the squadron – Smythe, Chalmers, even Knocker White – they chose me to stand up there and stick my neck on the line. You didn't see any of the Ruperts volunteering, mate. Oh no! They stuck yours truly up there to face the firing squad," replied Tetley.

"They seemed to think you had the OK from the rest of us, mate, which you did, including Knocker. You also seem to forget none of the Ruperts were at the FOB, so none of them were really in a position to talk on our behalf. You're the golden boy at the moment, even if you're a pain in the arse to them. The rest of us survivors are only here because you put your life on the line running to that ammo trailer, mate, and that's the truth. We all owe you our lives, and I, for one, am very grateful to you. My family will also be grateful to you, as will the families of the other lads, mate. I know you don't like all the attention, Tetley, but you are the hero of the hour, and I bet the head shed have no idea how to deal with the fact you're just an AEM. I suspect they would have been happier if some Rupert was hero of the hour so they could parade him in front of the media to show the officer class in a good light. You have put them in a quandary, mate; they have no idea how to treat you, and you're not making it easy for them either by standing up to them and calling them out. No Rupert would have done that; none of them have the balls, mate, and certainly not in front of the joint chiefs. Smythe and Chalmers sat there like good little boys at the top table and stayed shtum, just like Mummy taught them to.

"Tonight's going to be interesting, mate. What the fuck is the

PM going to talk to us about? He has been to the FOB site and seen all the bodies and body parts, no doubt. He can't imagine what that was like. I was there and I still can't get my head around it. It seems like a lifetime ago already! Yet here we are forty-eight hours later, lording it in London in some swanky hotel. Like what the fuck, mate?" said Muddy.

"I know what you mean, mate! Everything is happening too fast, Muddy. They are not giving us the time to digest everything ourselves first before they start parading us around the place. All we need is to get back to Yeovilton, and then we can speak with our families, let them know we are OK and put their minds at rest. Then maybe let us get hammered for a while, so we can digest what the fuck has just happened and after that, get back to business as usual at the squadron. I don't know about you, but I don't want to be meeting with the families of the lads who didn't make it or traipse around the country attending funerals. I don't think I can face it, mate. I can do the service at Yeovilton in the hangar, but after that, no more for me. If I get too depressed, I might never come out of it; better to stay away and keep busy," said Tetley, turning over on his side to face Muddy.

"Same for me, Tetley. I need to speak with my folks. Maybe spend a couple of days with them, then get back to work. I'll be glad to get tonight over with and get back to Yeovilton, mate. Now get your head down for an hour, you maudlin git, while you still have some time to sleep," said Muddy, as he pulled the bedspread over him from the bottom of his bed. "Yes, Mum," said Tetley, doing the same and tried to sleep.

Chapter 7

Tetley awoke about an hour and a half before they were due to leave for Downing Street. He rolled over and saw that Muddy was still snoring like a buzz saw. He bent down to the side of his bed and grabbed one of his trainers and hurled it at Muddy. It bounced off his shoulder, but he didn't wake up, so he bent down and grabbed the second one. This time it hit Muddy in the head, and he sat bolt upright, looked over at Tetley and shouted, "What the fuck, mate? What did you do that for?"

"Time to get up, mate. We need to shower and change into our best bib and tucker. We only have an hour and a half, and I want a brew first, so stick the kettle on; you're closest," he said, laughing at the state of Muddy. "God help any poor girl who wakes up to you in the morning, Muddy; you're a sorry sight first thing and not getting any better with age," he continued.

"You can talk, you ugly bastard! Take a look in the mirror when you go for a shit. Your ugly mug would scare the bejesus out of anyone, never mind some wayward stray you might manage to pick up in the darkest corner of some nightclub," replied Muddy, joining in the slagging. They both got up and Muddy filled the kettle in the bathroom with fresh water and switched it on to boil. Tetley got an Earl Grey tea bag for himself and some instant coffee powder for Muddy from the brew tray on the table and put them in the cups ready for the hot water. While they were waiting, Muddy asked Tetley, "What did you make of the speech Sir Robert gave about Henderson, mate? I mean, who the fuck is that guy?"

"When Sir Robert warned us off speaking about Henderson, I thought right away he must be a head spook, mate. Henderson probably isn't even his real name. If he has such high security clearance as Sir Robert claims, he must be MI5, just because they deal with internal security matters. He can't be MI6 because they deal with the spying shit abroad, and it would be very unlikely they would be involved with the FOB massacre," replied Tetley.

"You could be right Tetley," Muddy mused. "It sort of makes sense that MI5 would be involved in this mess. Whoever he is, he has some major clout with the military and, by the sound of it, with the politicians too."

"Right, I'm hitting the shower. You get the brews on the go and I'll be out in a tic, mate," said Tetley, heading into the bathroom. Muddy went over to the brew table when the kettle boiled and made himself some coffee, adding water to Tetley's cup so his could brew while he showered.

The room phone rang and Muddy answered, "War room, how can I help you?"

It was Smythe telling them to get themselves sorted and that transport would be ready in one hour's time.

"Yes, sir, we are already on the ball here. We'll be ready," answered Muddy. Muddy stuck his head in the bathroom and shouted at Tetley to get a shift on, as the CO was flapping already. Tetley finished his shower, brushed his teeth, ran a comb through his short hair and came out of the bathroom.

"All yours, mate," he said, and Muddy ran past him into the bathroom to shower himself. Tetley took a mouthful of his brew, then got his suit cover from the wardrobe and started to dress himself in his dress uniform. First, he put on his white front, which was the short-sleeved square-necked t-shirt with blue trim round the neck. Next, he took his dress trousers off the hanger and stood on a chair to put them on so that no lint from the floor was transferred onto them. After that, he took out his collar. He was issued this collar when he joined up and had looked after it very well. Inspecting the three creases, two raised and one reversed in the middle, he remembered his instructor from HMS Raleigh showing them how to iron the creases correctly, saying, "Two tits and a fanny lads, remember that and you'll never go wrong." This always made him smile.

His collar was one of the older types that was tied onto the body over his white front, not one of the modern ones that was attached to the jacket with velcro. It sat better on the jacket and, to him, looked much smarter. He finished off by putting on his white lanyard and tying his tapes in a neat bow with long tails at the front of his jacket. His shoes would not be put on until the very last moment. This was normal practice, as no one wanted a last-minute scuff on them after spending hours buffing them into a high gloss shine. Muddy had come out of the bathroom and was dressing himself in the same way that Tetley had; the main difference was the modern collar that attached to his jacket.

"See, you're still wearing that faded old collar, Tetley; when are you going to trade it in for one of these nice new ones?" asked Muddy.

"Never, mate, this is staying with me until they kick me out of the mob or it falls apart, whichever comes sooner. Now grab that sellotape and pat me down with it, mate, to make sure there is no dust or lint on my uniform. When you're done, I'll check yours."

Muddy wrapped the sellotape back to front round his hand and began checking Tetley's uniform, patting him down with the tape when he spotted any lint. Tetley then did the same for him.

Once they were both happy, they put on their gleaming dress shoes, grabbed their caps, left the room and headed for the dining room, where everyone was assembling. Nearly everyone was already there except for a few stragglers who drifted in over the next few minutes. They all stood a good distance apart, so they didn't mark anyone's kit or scuff shoes. That would be about the biggest sin anyone could make.

The doors opened and Henderson came in looking flushed. He went over to the acting CO Smythe and spoke quietly to him, then he left the room in a hurry again. Smythe called the officers together and broke whatever news Henderson had given him. They did not look happy. Then he turned to the lads, and by then the room had gone silent as they waited for whatever news Smythe was about to impart. "Gentlemen, I'm afraid I have some unwelcome news. It would seem that a group of family members have spoken to the press about the FOB incident and are apparently unhappy with the information they have been provided by the MOD. The media now has a list of names of the dead servicemen, and they are aware from the locals in Okehampton that there were some survivors. In fact, your whereabouts are now known to them, and there is a large media presence gathering outside this hotel. Mr Henderson assures me he has a contingency plan, which he is now in the process of activating. He will return here very shortly," announced Smythe.

"Well, that's us fucked now!" said PO White. "If the journos are waiting for us outside, they will take loads of photos of us as we leave the hotel. Our identities will be splashed all over the TV and newspapers this time tomorrow. We won't be able to do anything without those cockroaches following us with their cameras and microphones shoved into our faces." Smythe urged for calm in the room before he answered PO White.

98

"I'm sure Henderson's contingency plan will sort this out for us; he seems like a very capable man. Please remain silent and calm until he returns."

A few minutes later Henderson returned, looked around at the worried faces and addressed the room, "Gentlemen, I'm sorry the cat is now out of the bag, but I've always had a backup plan to fall back on and I will explain it to you all now if you will just give me a moment of your time. Plan B, as we shall call it, will work as follows;

"The hotel has been informed you are all checking out and heading to Yeovilton by coach. It has been arranged that one of the waiters will drop that little titbit to the awaiting press at the front of the hotel. The men I had guarding you have now been relieved and are getting dressed in Royal Navy tracksuits, the same as you were wearing earlier. The coach has been summoned and will arrive in ten minutes time, at the front of the hotel. The disguised security guards will then board the coach, and it will leave in the direction of the motorway heading west. This should appease the awaiting press, and should they follow the coach, they have been ordered to head for Tidworth Barracks in Salisbury, where they can disappear and return to duties. You, gentlemen, will follow me down to the hotel kitchens, which just happen to be in the building next door. That building also happens to have secure underground parking, and we can dispatch you as planned to Number 10 for your meeting with the PM."

Everyone looked at each other and nodded their approval of Henderson's plan. Tetley had to hand it to him; he was a wiley old fox and had their backs well and truly covered.

He had underestimated Henderson, and to his credit, he had come through for them.

They all remained in the dining room for a further thirty minutes until part one of the plan had been enacted. The hotel manager arrived to inform Henderson that the plan had succeeded and the media frenzy had died off once the coach containing the fake sailors had left the hotel. There were now only a few stragglers outside the hotel waiting for guests to exit so they could bother them for any information they could impart.

Henderson spoke with the CO, and then they all followed him out of the dining room to a staff lift at the end of the corridor. This lift took them straight down to the basement, where the entrance to a short tunnel connecting the hotel to its kitchen and laundry areas was revealed. Henderson led the way to another elevator that took the men to the underground parking area for the hotel staff. A number of cars were waiting for them all with very dark tinted windows and a tinted screen between the drivers and the passengers. It would be almost impossible to spot anyone inside those cars.

Henderson assigned the men to each of the waiting cars and then the first one left as soon as the passengers had boarded. Each car left in five-minute intervals and took different routes to the rear of Number 10 where the passengers were dropped off, before walking the short distance into the secure courtyard area away from any prying eyes.

There was half an acre of gardens arrayed in an L shape encompassing Number 10 and Number 11 Downing Street. Walking through the gardens, the men had not imagined that this existed, as all they had ever seen were shots of the front of the building. There was a large circular flowerbed in the centre, and flowerbeds lined the walkway that led to a large terrace at the back of the building. They were met on the terrace by some bloke in a dark grey suit who shook hands with Henderson, who then introduced the officers to him. He nodded politely and shook their hand but ignored the other men and asked Henderson and the officers to follow him inside. Henderson turned to the others and asked them to follow.

Once inside, they were led by the Muppet in a suit to what he announced was the Pillared Drawing Room. As they entered, he explained that it was created in 1796 and this was the largest drawing room in Number 10 and that many heads of state and other dignitaries had met the prime minister of the time in this room. He pointed out the large painting of Elizabeth The First above the mantle and explained it was often changed by the newly incoming prime minister. However, as prime minister Barrington was a direct descendant, he preferred the painting to stay in its proper place.

Two waiters entered the drawing room with large trays of wine, beer and some canapés. The Muppet announced the PM would be with them shortly and turned on his heels and left the drawing room. The officers took wine and the other men, and strangely, Henderson, took glasses of beer. Muddy and Tetley took a long drink of the beer before Muddy pronounced, "Not a bad brew, lads, I hope they have plenty in stock." Everyone laughed, even Henderson. *Strange*, Tetley thought. *Henderson seems much more relaxed now than he did earlier. Probably because he was in a flap about the journalists.*

Most of the lads had downed three or four glasses of beer before the door was opened by the Muppet in a suit, who then announced, "Gentlemen, the prime minister." Prime Minister Barrington entered the room and went straight to Henderson, shaking his hand and slapping him on the shoulder.

Henderson then introduced the officers in order of rank; then PO White, then the other ratings by name, leaving Tetley's introduction to the end. When the PM reached Tetley, Henderson introduced him as AEM Garside and the PM smiled and stuck out his hand, which Tetley took and shook. *The PM had a good, strong grip; it must be all that pressing of the flesh he does every day,* he thought to himself.

"Ah, Garside, I have been hearing great things about you from many people. It is my pleasure to meet you in person at last." The PM said as he shook Tetley's hand. The PM walked over to one of the waiters and took one of the beer glasses from the tray, held up his glass and spoke.

"Gentlemen of 845 Naval Air Squadron, it is my pleasure to welcome you all to this small gathering this evening, and I would like to propose a toast, 'The Royal Navy.'" Then he put his beer to his mouth and downed the whole glass.

The men arrayed around him smiled, raised their glasses, toasted "The Royal Navy," and downed their own drinks in one.

The prime minister smiled and requested the waiters to fetch more beer and wine. He took his turn talking to each of the men, spending around ten minutes with each before moving on to the next.

When he returned to Tetley, he looked him in the eyes and said, "Garside, if you will allow me, I would like to show you something that may interest you.

"Would you please follow me?" and he headed for the door. Tetley looked at everyone, then shrugged and followed. After all, he was the PM. He followed on behind the PM, who stopped and waited outside the door, then continued on along the hallway until he came to a large polished oak door, which he opened and stepped into the room. "This is the room I use each day as an office, Garside. Behind that desk, I make decisions that affect this nation and sometimes other nations. I send men to war, sadly, some I know will not be coming home to their families and friends. I sign trade agreements with many other like-minded leaders, and I have private one to one chats with other heads of state.

"Today, I have great pleasure ushering you into this inner sanctum. You have upheld the best traditions of great military leaders that have previously graced this room and this building. I have listened to and watched all the recorded debriefings that you and your colleagues undertook after the incident on the training grounds, and your name crops up many times as being the saviour of the moment. Your actions saved the men in that drawing room, Garside, and everyone I have spoken to or been briefed by, including the joint chiefs and Mr Henderson, have lauded your skill, leadership and your forthright action.

"Now I know you have been concerned about being exposed to the media, and I can understand why you do not want the limelight to fall on you. I agree and will endeavour to do my utmost to protect you and the other survivors to the best of my ability. Now there's something I wanted to show you."

The PM went behind his desk, opened a drawer and took out a slightly battered box. He came over to Tetley and opened the box and took out a medal, a Victoria Cross no less. He handed the medal over to Tetley and said, "Read the inscription on the back, please, Garside."

Tetley took the Victoria Cross and turned it over so he could see the inscription, "It says, Lieutenant Robert Hampton Grey RN on the rear of the suspension bar and 9th of August 1945 on the rear of the medal, sir," read Tetley.

"That is correct, Garside. What you are holding is the last VC ever issued to a member of the Royal Navy and, in a strange coincidence, a member of the Fleet Air Arm just like your good self. Now your squadron commanding officer, who was wounded during the attack and to whom you applied first aid until such a time as you were relieved by Commander Forbes, has recommended you for a commendation. Not just any commendation, but the Victoria Cross. This has been approved by all the joint chiefs, and I have on my desk the very document that will make it so."

He returned behind his desk and opened a dark blue leather document holder, lifted the Mont Blanc pen from its rest on the table and signed at the bottom of the document. With that completed, he closed the document holder and pressed a button on his desk phone.

A moment later, the Muppet in a suit appeared and the PM gave him the folder and said, "This is for immediate attention."

"Yes, prime minister," he said, taking the document holder and leaving the room.

The PM came round the table to face Tetley and thrust out his hand. Tetley took it, and the PM pumped his arm vigorously, slapped him on the shoulder and said, "Congratulations, Garside. I can honestly say that I have never met a man with your bravery before. This honour is richly deserved, and you are a credit to your parents, your squadron, the Royal Navy and to this great nation of ours. We shall be ever in your debt."

Tetley just stood there gobsmacked – he did not know what to say – for once in his life he was completely lost for words.

He eventually managed to say, "Thank you, prime minister."

The PM laughed loudly and slapped him on the back, then Tetley spoke up, "Prime minister, I wasn't alone in thwarting the attack on the FOB or in helping tend to the wounded or even raising the alarm. The other surviving members of my squadron in your drawing room played a massive part in that action too, sir."

"Don't worry, Garside, your colleagues next door will also receive recognition for their actions.

"They will each be awarded the Military Cross for their bravery and courageous action during the attack," replied the prime minister.

"You will all be required to attend a Medal Presentation Ceremony at Buckingham Palace three weeks from today.

"The awards will be presented by Her Majesty Queen Elizabeth, and you are welcome to invite your families to the presentation. I assure you now that this will all be kept under wraps.

"At some point in the future, knowledge of the incident and the awarding of medals will come to light, so you have time to prepare yourselves for that moment.

"I think we had better return to the drawing room; the others will be wondering what is going on."

Tetley gave the PM back the Victoria Cross Medal that he was still holding; the PM then returned it to its case and placed it back in his drawer. The PM led Tetley back to the drawing room, where the others went silent when they walked in. The PM went over to Henderson and the officers and began chatting.

Tetley walked over to the other lads who encircled him, asking where he had been and what went on.

"Give the man some breathing space, lads," said Muddy as he pushed into the circle and handed Tetley a glass of beer, which he gulped down as fast as he could.

He handed Muddy the empty glass and said, "Same again, please, mate." Muddy got another full glass and passed it to Tetley.

"What's the score, mate? Where did he take you?" asked PO

White.

"He took me to his private office, then took a Victoria Cross from his desk and explained that it was the last one presented to a member of the Royal Navy back in 1945. He then said I had been recommended for the VC by the boss, and the joint chiefs had approved it. He took out a document confirming his agreement and signed it in front of me. He then shook my hand, congratulated me and told me to be at Buckingham Palace in three weeks' time for the presentation from the queen," replied Tetley, before downing half the glass of beer in his hand.

"You poor bastard, think of all the shit functions you will be forced to attend now, mate," laughed Hammy. Everyone else started laughing and jokingly consoling Tetley.

Then he started laughing himself before he blurted, "That's not all lads, you are all getting gongs too, the Military Medal no less. Looks like we'll be on the celebrity circuit together, lads." He finished off his beer and went and got himself another. When he returned, all the lads just stood and looked at him.

"Are you sure?" asked PO White.

"I got the word from the PM himself, and not only that, you are all going to Buck House too," he replied, laughing. They spent another hour at Number 10 chatting with the PM and each other and drinking beers. Then the Muppet in a suit came into the drawing room with a photographer in tow and went over to the PM and had a quick chat before leaving the room again. The PM turned and faced everyone, then announced.

"Gentlemen, our official photographer has arrived, and I think it would be a fine idea for us all to have some record of this momentous occasion. We will start with some group photographs, me with the officers and then me with the rest of you men. After that, I think individual photographs of each of you and myself in front of the fireplace. I would also like to point out that none of these photographs will ever be published in any newspapers. These are to record visitors to Number Ten. Of course, you will all receive a copy for your own use. Now, if you would all gather round the fireplace, I think we will get started."

Everyone gathered in front of the fireplace with the portrait of Elizabeth The First keeping watch over them. The photographer organised everyone into the position that best suited his photo and began shooting pictures. He then asked the officers to remain and the rest to move out of shot. He organised the smaller grouping and took his pictures. Once he had completed this, he asked the officers to stand aside and the other men to gather next to the PM.

More pictures followed, and then he organised the individual portraits with the PM, starting in rank order, of course, and Tetley was once again last in line. When he stood next to the PM to have his photograph taken, the PM once again thanked him for his service and shook his hand. The photographer asked them to look in his direction while they were shaking hands, and he snapped away.

With the photographs completed, the PM lifted his glass of beer and thanked them all for coming to Number 10. He finished his beer and left the drawing room. Henderson asked them to finish up as the transports were waiting to take them back to RAF Northolt for the flight back to Yeovilton.

The lads knocked back their beers, and when everyone was ready, Henderson led the way to the rear of the building, out onto the terrace, through the ornate gardens and through the rear gates to the waiting vehicles. They each got into the same vehicle they had arrived in, and soon the cars left, making their way through the late London traffic and onto Northolt.

It took about an hour to get to the RAF base, and they were checked through security and driven onto the apron where the aircraft was waiting for them. They all boarded the aircraft as quickly as they could and took their seats. Tetley noticed that Henderson was coming with them and mentioned this to Muddy and Knocker, who were sitting next to him. Knocker thought he was just making sure his charges got back in one piece to Yeovilton, where he could hand over responsibility of them to the navy before returning on the aircraft back to London.

They were served tea and coffee as before, and the flight back was uneventful, with the lads either dozing or chatting about their visit to Downing Street and their impending visit to Buckingham Palace.

Chapter 8

When the aircraft landed at Yeovilton, it taxied to the visiting aircraft apron, where it shut down and the doors were opened. A bus was there to take them to the squadron HQ building, where the other members of the squadron, still in Yeovilton, were waiting to greet them. The officers and Henderson headed for the officer's ready room and the rest of the lads went into the ratings crew room. Someone had made a fresh brew in the tea urn, and they all grabbed a mug and shared the news with the others, who had not been invited to London.

There was great shock when they found out Tetley was to be awarded the VC, and the lads all came over one by one and congratulated him. Muddy held court and showed them the fancy kit they had been issued at the hotel in London and related the story of their exit away from the waiting media like it was from some Robert Ludlum spy novel. There was a knock on the crew room door, and Lt Chalmers stuck his head in and asked for Tetley to come with him. Tetley made his way through the excited mob in the crew room and stepped out into the corridor, closing the door behind him.

"Your presence has been requested upstairs in the briefing room by Henderson and Lt Commander Smythe, Garside. Don't ask me what it's about because I don't know," explained Lt Chalmers.

He led the way upstairs and knocked on the briefing room door. "Enter!" shouted Smythe, and he went in, followed by

Tetley.

Henderson and Smythe stood on one side of the flight briefing table, and Tetley and Chalmers on the other. Henderson spoke up first.

"Garside, I have a proposition I would like to put to you. You are under no obligation to accept. However, I have a feeling you will be very interested. Now, as explained by Sir Robert, I am charged with leading the investigation into the incident at the FOB, and he has given me full authority over all personnel involved, including military personnel and equipment. As you all know, we are not sure who attacked you at the exercise area, despite you providing many enemy bodies for us to check up on. There are many unanswered questions and lots of avenues of investigation to explore, and I need someone who was at the site who can walk us through exactly what happened step by step and who may also notice something that we may have overlooked as unimportant to the investigation. I would like you to join my team and help us find some answers as to exactly what happened, why and by whom. I think you may offer many insights that escape us civvy types.

"Would you be willing to join my team for the duration of the investigation, Garside?"

Tetley looked at Lt Chalmers and then at Lt Commander Smythe, then answered Henderson, "I'm not exactly qualified as an investigator, Mr Henderson. However, I must admit I would like to find out who was responsible for killing our mates and why. If you feel I have something to offer that investigation, then with the permission of my CO, yes, I would like to be involved."

"Very good, Garside," replied Henderson. "I've been invited by your CO to spend the evening here in Yeovilton, so I think we'll start first thing in the morning, say 08:00 hours. Pack a bag with whatever uniform you need for working in the field and some informal civvies, plus any other kit you feel you may need. Bring it along, as you may be gone for some time." Tetley nodded and left the room, going downstairs and back to the crew room. He found Muddy, Hammy and Ginger deep in conversation with Stinker and Knocker.

"What did they want, Tetley?" asked Knocker.

"Henderson wants me to join his investigation into the attack. I agreed, and we leave in the morning. He said to pack some kit as it may be some time before I return," explained Tetley. "Anyway, I'm heading back to the mess. I need to pack, and the walk back will do me some good," he continued. The others decided to call it a night and accompanied him back to the living quarter's side of the base. Knocker said good night, wished Tetley well, told him to keep in touch and headed for the PO's mess. Tetley promised him he would, and with the others, headed for their room in Yeovil block. When they got there, they all changed out of their number one uniforms and into jeans and t-shirts before stretching out on their beds and watching Tetley organise his kit, ready to join Henderson the following morning. He packed two sets of civvies, two sets of combat clothing, boots, trainers, cleaning kit and his shaving bag. When he had finished, he stretched out on his bed and chatted with the lads about the events over the past few days and what may happen in the near future.

Hammy made a brew for everyone. Then they decided to get some shuteye, as it had been an eventful day.

The following morning, the lads were up at six to shower and shave, then they all headed to the galley for breakfast. When they walked in and joined the queue of lads waiting to get fed, the place went silent; everyone stopped eating and stared at the four lads in the queue. There were about fifteen lads and wrens in the queue in front of them, and they all moved to one side, with the lad on the end, telling them to go to the front. Muddy asked him, "What's the score, mate?"

He replied, "You lot are war heroes. Heroes get served first in this galley." They walked to the front of the queue and lifted a plate each from the counter, walked along the line serving themselves with whatever they wanted from the heated buffet trays, then poured themselves brew from one of the urns at the end, found an empty table and sat down. There was a spontaneous round of applause from all the men already seated, and all four of them blushed to their socks. It soon quieted down, and a few lads came over and asked if the rumour was right that Tetley was getting the VC and the others the Military Medal. Muddy nodded in the affirmative, and they congratulated them all and left them in peace to eat their breakfast.

Hammy asked Tetley, "Where is Henderson taking you this morning, Tetley?"

"Not sure, mate, but I assume they have an incident room setup beyond the boundaries of the FOB site, and that is where we are headed," replied Tetley.

"Not sure if I would want to go back to FOB, mate, not with all the bodies still there. Even if they were not there, I'm not sure if I want to return any time soon," said Muddy.

"I know what you mean, Muddy. I'm not one hundred percent sure myself if I want to walk through that place yet. However, I think Henderson is right in that I may spot something out of place that they may have all overlooked. I'll just have to take a deep breath and get on with it," replied Tetley.

The lads ate their breakfast and drank their tea and coffee in silence, then Tetley picked up his bergan and headed out of the galley with the others and headed for the squadron buildings. When they arrived, they went to the crew room as normal until all the squadron personnel on base had reported for duty. PO White came in with his clipboard and assigned all the men to various tasks relating to aircraft maintenance and also getting them fitted out ready to be on fifteen-minute standby. He told Tetley to wait until Henderson came to fetch him. All the lads came and wished Tetley well before they headed for the hangar, and Muddy said, "Watch your back, mate; you can't trust spooks," before slapping him on the back and following the others out.

Henderson arrived with Lt Commander Smythe and Lt Chalmers and asked him if he had everything he needed.

Tetley replied, "Yes, sir," stood up, grabbed his bergan and walked towards them. Smith and Chalmers shook his hand, wished him well and told him to be careful and accompanied them out to the front of the building, where a car was waiting for them. Tetley threw his Bergan in the boot, turned, saluted the officers and got in the back of the car. Henderson shook their hands, then climbed into the front passenger seat and instructed the driver to drive on.

Chapter 9

They were taken to the aircraft they had arrived in the previous night, and they both boarded. The co-pilot showed them to seats in the middle of the aircraft, and Tetley noticed that all the window blinds had been pulled down, making it impossible to see out.

The co-pilot closed the door and asked them to fasten their seat belts before heading for the flight deck. The engines whined; they went through the start-up procedure, and before too long, they were taxiing towards the runway. They turned onto the runway and stopped as the pilot increased thrust before releasing the brakes, and the aircraft shot down the runway and then smoothly into the air. Henderson turned to Tetley and explained, "The blinds are closed on my instructions, as we're heading to a secret location that you currently do not have the required security authorisation to know its whereabouts. When we land, a waiting vehicle will take us to our destination." Tetley nodded his understanding and closed his eyes to relax, thinking, *What have I let myself in for?*

The flight lasted about forty minutes, and the aircraft landed quite steeply and pulled up very quickly. Tetley surmised that the runway must be very short, hence the abrupt landing. The co-pilot appeared from the flight deck and opened the exit door, then deployed the built-in staircase. A Range Rover was waiting for them, with a female driver at the wheel. Tetley threw his bergan in the boot and climbed in the back beside Henderson. The car took off, and about five or six minutes later, they entered a tunnel, and the sound of the engine changed and echoed around them as they drove along. A few minutes later, the car stopped and the driver exited the vehicle. Henderson got out, and Tetley followed, grabbing his bergan from the boot space. The driver led the way to a set of re-enforced steel doors.

Henderson inserted a key card into the slot on a panel he opened on the wall to the side of the doors, and when the doors opened, revealing a lift, the driver, Henderson and Tetley stepped in. Henderson pressed one of the buttons on the panel, and the lift descended for a good few minutes. When it stopped and the doors opened, he was led out and along a corridor with a stone floor, then Henderson opened the first door they came too on his right. Using the key card again, the door opened and he was led inside. The room was a large office that contained a desk and three chairs, two in front and one behind the desk.

"This room is our induction room, Garside; there is some paperwork for you to complete before you can continue further into this facility. You probably think I work for the security service, but you would be wrong. I work for a small government organisation that takes on work from many international partners.

"The paperwork on the desk in front of you contains a copy of the Official Secrets Act, which I know you have already signed as a member of Her Majesty's Royal Navy. However, this copy will give you far greater security clearance. The other documents are a mere formality for this organisation so that we can issue you access cards to this facility and the various rooms it contains.

"Once you have completed these documents, we will move on to a briefing room where I will introduce you to the other members of my small team. I will leave you now to complete the documents. It should not take you any longer than about twenty minutes. When you are happy they are completed, press the buzzer on the desk and I will return and fetch you."

Henderson turned, swiped an ID card on a reader beside the door that unlocked it, and left the room. Tetley went round the desk, sat in the chair and picked up the first document, which was the Official Secrets Act. He read it thoroughly and noticed that he would be getting top secret and highly confidential security clearance if he signed this. He also noticed the penalty for breaching it would be life in prison. He thought for a moment if he was doing the right thing before picking up a pen from the desk and signing it. He waded his way through the other documents, reading and signing them in turn before setting them on the table, then pressed the buzzer.

A few minutes later, Henderson arrived, went to the desk, picked up the documents and examined them. Happy that they had all been signed correctly, he shook Tetley's hand and said, "Welcome to the Foundation, Garside. Do you have any questions at this time?"

"Yes, sir, just one, can you please call me Tetley? Garside is a bit too formal if we are to be working closely together, and this is not a military outfit," replied Tetley.

"I think that can be arranged, Tetley. Remind me to ask you how you came by that nickname at some point," said Henderson, as he swiped his key card to release the door lock and beckoned Tetley to follow him. They continued down a long, wide concrete corridor, wide enough to drive a vehicle down, until they came to the next door on the right side, marked 'briefing room'. Henderson used his ID card to swipe the electronic lock, opened the door and stepped in. Tetley followed him in, and Henderson pointed at a row of comfortable chairs in front of a large screen and told him to sit down.

116

"I'm just waiting for the rest of the team to arrive, and then I will introduce you and provide you with a short overview on our operation here and what progress we have made so far in the investigation. I will then give you the grand tour of our facility and show you where you will be living for the duration of this investigation," explained Henderson.

Tetley sat himself down and set his bergan next to his feet. Just then, the door opened and three men and two women entered the room, all carrying mugs of tea or coffee and made themselves comfortable in the easy chairs.

Henderson asked Tetley to step up to the front and stand beside him, then addressed the others, "I would like to introduce you to AEM Andrew Garside from 845 Naval Air Commando Squadron based out of Yeovilton. He prefers to be called Tetley for some reason, which, I'm sure, will be made clear later. I know you are all familiar with his exploits during the attack on the FOB, from our investigation. However, I've managed to get him to agree to work with us to help find the answers the government is so urgently demanding.

"I think you will all agree he can give us a real perspective of the events of last Friday morning." Henderson looked at the others seated and asked them to stand and introduce themselves when he called their names out.

First was Melanie Rymes. She was about five feet, six inches tall with dark brown, shoulder-length hair. She was dressed in jeans and a long-sleeved top open at the neck.

"Hello, Tetley, I'm Melanie Rymes, and I'm currently the number two in this operation. I was recruited from MI5, where I was a case officer working in Germany."

She sat down and Henderson called Stephen Allen to stand and introduce himself. He was around six feet, six inches tall,

117

wearing jeans and a polo shirt and very athletic-looking. It seemed to Tetley there was not an ounce of fat on his body. "Hi, Tetley, nice to meet you. I'm Stephen Allen. I was recruited from 22 SAS Regiment into this band of merry men and women." Stephen sat down.

Then Henderson called Sam Boscombe to stand and do the honours. He was around six feet tall and muscular, but slight compared with Stephen, but again, there was hardly an ounce of fat on his body. Like Stephen, he wore jeans and a long-sleeved polo shirt.

"Hello, Tetley. I was recruited from the Special Boat Service, and before that, I was a Royal Marine in 42 Commando." He sat down, and Henderson asked Bill Ashton to stand. He was about five feet, six inches tall, skinny to the point of looking anorexic and quite pale, like he had not been out of this bunker for months.

"Hello, Tetley. I'm Bill Ashton, and I am the main data analyst on the team. I was recruited from GCHO to join this operation."

Next up was Anita Keys. She was a small woman, about four feet, five inches tall, with unruly red curly hair.

"Hello, Tetley. I'm Anita Keys, and I am in charge of the IT and comms systems in this facility. I have a small team of four working with me to keep everything running 24/7."

When she sat down, Henderson thanked them all and explained that he was going to show Tetley around the facility, then they would go to the dining hall to eat.

"Anita and Bill," he said. "I would like you both to show Tetley the 3D map of the FOB after we have all eaten later to see if he can offer any insights. Thank you all for your time, you may now go back to whatever you were doing before."

They all got up and left the briefing room, then Henderson

asked Tetley to follow him on the grand tour. Tetley grabbed his bergan and slung it over his shoulder and followed Henderson out into the corridor. They turned right and the first door they came to was the weapons store. Henderson swiped his card and entered, with Tetley close behind. When the door closed, Tetley saw there was an array of weapons stacked in racks along the walls, some of which he recognised and others he had never seen before.

"This is where we store all our weapons for use in the field, Tetley. The store is run by Stephen, and we all have our personal weapons provided along with some other exotics you see racked here for special purposes. We are lucky in that we have access to the latest weapons available, including some that are not on general issue to the military forces yet. Stephen will brief you on weapons use and provide you with a personal weapon; he will also take you through weapon drills in the ranges on the third floor." They went to the other side of the wide corridor, and Henderson opened the first door nearest another lift. "This is the dining hall; I believe you naval types call it a galley. We have a chef and three staff who man this area most hours. They sleep in a bunk room at the back of the kitchens and will be happy to make you some food at any hour when needed." They left the galley, and he pointed at the next door, stating it was the food storage area, but not entering it.

Next up was the comms room. Henderson swiped his card and entered. Anita and her staff were sat at computer workstations typing away, and on the main wall there were a number of large plasma screens displaying what looked like real-time satellite footage of the FOB area. Tetley stopped in his tracks and just stared at the screens. Henderson explained they had access to a number of satellites and drone footage when required, and what he was seeing on the screen was indeed real-time footage. Tetley just looked at him, slightly shocked, and Henderson suddenly said, "I'm sorry, Tetley. I should have warned you before entering this room what would be on the screen. I just realised that this is the first time you've seen footage of the area since the attack. I should have realised."

"It's OK, Mr Henderson. I knew at some stage this would happen, but I presumed it would be on the actual exercise area, not via satellite on a big screen. It just took me by surprise, that's all," replied Tetley.

"Let's move on," said Henderson, heading for the door. "I think I'll show you where the toilet facilities are on this level, and then I'll show you where you can put your kit."

Henderson left the room and turned right, pointing down another corridor. "Down there on the left are the toilet facilities, and further down on the left at the end of the corridor is our conference suite, where we will all be meeting later."

He led the way to a lift, pressed the button and the doors opened. They stepped inside, and Henderson pressed the button for level two and the lift descended to the next floor. When the doors opened, he stepped out with Tetley following and turned right, then left down the first corridor. "This is level two, Tetley, and is taken up with living quarters and a hangar area for helicopters that would use this facility in a time of emergency. There is a large helipad on the surface that can only be located with precise instructions as it is camouflaged. When a helicopter lands on the pad, the lift can be activated from the comms room, from the conference room, or using a handheld remote-control device. A hydraulic lift similar to those used on an aircraft carrier can bring the aircraft into the hangar here on this level for storage. Then the opening is closed by raising the lift, and it is strong enough to withstand a nuclear blast. A secondary door camouflaged to match the area above closes over it. If you follow me over to the far end of this floor, I will show you your room." He led the way down a narrow corridor to a number of rooms lined on each side. As they walked along the corridor, he explained, "You can see each room has a name tag on it for each member of the team, including myself; your room is located at the far end on the left side." Tetley walked along until he saw a door with his name on it and tried to open the door, but it was locked.

"I'm afraid you need an access card to access any room in this facility. This allows us to track who is where, should we need them urgently, or in the event of an emergency," explained Henderson. He used his card to swipe the door open and stepped aside for Tetley to enter first. On the bed was a box containing an ID card with Tetley's photo on it and some more paperwork for him to fill in.

"The card will give you access to all rooms in the facility, Tetley. Please keep it on you at all times, and for God's sake don't lose, it. This is your own private quarters, and only you have access to it. You have an ensuite shower room at the rear, and you have a television, DVD recorder and tea and coffee making facilities for your own use. Just speak to the dining room, staff and they will get you supplies of your preference. There is a common room on the first floor that I'm sure the others will show you later. I think that is enough for now. The level below us houses the weapon ranges and the power room for the facility. You can check that out another time. Make yourself at home, unpack your kit and change into civvies, food will be served in the dining room in about forty minutes. When we have all eaten a good meal, we will head to the conference room, where we have something to show you."

Henderson left the room, and Tetley looked around his new home. There was a large, comfortable double bed, new bedding, a wardrobe, a chest of drawers and a desk and chair. He wandered into the ensuite, and there was a walk-in shower, sink, toilet and hanging space to dry stuff. *This would do indeed,* he thought as he walked back into his bedroom and started to unpack his bergan.

Forty minutes later, Tetley made his way back up to the first-level galley and swiped himself into the large room. There was one large refectory table and chairs at the front, behind that was a help-yourself serving area similar to that on most military bases. Beyond that was the kitchen and food preparation area, where he could see the chef and his team working away. Most of Henderson's team were there already, so he went up to the service area, grabbed a plate and helped himself to a rib steak, chips, mushrooms and onions with a side portion of gravy. He went over to the refectory table and sat in a chair beside Stephen and Sam, facing Melanie and Anita; the only missing people were Henderson and the analyst, Bill. Everyone said hello, and Sam turned and said, "Tetley, mate, you're in for a treat eating in this galley. It's not like pusser's grub, this is more like eating at the Ritz. The chef is fantastic, and he knows how to cook good grub. Enjoy! And by the way, congratulations on being awarded the VC, mate."

The others congratulated him too, and he replied, "I'm not sure I warrant a VC, but thanks anyway, everyone."

There was no urn at the counter. "Where can I get a decent brew around here, Sam?"

Melanie started laughing, and Tetley looked at her and said, "What's so funny, Melanie?"

"It seems you have a story to tell as to why they call you, 'Tetley'. Henderson arranged for Earl Grey tea to be available, especially it seems for you. It's over there on the dresser beside the kettle." Tetley reddened, got up and went over to the dresser. Sure enough, there were four boxes of his favourite brand of Earl Grey tea. He smiled as he opened a box, set the kettle to boil and started making himself a mug of tea.

When he came back to the table and sat down with his brew, Stephen urged him, "Come on, Tetley, tell us the story behind the name."

"Not much to it, really. I was on a run ashore in Singapore when I met the pilot of my aircraft, and he offered to take me to Raffles Hotel. The lads could not get in as they had been pre-warned about our ship coming in, and the lads would be heading there for a taste of a Singapore Sling or three.

"The last time a Royal Navy ship was in port, the bar was wrecked when they ran out of booze to serve the lads, so this time we were all barred except the Ruperts. So, when my pilot offered to get me in, I went along. When we arrived, the visitor's bar was not open yet and the other bar was only open to guests. It would be an hour before the visitor's bar would be open, so we had time to kill. The pilot suggested getting a brew and waiting in the lobby, so I agreed. He ordered Earl Grey and I asked for Tetley tea. The waiter told us he only had green tea or herbal teas, so I went along with the Rupert and had the Earl Grey. Now I'm hooked and carry it with me everywhere I go. The lads are always looking for a way to take the piss, so when they heard the story, they started calling me Tetley, and it stuck," explained Tetley.

The others looked confused when Anita asked, "Why didn't they call you Earl Grey?"

"Royal Navy humour, Anita, because I had asked for Tetley

Tea and they had none in the poshest hotel in Singapore," he expanded.

They all laughed before Stephen said, "All joking aside, Tetley, that was some feat of bravery last Friday and no mistake. I have been in the regiment and been involved in all sorts of shit, but nothing compares to what you did. I, for one, am looking forward to working on this investigation with you, mate."

"Cheers, Stephen! To be honest, I did what I did just to survive. I could see no other options. I mean, can you imagine being bombed the hell out of and waiting for the final enemy mop-up operation sat in a wet and muddy trench with a weapon loaded with blank ammo? Just brings me out in a sweat thinking about it. I had three choices as I saw it; one, run away if I could. Two, sit where I was and wait for the kill shot, or three, do something that might give me a chance to survive. Never underestimate the basic human instinct of survival," said Tetley.

Melanie looked round the table and said, "We are all looking forward to showing you something in the conference room, Tetley, and it has to do with the FOB site, so before we go in there, I want to ask you, are you OK with reliving the details of that day again and again? We will understand if this is asking too much of you so soon after the incident."

"No problem, Melanie, I want to find answers probably more than anyone else in this team. I'm happy to help where I can. I promise if it all gets a bit overwhelming, I will let you know, but I'm here to find out who those fuckers were and who sent them. I owe that to the lads who did not make it home with us," replied Tetley.

When they had all finished eating, they put their plates and mugs in the washing trays, and Melanie led the way to the conference room across the corridor. She swiped the lock on the door with her access card, and everyone else did the same before entering. Stephen reiterated it was for location purposes in case of any emergency. The room was huge with comfortable seats at one end arranged in a semicircle in front of a small podium and behind that, a large cinema-style screen. In the middle was a large electronic table and Henderson and Bill Ashton were stood to one side of it. They all gathered round the table, and Henderson asked Tetley to stand next to him, then went on to explain what was about to happen.

"This is a special bit of kit that we have managed to borrow from GCHQ. It's an electronic 3D rendering table used to replicate anything that has been specifically scanned and mapped by lasers. The computer systems then create a three-dimensional representation of the item or area that has been scanned and it is displayed on this table. For the past eighteen hours, the team has been at the FOB site scanning the area with lasers and that will be displayed here for us all to see in every detail. I must warn you first, Tetley, that this was completed before the bodies were removed from the site, and they will all be displayed here, so prepare yourself. Are you OK to proceed?"

"Yes, sir, I am," he replied.

Henderson nodded to Ashton, and the machine was switched on.

Very soon, a complete replica of the FOB site and the Marines encampment was displayed in amazing detail in front of them. Tetley took it all in before looking up and noticing that the others were all looking at him and not at the display. He looked at each one of them and asked, "I assume, as you're all looking at me, that you have all seen this before? This is amazing technology. I didn't know this sort of kit existed. I assume you all have some questions for me, so please ask away."

Henderson spoke first, "Tetley, if you would, please take us through the events from your perspective." Henderson passed him a pointer that he could use to highlight areas on the display.

"Sure, not a problem," he said. Tetley picked up a laser pointer and ran through the timeline of events again for all the foundation team and finished by explaining, "I organised a search for survivors, sent two guys for help in the bowser to Okehampton, then set up a small security perimeter. We tended to the wounded, although we had little but field dressings, and placed them in the body of the last aircraft as some cover from the elements. Help soon arrived, and I waited until all the wounded and survivors had been loaded on the aircraft before I got a ride back to Yeovilton with the rest of the survivors."

The room was silent, and everyone took turns looking at the display, then at Tetley, then back to the display.

"I tell you what, Tetley," said Melanie. "That is the most comprehensive briefing of any incident I have ever been involved with." Henderson concurred and congratulated Tetley on his bravery and his ingenuity to be able to fight back against all odds. Sam just whistled and slapped Tetley on the back. Stephen came over, shook his hand and said.

"Tetley, mate, you would be welcome at Sterling Lines anytime. Nice work." Bill just looked at him like Muddy had when he said he was going to try and get the live ammo. It said 'You're a crazy bastard, Tetley', without saying anything at all.

"Do we know who the attackers were yet?" Tetley asked Henderson.

Henderson held his hand out and pointed at Melanie, who replied, "We have identified some of the attackers as British Muslim extremists who were actually on a watch list. They had disappeared about six weeks ago, and now they are dead at the

FOB. One other is a Chechen rebel who had been fighting the Russians in Chechnya until he turned up at the FOB; the others we are having difficulty finding out who they are. As for whom they were working for, we are not sure, but Bill is trawling through piles of data from GCHQ, hoping to find some telltale signs of their activity before the incident."

Henderson turned to them all and said, "All the bodies will be removed from the site tomorrow and taken to the morgue at RNAS Yeovilton; when that happens, the cat will be well and truly out of the bag, and you can bet there will be huge political pressure on the PM, then on us to find answers. The attackers' bodies will be removed separately and flown to the morgue at Tidworth Barracks, not too far from here. Work will continue to identify them all and to find out who planned and financed the attack. So far, no one has claimed any responsibility, but you can bet every nut job organisation will take responsibility, once the news gets out there. Let's call it a night and start fresh in the morning; breakfast is at 06:00."

The following morning, they all gathered for breakfast in the galley. Tetley helped himself to a good old-fashioned fry-up and made himself a mug of Earl Grey tea. He sat beside Melanie and tucked into his breakfast. She looked at his plate and then at her own breakfast choice, which was a bowl of muesli and a yogurt with orange juice to drink.

"How can you bring yourself to eat that first thing in the morning?" she asked Tetley.

"Years of experience," he replied. "The first rule you learn when you join the military is to eat and sleep when you can because you don't know when you will get the chance to do so again. A good old fry-up sets you up for the day, not just the

127

morning. Push comes to shove; as long as I get a brew or two throughout the day, I'm sorted and ready for anything. What's the plan for today?"

Melanie nodded across the table at Bill Ashton. "Bill is going to sit in on a morning briefing from GCHQ to see if anything has been picked up on electronic intercepts or other intelligence gathering. I thought the rest of us could go back to the FOB site and collect the weapons the enemy used to see if we can trace their origin, which may give us some other leads to investigate. Henderson is going to London to brief the PM at a COBRA meeting, then he will meet us back here to see if we found anything."

When breakfast was over, they all headed for the large conference room, where the plan was laid out in more detail. Henderson was going to use the aircraft to get to London, so they would have to await its return before they could head for Exeter and onto the FOB by car.

"Why don't we use 845 Squadron for transport to and from the FOB? They are currently on fifteen-minute standby, and the lads will be eager to get involved in some form to help find the mastermind behind the attack on their mates," asked Tetley.

"I'm not sure that's a good idea," replied Henderson. "They are too close to this."

"Of course they are too close to this, and so they should be; they lost a lot of good friends in the attack, but keeping them on the sidelines the whole time will drive them mad. They are front-line troops and need to be used as such, even if all they are doing is taxiing us around from point A to point B. They will feel they are helping find the culprits in some way, and with the aircraft flying, there will be more maintenance to keep them busy." Tetley answered.

"OK, I suppose you're right, Tetley, we do need transport as and when required, and I take your point about helping your squadron's morale. I'll leave the organisation up to you, as you are the naval airman in this team. However, I must insist that they land at the airfield rather than the helipad above us. The security of this facility must be maintained. You can use the comms room to organise the pickups. The aim today is to collect the weapons used in the attack, forensics dusted them for prints and they are awaiting collection at the incident centre at the FOB site. While you are there, feel free to walk around the site with Tetley to get a feel for what happened. Tetley gave us all a blow-by-blow account in great detail, but nothing beats checking the actual scene out to get a real perspective on things. Tetley, if at any time this proves too big an ask, please return to the aircraft and wait for the others to finish up," said Henderson.

With the briefing over, Henderson left to catch his flight to London, and Tetley headed to the comms room to contact his squadron HQ. Anita accompanied Tetley to her workspace in the comms room, stopping at the galley to top up a flask of coffee to keep her going for the morning ahead. When they arrived at the comms room, Anita swiped in and Tetley swiped his card too, as instructed the previous night, so that everyone's location within the complex was known at all times. Anita's staff were already in the room and attending to their jobs at various terminals. She showed Tetley to a secure phone that was linked through GCHQ, where he would be able to contact his squadron HQ.

Chapter 10

Tetley picked up the phone and dialled the number of the flight line office. PO Knocker White answered the phone and was surprised to hear Tetley's voice.

"Hi, Tetley, are you missing us already, mate?" he said.

"You know what it's like, Knocker. I like to check up on you guys to see if you managed to get out of bed in the mornings," replied Tetley.

Knocker laughed down the phone, almost bursting Tetley's eardrum, then he asked, "What do you really want, Tetley?"

"Can you patch me through to the CO's office, Knocker? I might have a little job for you all," answered Tetley.

"No problem, mate, just hang on the line while I transfer you," said Knocker, all excited.

The phone in the CO's office rang and he picked it up. "Lt Commander Smythe, Acting CO, 845 Squadron, how may I help you?" he answered.

"Morning, sir, it's AEM Garside. I am calling from Henderson's HQ, and we need some assistance from the squadron, sir." Tetley explained that they needed an aircraft to get them from a specified location to the FOB site in Dartmoor and to wait around for a bit, then to get them and their cargo back again. Smythe asked for the pickup location, and Tetley gave him the coordinates for the airfield on where he landed the previous evening and asked how long would it take for an aircraft to arrive.

"I would have to task two Merlins, Garside. One for your

party and another rigged as a gunship for security cover due to the current alert status. We could be with you within the hour. Are you sure the coordinates are correct? It seems to be in the middle of Salisbury Plain."

"Yes, sir. The coordinates are correct, and I will have the official tasking document sent to you ASAP," replied Tetley.

"Very good; we will be there on time and, Garside, thank you for getting us in on the investigation."

"You're very welcome, sir," said Tetley and hung up.

That organised, he went to join the others in the conference room and explained the Merlins would be at the airfield within the hour. Stephen explained he would be leading the team with Melanie, second-in-charge. Sam and Tetley would be the only others going to the FOB site. Bill Ashton would continue to work with GCHQ hunting intelligence, and Anita would be manning the comms centre with her team. "I suggest we change into combats for this trip, and when you're sorted, come to the ammo store and I will issue you weapons. We'll be carrying live ammo, so be aware of your weapon drills at all times. Tetley, I have not had the chance to get you onto the range, but as you have been trained in using an SA80, that's what I will issue you for this trip. OK, go get sorted, and I'll meet you at the store," said Stephen.

They all headed to the accommodation on the third level to get changed into their combats and to pick up any other personal kit they needed. Everyone had certain items they all liked to carry in certain situations, and military personnel are no different. Although they are all issued with the same kit from the quartermaster's stores, they usually buy supplemental kit they feel best suits their needs in a particular environment. Tetley always had a tobacco tin that contained a whistle, plasters, cortisone ointments and some dextrose glucose tablets that could be eaten for energy or melted in hot or cold water for a drink. He also carried waterproof matches and a Mini-Maglite torch with spare batteries wrapped in tape so they would not rattle. His favourite bit of kit was the pilot's boots he managed to barter from a good contact in the stores at Yeovilton in exchange for a flight in a Merlin. The boots were made of softer leather than the combat issue boots and more comfortable to wear for long periods of time.

Once he was all sorted, Tetley headed up to the ammo store, where some of the others were already getting issued weapons from Stephen. There were a variety of weapons being issued, but most carried SIG Sauer P226 9mm handguns. In addition to the hand guns, he noticed Sam and Stephen carried Heckler and Koch HK53 rifles and a multitude of magazines strapped to a harness worn over body armour. When his turn came, Stephen gave him a chest harness for his SA80, then handed him the weapon, which he checked was clear, then strapped to the harness. Stephen gave him four mags of live ammo and told him to load the weapon and apply the safety catch once outside the tunnel entrance. "What knife do you want to carry?" asked Stephen.

"No need, mate, I already have one," replied Tetley as he pulled open a flap on his combat trousers to reveal a Fairburn Dagger in a sheath strapped to his leg.

"Nice bit of kit you have there, Tetley. How on earth did you manage to get issued one of those? I wanted one of those in the regiment, and even they could not get hold of them," said Stephen incredulously.

"The mob is about who you know, mate. Bartering is a way of life in the navy," answered Tetley, smiling.

Once everyone had been issued weapons, they made their

way to the lift and the tunnel entrance. It was a fine day, and the four of them blinked from the bright sunshine after coming out of the dark tunnel. Melanie led the way off to the left, where there was a camouflaged area hidden by a deep cut in the landscape. When they got there, there were six four-wheel-drive Range Rovers parked under the cammo nets, hidden from view.

"Nice wheels, better than the old Land Rovers we get issued with," remarked Tetley.

"And more comfortable, too," replied Melanie. They stored their weapons on a rack in the boot of the first Land Rover, and Melanie and Stephen got in the front, leaving Sam and Tetley to get in the back. It did not take too long to get to the airstrip and right on time, two Merlins appeared in the distance, heading towards them. One of the helicopters peeled off and circled the landing strip, providing cover for the Merlin that landed close to the Range Rover. The occupants climbed out of the Rover and went to the rear to retrieve their weapons, then ran to the rear of the Merlin, where the troop ramp had been lowered for them to board. In the back, was the crewman PO Thomas and Tetley's best mate, Muddy. They busied themselves with getting the four seated and strapped in. Thomas spoke to the pilot on the comms headset, and the aircraft took off vertically into the sky. He raised the ramp just enough, so it was horizontal with the floor, then took up position at the rear. Muddy handed each of the four a headset with a boom mike attached and showed them where to plug into the aircraft's comms system.

Once they had plugged in, Muddy pressed a pressel switch on the cable attached to his headset and spoke to them all.

"Welcome aboard Commando Airways; if the aircraft crashes, we're all fucked! If we ditch in the sea, we get to swim home! Emergency exits are at the rear and side doors, and the windows can be kicked out if needed. Sorry, we don't have an inflight menu service. However, as assigned entertainment manager, I can tell a good few sea stories, if you would like." By this time, he was laughing hysterically, and Tetley forced him to release the mic switch.

He then told the others, "This is my best mate, Muddy Waters. He thinks he's a comedian, but in all fairness, he's a good lad to have around in a crisis. He was in the trench with me at the FOB, and he can shoot straight too."

The others all waved to Muddy, who took a bow. The pilot was Lt Commander Smythe, and the co-pilot was Lt Chalmers.

Smythe came over the intercom. "Welcome aboard, everyone. Good to see you again, Garside. Our flight will take about forty minutes, and we have been directed to land close to where the Marines had their camp; from there, it's a short distance to the FOB site. When we land, this aircraft will remain on the ground, ready to return you to Salisbury Plain. Our protective cover will remain airborne, looking for any threats to us on the ground. The ground is controlled at present by Major Barnes Royal Marines, and he has arranged for a driver to meet you when we land and take you to the incident room. Major Barnes will brief you on the current situation at the site. Sit back and enjoy the ride."

They all sat back and relaxed. Tetley and Muddy chatted over the intercom with Tetley, asking how things were back at Yeovilton. Muddy explained that they were all glad of the tasking Tetley had arranged, as they were getting restless, being kept in the dark on the investigation. At least with aircraft in the air, it meant there was more maintenance to be done when they landed, which would keep the lads' heads in the game. Yeovilton was busy as they were providing a base for any troops manning the cordon at the FOB site, as well as tasking Harriers and now the Merlins for support. Muddy was dying to ask Tetley about his new role, but he bit his lip as he did not want to embarrass his mate in front of his new colleagues. He did nod over in the direction of Melanie and winked at Tetley, who just shook his head in exasperation.

Before too long, Smythe came back on the intercom and informed them they were five minutes out and prepare to disembark. The Merlin came in fast and flared at the last minute and touched down gently. They all took off their headsets, grabbed their weapons and headed down the rear ramp to a waiting Land Rover and driver. Melanie climbed in the passenger seat, and the others climbed in the back. Once all were on board, the driver took off for the incident room and Major Barnes. They did not have far to go; about two kilometres before they crested a small rise, and in front of them were a number of Portakabins. Some were joined together, making larger compartments, and others stood alone.

The driver pulled up in front of one, which had Command HQ on a sign outside. The door to the Portakabin opened, and Major Barnes stepped out to welcome them all. He went straight over to Tetley and held out his hand, and Tetley shook it.

"Good to see you again, Garside. I'm just sorry it's under such bad circumstances," he said.

"Good to see you too, Major, said Tetley; we have yet to have that drink. Maybe when all this is over," replied Tetley.

"Sounds like a plan," he answered back.

"I'll introduce you to my new colleagues, Major," continued Tetley, walking over to the others and stopping in front of Stephen. "This is Stephen Allen; he is in charge of our merry band here today."

135

Barnes shook his hand, and then Tetley introduced the others in turn. Barnes shook each of their hands and then invited them into the Command HQ Portakabin. He had an overhead photograph of the FOB area, and he explained that earlier that morning, the bodies of the naval personnel were removed and taken to Yeovilton under the cover of darkness to avoid any press photographers.

"The bodies of the attackers have been taken to Tidworth Barracks. The attackers' weapons have been examined by forensics, and they are secured and guarded in one of the other Portakabins. They are ready for your collection, as and when." Tetley told him they would like to walk the FOB site to see if anything new came to mind. He explained he would also like to take Muddy Waters with him as he was a survivor of the attack and he might notice something others would miss. Barnes and Stephen agreed that would be a good idea, assuming Muddy was up for it. Sam and Stephen said they would accompany Tetley and Muddy but hang back from them so they would not disturb their train of thought. Melanie said she would stay with Major Barnes and arrange for the transfer of the weapons, filling in the necessary paperwork to ensure the chain of evidence was not broken.

Tetley excused himself and went to look for the driver that drove them from the Merlin to the site. He found him standing with a group of other Bootnecks having a brew and a fag break. He went over and asked him if he could have the keys to the Land Rover so he could fetch someone from the aircraft and bring them back. The driver threw the keys to him, and Tetley headed for the Land Rover, climbed in and started the engine. He stuck it in gear and headed back to the Merlin landing site. When he got there, he found the crew all gathered outside the aircraft having a brew from a couple of thermos flasks they had brought with them.

"Hey Tetley," shouted Muddy, "are you all finished at the FOB site already?"

"No, mate! I came back to ask you a favour. Would you be willing to walk the FOB site with me to see if it throws up some hidden clues that we have missed so far? I know it's a lot to ask, mate, but this could help us get the answers we need much sooner. Just say the word if you don't want to do this, mate. I completely understand? Just so you all know, the bodies of all the squadron lads have been removed early this morning under cover of darkness and flown to Yeovilton," replied Tetley.

"Sure, mate," said Muddy. "I will help wherever I can, Tetley."

Chalmers and Smythe looked at each other, and then Smythe asked, "Garside, any chance we could tag along, please? It would help us better understand the situation and also help when we are talking to the other survivors about their experiences. It would also help when we have to speak with the families of the dead, too."

"You can come back with me to the incident room and speak with Melanie Rymes, sir. I am not authorised to make those calls, but she is second-in-command of the investigation, and she is authorised," replied Tetley.

Smythe instructed the crewman to mind the aircraft in their absence and jumped in the passenger seat of the Land Rover. Chalmers and Muddy climbed into the back, and Tetley drove back to the incident room. He handed the keys of the Land Rover to the driver, thanked him and asked him to stick around, then led the others to the incident room in Portakabin. He knocked on the door and Sam Boscombe opened it and invited them in before closing the door again. Tetley went over to Major Barnes and

Melanie, who were in the process of filling out the paperwork for the weapons transfer.

"Sorry to interrupt Melanie, but Lt Commander Smythe, who is currently acting CO of 845 Naval Air Commando Squadron, would like a chat with you," explained Tetley. Melanie stopped what she was doing and followed Tetley over to where the officers were waiting.

Tetley introduced her to the two officers, then Lt Commander Smythe asked her, "Garside explained he and Waters are going for a walk around the FOB site to see if any memories throw up some new clues. I would like to request that Lt Chalmers and I accompany them to give us a better understanding of what happened here so that we can better serve the men that survived and the grieving family members. I know this is a little unorthodox, but seeing the layout of the site would truly help. Garside explained that we would have to get permission from yourself as you are the ranking officer on site."

Melanie looked at Tetley and the others in the Portakabin before she answered, "If you follow all directions from Stephen and Sam here," she gestured towards the two men, "You must not touch anything on the site, and walk where directed; then I can't see you accompanying the men being an issue. You will have to sign some papers here with Major Barnes, so we have documented knowledge of who has been on the site. When that has been completed, then you're ready to go."

"Thank you, Melanie, we truly appreciate your understanding," replied Smythe.

"We'll meet you outside and I'll brief you what we are going to do," explained Tetley as he opened the door of the Portakabin and stepped outside with the others.

It took only a few minutes for the paperwork to be completed by Smythe and Chalmers, then they came out of the Portakabin and joined the others, who were standing in front of a Land Rover.

"Okay, this is what I would like to do," started Tetley. "Muddy and I will walk around the Bootnecks' camp site first. I, for one, would like to see where the mortars were launched from. From there, we will head down the hill and veer off to where Muddy and I were in our trench prior to the start of the attack. My plan is to walk through the route I took to the ammo trailer and back to the trench, then follow on from there with the path we took in the counterattack. I would like all you guys to stay behind us and listen to our conversation as we walk. If you have any questions about what you hear or see, ask us to stop and we will try to answer those questions. Sam, would you, or Stephen, take notes as we go along so we have some documentary evidence we can refer back to later on?"

Everyone nodded their understanding, and Stephen took out a small recording device from one of his pouches and explained he would use that to record the conversation during the walk. Tetley and Muddy headed off the short distance to the Marines Camp site. When they arrived, they had a walk around and found the marks in the ground where six mortars had been placed. Stephen suggested that each of them stood on each particular mortar location and face the FOB site below to get a better perspective of the spread of the launchers and their trajectories. When they were all in place, Muddy turned to Tetley, who was standing on the closest spot to him and said, "Looking from here, mate, the lads didn't stand a chance. The spread of the mortar launchers really covered all angles of the FOB defences. This was a duck shoot, mate."

"I agree, Muddy. Thank fuck we were in those camouflaged

trenches! Even now in full daylight, it is still hard to pin point them from here, never mind the early morning daylight last Friday morning. OK! Let's head down the hill and over to our trench." They started down the slope, then veered off to the left and headed for the three secret trenches they had dug the previous week.

When they got there, Tetley and Muddy jumped down into their trench, then turned to the others, who stood back a little and Tetley said, "As I've explained before to you all, this was our position on the morning before the attack. This was meant to be a double cross on the Bootnecks, who always won the Friday War on these exercises. We had decided this time the navy would come out on top. The plan had been to wait until they attacked the FOB main positions over there, and then we would spring our ambush, turning the tables on them. However, what happened was rain from hell started at 06:45. Stephen, make a note that somehow they knew the plans of the Friday War. They knew we would be in position in the trenches before 07:00, when the attack was planned to take place. How did they know that in advance?"

"Very good point," said Stephen, looking at the others. "We may have a mole in our midst. We need to find out who knew the plans of this exercise and check each of them out," he continued.

Lt Commander Smythe said, "All the squadron officers taking part in the exercise had been briefed along with all the NCOs and men. These exercises are fairly common, taking place three or four times a year and always around the same area. I cannot speak for the Royal Marines, but I'm pretty sure the information will be limited to the training team and the participants."

"We will have to follow up on this query later with Melanie and Henderson," said Sam. Tetley and Muddy got out of the trench and headed over to the track edge where Tetley had taken cover, they stopped and looked around, "Jesus, Tetley, there is very little cover over here, I'm surprised you were not spotted from up the hill," said Sam.

"You have to remember, Sam, it was just daylight; mortars were exploding all around the FOB and the air was thick with acrid smoke from the exploding shells. It seemed about three feet of ditch above me that morning, not the couple of inches it really is," explained Tetley. They moved on towards the aircraft where Tetley's next halt was.

The Merlin was badly damaged, holes and rips all over the skin. The windows were blown out and the undercarriage was leaning to one side where it had been torn away in a blast. Tetley moved on to where the fuel bowser had been parked, and explained to the others this was where he had stopped to gather his breath before heading for the ammo trailer a hundred yards away. He explained, "I crawled under the bowser just here, risky, I know, as shells were landing all around me. This was the only cover available to me. If it took a direct hit, it was game over!"

Muddy looked at Tetley and said, "You mad bastard. The most explosive thing here next to the ammo trailer and you took refuge under it?"

"Look around, Muddy, there was nowhere else to take cover. This was my only option," replied Tetley.

He then started towards the ammo trailer, his destination that morning, and stopped about halfway there. "A shell hit close by and I was thrown about fifteen or twenty feet over there," explained Tetley, then headed in that direction. "Thankfully, other than a few bruises, I was not injured." There was a hollow in the grass and Tetley recognised that this was where he had landed and told the others, "I lay here for a while before I ran to the trailer over there." He pointed and headed over to the trailer. "When I got here, it was locked, so I broke it open with my rifle."

He unhooked his rifle from the sling and demonstrated to the others.

"I took off the blank firing attachment from my rifle and unloaded the blank ammo from my two mags. I then opened a box of ammo and loaded my mags with live rounds. Then I grabbed two boxes of rounds and two boxes of anti-personnel grenades and headed back the way I came." He headed back in the direction he had taken. When he got to the last aircraft, he continued, "I was taking a breather here when the middle aircraft took a direct hit from a mortar shell. I threw myself under the aircraft and tried to dig in with my hands." He crawled under the aircraft to demonstrate to the others, "The damage to this aircraft was done when that shell hit; this cab was torn to shreds by the shrapnel from that explosion. When that died down, I crawled out and headed back to the trackside ditch." He crawled out from under the cab and headed to the ditch. "I caught my breath here, then ran the last bit and dived in on top of Muddy, taking cover in the trench." They walked back over to the trench and they both jumped in again.

"I asked Muddy to sort his own weapon and ammo out, then sent him over to the other lads in trenches two and three and got them to do the same. I instructed him to tell the others that when the enemy came down that hill to finish off the lads in the trenches, I would shout 'NOW' and we would all open up on them.

"When Muddy spotted the enemy coming down the hill towards the FOB main defensive positions, I waited until they had passed us, then I shouted 'NOW' and opened fire on them. The other lads followed my lead.

"After a short while, I climbed out of the trench and shouted for the lads to follow me, and we charged at the enemy, shooting and throwing grenades until they were all dead."

Tetley and Muddy got out of the trench, and Muddy turned to Tetley as they followed their footsteps from the previous Friday and said, "I don't mind telling you, mate, I was shit scared and so were all the other lads. You just leapt out of the trench shooting and waved for us to follow, and blow me if we did follow you. We must all be raving mad."

"It seemed to be the right thing to do, mate. Kill them first before they realised what had happened and regrouped. Anyway, you were like a pig in shit, mate, shooting from the hip and chucking grenades at them like fucking John Wayne," said Tetley.

"Maybe we were more scared of you than them, mate," Muddy said, laughing. The others started laughing too. Sam said, "You sure you were not a master at arms in some other lifetime, Tetley?"

Muddy started crying; he was laughing that much, then he managed to say between sobs, "God forbid, mate." Muddy was laughing so much now that he was gasping for breath. His laugh was infectious and soon they were all laughing, including Tetley. When things died down, Tetley started walking towards where the enemy had been mowed down.

"The thing that puzzles me is that when they attacked coming down the hill, they were all grouped close together. They did not move tactically in any shape or form. They obviously had weapons training, but they had no tactical training of any sort, or so it seemed to me. It made it easier for us when we counterattacked; they were like rabbits caught in headlights. We need to find out who they were, how they knew about the details of the exercise and who financed and sent them here. Their weapons should help us with some of that; they didn't wear gloves, so there should be prints and DNA. The weapons will have serial numbers, so hopefully we can trace their origin and how they came to be in their hands. This place is a mess and will take some cleaning up. I assume all this will be done before the media are allowed anywhere near the place."

Stephen replied, "We can ask Melanie and Henderson when we get back. I can't imagine they will allow any media onto this site while it looks like this. It would be very unfair to the families of the fallen. Let's head back up to the incident room and regroup."

They all walked back up the hill through the Marines' camp and towards the Portakabin Incident room. When they arrived, Smythe turned to Tetley and said, "Thanks for including us on your walk around the FOB site, Garside. It blows my mind what happened and how you managed to salvage something positive out of the carnage. I had been originally tasked to lead this exercise, but I was included in a promotion board hearing at the last minute and the CO took my place. It makes you think how fragile life can be.

"Garside, you deserve the Victoria Cross for what you did here last week; maybe even that is not enough recognition. You have proven yourself a leader of men, and that needs to be addressed somehow. We will return to the aircraft and await your return. Thank you once more."

"Sir, I am a product of how good the Royal Navy trains its men. I have served with this squadron four times now in various hot spots around the world. We were all trained to do these things. We had good weapon instructors, excellent NCOs and officers training us to be first-class engineers, and above all, we developed a great camaraderie which enables us to operate as a team. Without those things in place myself, Muddy and the other

144

survivors would not be here today. It is all our job to ensure that training continues and improves, that lessons be learned from this tragedy so that we can honour the guys who did not return home.

"When we all signed on, we knew that at some point in our careers we would probably be sent into harm's way. That is our job. That is why we train so hard and that is why we will continue onwards. When this investigation is over, the squadron will return to normal operations. New men will fill the billets of the fallen, and life will go on. We joined up despite those things, and men will continue to volunteer for the military. I am just an AEM and am happy with my lot. That will not change either, sir. I am where I belong, fixing aircraft and shooting bad guys."

He shook Smythe's and Chalmers' hands when they were offered and watched as they walked over to the driver who was waiting for them. He turned and headed for the incident room.

When they entered, Melanie looked up from the paperwork she was filling in and asked them, "Did anything pop up during your walk about?"

Stephen answered, "A few questions were raised. Do we know if any prints or DNA were lifted off the weapons?"

"The forensics reports will be sent to our HQ for us to look over when we get back later," she replied. "Tetley noted that they seemed to have weapons training but had no tactical knowledge. They attacked the FOB, grouped closely together. That means these guys did not fight in other military units around the globe before gathering here for this attack. There is a good chance that a lot of these guys are UK natives, and we may be able to track down where they came from."

"What about the weapons? Did they still have the serial numbers on them?" asked Sam.

"Again, the forensics and ballistics reports on the weapons should be sent to us later today; with any luck, they will be waiting for us on our return to HQ," replied Melanie.

"I think we are done here," said Tetley, looking at the others. They all nodded in unison.

"Major Barnes, thank you for your assistance today. We will head back to our HQ and hopefully pick up some small thread we can pull on to move us forwards," said Melanie.

"My pleasure. If there is anything you need, please feel free to contact us here," he replied.

They all gathered their gear and left the Portakabin and headed for the Land Rover, which had returned and was waiting for them outside. Melanie climbed in the front as before and the others all climbed into the back, then they headed for the waiting Merlin. As soon as they arrived at the aircraft and boarded via the rear ramp, Smythe started the engines and when they were fully wound up, he released the rotor brake, getting the blades turning. Once the blades were at maximum rotation, he lifted off and was joined by the accompanying gunship, then started back for the airfield on Salisbury Plain. Everyone slept most of the way back, including Muddy. When they landed and the ramp was lowered, they took off their headsets and made their way off the aircraft to the car they had driven to the airfield. Tetley shook Muddy's hand and told him he would keep him in the loop when he could. The Merlin lifted off, turned and headed back to Yeovilton before they had even got into their car for the short journey back to the bunker.

Chapter 11

They were all tired and hungry, so the journey back to the bunker was silent. When they arrived and had parked the car under the cammo nets and walked down the tunnel, they swiped in to open the lift doors, then after reaching the first level, they headed straight to the ammo store, where Stephen signed their weapons and kit back in and stored it on the racks.

Sam said, "I'm going for something to eat. Anyone care to join me?"

They all nodded and headed for the galley and some well-needed food.

While they were eating, Anita Keys came in and told them there had been a breakthrough. Bill Ashton had found a link between one of the British Muslims and a radical cleric in Bradford. "Henderson is on his way back and should be here within the hour and he wants to hold a briefing in the conference room with everyone," she said.

"Cool," said Sam, "that gives us time for a shower and change into civvies. I suggest you all do the same." Once they had finished their meal, they all headed down to the second-level accommodation to sort themselves out before Henderson returned. Tetley showered and changed into his jeans, sweatshirt and trainers so he would be more comfortable, yet warm enough, in the cold concrete bunker.

It was typical of military accommodation; you were either too hot or freezing cold; rarely was it comfortable. This old bunker was cold; there were air ducts in every space, but only cool air came through. *There seemed to be no heating system in there, but I doubt that,* he thought, this was designed for the VIPs who were worth saving in a nuclear war. They would want to be warm and cosy down here, not freezing to death. When he was sorted and had packed his other kit away, he headed back up to the first-level conference room. He swiped himself in and saw that Anita, Bill and Sam were already there and drinking coffee. Bill told him, "The urn is hot if you want to make yourself a brew, Tetley, Melanie is picking up Henderson at the airfield and Stephen should be here in a moment."

"Cheers, Bill, that's just the ticket," replied Tetley as he wandered over to the hot water urn to make himself a fresh mug of Earl Grey tea.

Just as he was finishing up, Stephen came in the door to the conference room and shouted at Tetley, "Make mine white, mate, with two sugars." Tetley laughed and turned back to make Stephen a brew and then handed it to him. Stephen took a sip of his tea, then made a face and said, "Jesus, mate, what is this shit you've given me?" He sniffed the contents of the cup and said, "Is this that flowery shit you drink?"

Tetley laughed as he told him, "You asked for it; white with two sugars, and that's what I gave you."

The others were laughing now as Stephen said, "I meant a proper brew, not this flower power crap." Just then, the door to the room opened, and in walked Henderson and Melanie.

"Stephen, if you're doing the honours, I'll have coffee black please and tea white with one for Melanie," said Henderson. Everyone just burst out in hysterics as the tables were turned on Stephen, who now had to play mother. He took it all in good cheer and returned to the table and handed the cups to Henderson and

Melanie before going back for his own fresh cup of real tea.

"Right." Henderson started to get everyone's attention. "It seems we are making some progress. Melanie has been going over the forensic and ballistic reports and it seems we are now able to identify all the attackers from the FOB site. Ballistics has also confirmed that the weapons used in the attack were from a shipment sent to Syria from NATO armouries last year and stolen soon after arrival in the country. I have spent the day with MI5 and MI6, they had been working to find these weapons since then, but they just disappeared off the radar. Until now!

"They could also tell me that most of the attackers are linked to a mosque in Bradford famed for having a radical cleric who MI5 suspects is tied to Al-Qaeda. They are planning to raid the mosque tomorrow along with all the homes of the attackers who were living in the UK. The plan is to hit them all at the same time so no one gets a heads up.

"Now, I believe Bill has also found some intelligence. Over to you, Bill."

"Thank you. I've been trawling through some electronic intercepts that GCHQ thought were pertinent to our investigation, and a name keeps coming up in them. The name is William Connors, an Australian citizen, whereabouts unknown at this time."

Tetley interrupted, "I know a Billy Connors who is an Aussie. He was a chief petty officer bomb head on the squadron about eight years ago. If my memory serves me right, he did time in Colchester Military Detention Centre for two years before being dishonourably discharged from the mob. He was sent down for stealing ammo from the ranges, then selling it online. Surely it can't be the same bloke?"

Bill looked at him, then at the others and replied, "It doesn't mention any of that here, Tetley, but it does seem to be a bit of a coincidence."

"I don't believe in coincidences, Bill. Chase this up right away. We may have our first major breakthrough! Melanie, can you get onto MI5 and MI6 to see if they know the whereabouts of this gentleman?" interrupted Henderson.

"Right away," said Melanie as she and Bill left the room and headed to the comms room to make their calls.

"Well done, Tetley. Obviously, the Earl Grey stimulated the little grey cells," Henderson said, smiling at everyone.

"When I knew him, he was an all right bloke. Nobody knows why he started stealing ammo from the ranges, then one day the Reggies came for him and carted him off. We never saw him again after that. We heard he got time at Colchester and was booted out. It sort of blotted the squadron's copybook," replied Tetley.

"Not wanting to seem stupid here," said Melanie, "but what is a bomb head?"

Tetley smiled then said, "A weapons loader and armourer on the squadrons. I'm a mechanic, and we are called Grubbers; electricians are called Greenies, avionics mechanics are called Pinkies, re-fuellers are called Badgers and aircraft movers are called Chockheads. The military has nicknames for everything," answered Tetley.

"How did your trip to the FOB go?" asked Henderson.

Stephen answered, "That place is a mess. I know we saw it on the 3D graphics, but seeing it up close is a different kettle of fish altogether. Tetley and his mate, Muddy, walked us through their movements on the day and, if I am being honest, I have no idea how so many of them survived. The mortars chewed up everything, including the aircraft. Tetley manoeuvred across the site under heavy mortar fire and made it back before launching an attack of his own, killing the enemy. I really don't know how he did it and survived. He certainly earned that VC three times over; the SAS or SBS would love to have an army of Tetleys." They all agreed, and Tetley just stood there and blushed.

"OK, I think that's us for now until we get some more feedback from the intelligence agencies. I think we will call it a night and reconvene at 08:00 here in the morning," announced Henderson. They all wandered out of the room and headed for their own quarters on the second level.

The following morning, over breakfast in the galley, Bill explained to Tetley that the William Connors he had found was in fact the Billy Connors from Tetley's past, and he could be the link to the weapons the attackers had used at the FOB.

"It seems he is a small-time arms dealer and does not seem too fussy who he sells his merchandise to, or where he procures it from in the first instance."

Tetley was surprised. "You would think he would have learnt his lesson first time around. Maybe he likes the money," he said to Bill.

"Hopefully, Melanie will have some more intel when we all meet in the conference room after breakfast," replied Bill.

Sam and Stephen were the last to arrive in the galley along with Henderson, and they helped themselves to a full English with a mug of proper builder's tea, as Stephen called it. Bill gave them the same news he had given Tetley, and Henderson seemed very happy. "Looks like we are on the right track. if we can find Connors, we may be able to find out who was behind this attack and why. We might even find out how they knew the details of the exercise in the first place," he explained.

When they had all eaten their fill of the fried food, they

topped up their mugs with a fresh brew and headed for the conference room to meet with the full team. Anita and Melanie were already there and sitting, having a cup of coffee and chatting away to each other, when the men walked in. They all gathered round the table, and Henderson asked Bill to bring the women up to date on the information he had gotten from GCHQ. He then asked Melanie and Anita if they had found out anything new from MI5 and MI6.

Melanie spoke first, "I have spoken to my colleagues at MI5 and they had a file on Connors that was fairly substantial. It seems Connors got into the arms dealing game soon after he came out of Colchester Military Detention Centre. It seems he buys most of his arms from Eastern Europe and sells them mainly to the Middle East and African nations. He is not fussy about whom he sells to, and it seems even MI5 and MI6 have used him to procure weapons for off-the books black operations. MI6 are also hearing chatter that the attack is being claimed by 'The Janissaries'. They have only heard rumours of this Turkish extremist group, and apparently, they were suspected of attacking an American military convoy in southern Turkey four years ago. However, this has never been verified."

"If this group is Turkish, why would they attack us in the UK? Aren't we allies and both members of NATO?" asked Tetley.

"Technically yes, but the Turkish government is becoming more and more radical in their actions, mainly due to the Turkish President Aagha Akbas pushing for a greater swing to the Muslim world and aligning himself with Iran and Russia. When the UK supported the Kurds in Syria against President Assad and his Russian backers, they prevented Turkey trying to wipe them off the map. We even shot down two of his military aircraft in the process," she explained.

"It seems to me we have our main suspects, Connors, the arms dealer and the Turks, who seem to have motive enough to pull the trigger," said Sam. Henderson had stayed quiet through the briefing, listening to the arguments being put forwards, finally he spoke up.

"I think the first order of business is to locate Connors. The other agencies are raiding the mosque and the homes of the attackers this morning. With any luck, we may have some more information to go on by the end of the day. Melanie, do we have any possible location for Connors?"

"I'm afraid not. His last whereabouts put him in Manchester about two years ago. He slipped through a raid on a warehouse during which four others were arrested and eventually sentenced for terrorist activities. Two of those are in the scrubs in London and the other two in a max security prison on Portland," answered Melanie.

"I think we should split up today. Tetley, you and Sam go to the prison on Portland and question the two imprisoned there. Stephen and I will go to London and interview the two in the scrubs. Melanie, can you pass the details of the prisoners' files to each relevant group? Hopefully, we'll get a lead on Connors. He is the key to solving this case. Stephen and I will use the jet. Tetley, can you call your squadron and rustle up an aircraft for your use?" ordered Henderson.

Given their tasks by Henderson, they all went to organise themselves, and Tetley went to the comms room to contact his squadron again. This time he got the duty line chief, who transferred his call to the Acting CO, Lt Commander Smythe. Tetley explained what he needed and told him authorisation was being faxed to him now. Smythe told him the aircraft would be with him within the hour, and he hung up to go spin up the two alert Merlins.

Tetley went to the accommodation block and knocked on Sam's room door; it opened and Sam invited him in. "Have you ever been inside a prison before, Sam?" Tetley asked. "Never, mate, this is a new experience for me, what about you?"

"No, first for me to Sam. They will send us a car and driver to take us to the prison and return us back to the aircraft when we have finished. We'd better head back to the conference room to read up on the prisoners we have to question. We can grab another brew while we are at it," replied Tetley.

They grabbed their daysacks and headed for the lift to take them to the first level and the conference room. When they exited the lift on the first level, they met Henderson waiting as the doors to the lift opened. "I need to speak with you both before you head off to Portland," he said as they walked in the direction of the conference room. When they had swiped in, they went over to the tea and coffee tray and helped themselves to a brew, then sat down.

"I was thinking, Tetley, we are using your squadron's aircraft on a more regular basis, and I have to admit it's a handy option to be able to call on at short notice. As you know, we have the facilities for housing two aircraft in our own hangars on the first and second level and our own hangar lift similar to that used aboard aircraft carriers. Do you think your squadron would base two Merlins here for the duration of this investigation? It would certainly benefit us greatly. What would we need here to make that happen?" continued Henderson.

"We would need two aircrews consisting of three men per aircraft. One flight of ground crew consisting of five men of different trades, plus a tractor to move the aircraft in the hangars.

If the cabs need major maintenance, they can fly back to Yeovilton. Minor stuff can be done here by the maintenance crew."

"What about the secrecy and security of this base?" asked Tetley.

"Well, you pick the ground crews and Smythe can pick his aircrew. Between you both, you have a wide knowledge of the men on the squadron. They will all be briefed and be required to sign the Official Secrets Act, as you were on arrival here, and their security passes will only let them use certain spaces. We have no other accommodation available, but they can use the third-floor empty space if they bring their own kit. I have a feeling this could become a more permanent arrangement further down the line if this all works out," answered Henderson.

"OK," replied Tetley. "When we've finished up at Portland, we'll fly back to Yeovilton with them and put the proposal to the CO. You may have to involve Captain Standen and Rear Admiral Fleetwood, as they are his direct superior officers at Yeovilton. I doubt he'll agree without their prior agreement."

"Don't worry about that, Tetley. I will clear it with Sir Robert when I'm in London today. Tell Smythe I need them here tonight, if possible, tomorrow morning at the latest. I have a feeling we'll need them sooner rather than later," said Henderson.

Chapter 12

Henderson got up to find Stephen and then headed for the airfield.

Tetley and Sam picked up the files of a prisoner each and started reading, trying to prepare for the face-to-face with the terrorists in Portland. They took about thirty minutes to read the files, then they headed for the airfield to catch their flight. The Merlins were just arriving when they got to the airfield. As before, one stayed aloft on watch while the other landed to pick up Tetley and Sam. The rear ramp lowered and the crewman waved them onto the aircraft. Before they got settled, the cab was in the air and the ramp rose to its horizontal position. Ginger Baker was in the cab this time, and he handed out the headsets so they could communicate with the aircrew. Once Sam and Tetley had got plugged in, Ginger welcomed them aboard and handed them a flask of coffee and two plastic mugs.

Lt Commander Smythe was pilot as before and Chalmers was his co-pilot, and once they got under way, he came on the intercom and asked Tetley why they were heading for the old Portland Naval Air Station.

Tetley looked at Sam, who shook his head as if to say don't tell them, then answered, "We have an important meeting nearby, and this was the closest and quickest method to get there." Sam gave Tetley the thumbs up before Tetley continued, "Sir, we will both be flying back with you to Yeovilton after this, and we would like to have a meeting with you and Lt Chalmers."

"Can you speak now while we are in the air, Garside?" replied Smythe.

"Sorry, sir, no can do; it will have to wait until later," explained Tetley.

The flight to Portland did not take too long, and they soon landed on the old airfield and taxied to the old apron area that Lynx helicopters of the small ship's flights had used when not at sea. The Merlin sentry continued to do racetrack circuits around the area while the other cab shut down. Ginger was there as a ground engineer and sentry while the cab was on the ground. He was armed with his SA80 rifle and patrolled around the aircraft. A car and driver appeared and Ginger stopped and challenged him. It was the car designated to pick up Sam and Tetley, so he waved him past. Sam asked the driver for some ID and once he was happy, they both got in the car, Sam in the front and Tetley in the rear.

Portland Naval Air Station was now closed but was the base for anti-submarine hunting helicopters that operated from the decks on the rear of Royal Navy Frigates and Destroyers. It was sad to see the base in such disrepair and was a reminder of just how small the Royal Navy had become due to cuts year after year.

The peninsula of Portland is only 6 kilometres long and 2.7 kilometres wide and sits just south of the southern seaside town of Weymouth. From the airfield to the prison was just a short drive.

HMP The Verne was a maximum-security facility and housed some of the most dangerous criminals and terrorists caught in the UK. As they drove through the gates into the parking area in front of the main administration building, Tetley was more than a little apprehensive, and looking at how pale Sam was, it looked like this experience was not one he was relishing, either. The driver got out and asked them to follow him to the governor's office.

He explained as they walked that they would have a guard accompany them at all times when on the premises, the only exception being that the guards would remain outside the interview room when they interviewed the inmates. It took nearly twenty minutes to get to the governor's office through a number of security doors, which, when opened for them, had to be closed fully before they could continue to the next one, and so on.

The governor was waiting for them when they entered his office and introduced himself as John Wilson. Tetley just introduced himself as Mr Garside and Sam as Mr Boscombe. The governor said, "It was a very strange request that we received. It came in late last night, close to midnight and was couriered down from the Ministry of Justice. It also stated that I have to give you gentlemen complete co-operation and that no request, no matter how strange, was to be refused. I see you have come to see Jamal Ahmed and Ibrahim Izzari. Both of these gentlemen are incarcerated for terror offences and are both serving full term life sentences. They have both been remanded in solitary confinement with one hour's exercise outdoors in the yard each day. They may exercise at the same time as some other prisoners, but are not allowed to converse. Can I ask why you would like to interview these prisoners?"

"Sorry, Governor Wilson, we cannot discuss that with you or anyone else at this facility. Can you please place each of them in interview rooms close to each other so that Mr Garside and I may step out of the rooms to confer?" requested Sam.

"That can be arranged, Mr Boscombe. If you would like to be seated for a while and have a cup of tea or coffee while we move the prisoners to the interview rooms for you. It should only

158

take about fifteen minutes or so," asked the governor.

Sam and Tetley sat down in front of a coffee table that had a pot of tea and a pot of coffee and helped themselves while the governor organised the prisoner move.

It took closer to forty minutes before the phone rang, and the governor informed them that the prisoners were ready. Four guards accompanied them through the prison to the interview rooms, two leading and two following them. When they got to the interview rooms, Tetley asked one of the guards if there was another empty room nearby. The guard pointed down the corridor to the third door on the right and explained this was a small meeting room for solicitors. Sam and Tetley entered the room and the guards took up positions in the corridor.

"How do you want to play this, Sam?" asked Tetley.

"Well, the key information we need is the whereabouts of Connors. So maybe we ask them about their previous weapons' purchases, who they met, where and when.

"We don't have anything to offer in trade except maybe some contraband goods or maybe a meeting with a family member if we get what we really want. This is not going to be easy; they may not speak at all to us. In fact, that is probably what is going to happen; I have no idea what we can do then," explained Sam.

"If we get to that point in proceedings, I have an idea, but I will need to speak with Henderson first before proceeding," answered Tetley.

"OK," said Sam. "I will take Ahmed and you take Izzari. If after an hour we get no joy, we can swap and see if that changes things. After that, it's down to your call with Henderson."

They left the meeting room and headed for the interview rooms, holding the prisoners. Before they went in, the guards

159

briefed them on using the panic bar should the prisoners get violent. The panic bar was a strip of electronic cable at chest height all around the room; pressing it set off an alarm and flashing red lights outside the interview rooms, to which the guards would react by entering the room.

"I doubt we'll need that. If they try to cause trouble, we can handle it ourselves. Under no circumstances are you to enter the rooms unless we call you in. Understand?" explained Sam.

All the guards looked at each other before nodding their understanding to Sam and Tetley. Tetley opened the door to his designated interview room, and Ibrahim Izzari looked up from the table and straight into Tetley's eyes. Tetley held his stare even when closing the door and walking over and sitting in the chair opposite him. He continued to hold his gaze and stayed silent the whole time until, finally, Ibrahim looked away.

One nil to me, thought Tetley.

Tetley just sat there for almost thirty minutes without saying anything, just looking at straight Ibrahim, not even moving in his chair. Finally, Ibrahim asked, "Why am I here?"

Tetley looked at him and said, "I need some information and I think you can give it to me. You are in this dump being held in solitary confinement with no privileges for a full life term. How many of those years have you done so far? Just four, according to your file.

"Did you know people are now living to well over one hundred years now in the west, thanks to modern medicine? Some experts think the average years people will live will soon be one hundred and twenty years old. Can you imagine that? You're thirty-six years old now, that leaves you with sixty-four miserable years alone in a six-by-six cell with only your own thoughts for company. I think you'll be a raving mad lunatic in

160

ten years. They'll just put on a straitjacket and throw you back in your cell, mate."

"What information do you want?" asked Ibrahim.

"I know you bought a shipment of weapons some years back. Who did you buy them from? Where did you buy them? How did you first contact the arms dealer? Do you still have a way to contact the arms dealer?" replied Tetley.

"That is a lot of questions, my friend. I have never answered any questions the authorities have asked me since my arrest nor since my imprisonment. Believe me, many have tried to make me talk and failed. What makes you think I will answer your questions?" spouted Ibrahim with disgust.

"Well, Ibrahim, you are not my friend, but you have never met anyone like me before. I cannot offer you very much, but in the spirit of trading with you, I can offer you some contraband or even possibly one day per week exercise with another prisoner of your choice where you can converse for an hour. I cannot get you out of solitary, sorry that one's on you. I cannot get you moved to a different prison; again, that one is on you. What do you think?" offered Tetley.

"You do not scare me, friend, I am happy with my lot. I will not betray my kin by trading with you. I will not tell you who we bought our arms from."

Ibrahim was about to continue when Tetley banged on the desk very loudly with both palms of his hands and shouted, "William Connors," straight into Ibrahim's face. Tetley saw a glimmer in Ibrahim's eyes that he recognised the name of the arms dealer, so he said it again, this time even louder, "WILLIAM CONNORS!" Again, there was a flicker of recognition before Ibrahim hid it behind a blank look and stared at the walls in front of him.

161

"How did you contact him, Ibrahim? Where can I find him?" Tetley continued. Ibrahim just looked straight ahead and didn't speak. Tetley went round the desk to him and whispered into his ear, "You should be afraid of me, Ibrahim. I have nothing to lose and am willing to do just about anything to get the answers to my questions."

Tetley kicked Ibrahim's chair over and then went to the nearest wall and pressed the panic bar. The alarm began to ring very loudly in and outside the room as Tetley just circled Ibrahim. Tetley had to shout to be heard over the loud alarm, "See Ibrahim, no guard is coming to save you, it's just you and me. Your life is in my hands and I am free to do whatever I wish. You should be afraid of me, Ibrahim."

Ibrahim was terrified, but still managed to keep his mouth shut. He closed his eyes so he could not see the madman circling him like an eagle waiting to pounce on its prey. Tetley opened the interview room door to see all the guards and Sam gathered outside.

"Shut that bloody alarm off, please someone," he shouted. A guard went to the last room in the corridor and switched off the alarm.

"He knows something all right, but I cannot scare him enough to make him talk. How did you get on, Sam?" asked Tetley.

"Jamal did not say one word the whole time I was in there. I dropped Connors' name into the conversation, but it did not seem to register or I missed it. No point in us swapping prisoners now, mate."

"What about that idea you wanted to pass by Henderson?"

"I think it is something I need to discuss on a secure line, Sam, and I also need the squadron on board to make it happen. I think we can call it a day here, but with a proviso we can return tomorrow morning to see Izzari again. Let's brief the governor and get out of here," said Tetley.

They told the guards they were finished with the prisoners and that they needed to go back to the governor's office. As before, two led the way, with two following behind until they arrived at the governor's office and entered. He was sat behind his desk and did not look very happy.

"What's the idea of setting off the alarms in the interview wing? It has caused chaos. We have locked the prison down and all prisoners have been locked in their cells," he said, exasperated.

"It was just an interview method. Nothing happened to any of us or the prisoners, so calm down. We may be back here tomorrow morning just before first light, so please be here and have Izzari ready," explained Tetley.

"Ready for what?" asked the governor.

"For us," answered Tetley as he left the office with Sam in tow and the guards rushing to catch up. Once out of the prison, the driver took them back to the old naval base and the waiting aircraft. Before they boarded the Merlin, Tetley turned to Sam and said, "I have a busy night ahead of me. I have to convince Henderson of my plan and also get Smythe and the squadron to agree to its application. I could kill a pint now and know just the place. You up for one?"

"Always," said Sam.

They boarded the aircraft, and Smythe had it set for takeoff in no time, then they lifted off and turned in the direction of 'home' Yeovilton. No one spoke on the flight to Yeovilton other than Smythe, Chalmers and the Crewman as they spoke to the tower and guided the helicopter to 'Points West' a taxiway for landing helicopters on the west side of the runway. The Merlin taxied up to the parking apron in front of the squadron HQ and stopped when instructed by the ground crew. The rotors stopped and the engines shut down before everyone on board disembarked and headed for the office space. Some of the lads had gathered to welcome Tetley back to the squadron, and he introduced them to Sam, a bootneck. The lads all shook his hand and welcomed him to Yeovilton, asking Tetley how long they would be here for. "Time enough for a pint and then I have to be back here early tomorrow morning. Anyone up for a pint at the Podymore, say about 21:00?" Tetley asked the lads. They were all up for it and said they would meet him there when their shift finished. Tetley excused Sam and himself and went over to see Smythe, who was signing the Merlin in and completing all the flight documentation.

"Excuse me, sir, is there somewhere I can make a secure call to Mr Henderson? Then, if possible, I would like to meet with you alone to discuss something very important and of the utmost secrecy."

"Very sneaky beaky, Garside." laughed Smythe. "I think the briefing room has a secure phone you could use; then we can meet in the CO's office when you're done. How's that?"

"Perfect, sir, thank you."

Tetley led Sam upstairs to the briefing room and slid across the door sign from 'free' to 'engaged', then closed the door behind them.

Tetley picked up the scrambler phone that allowed private and secure point-to-point calls, assuming each end had a secure scrambler. The comms room at the bunker did. Tetley remembered Anita showing it to him, and she also gave him the number just in case it was needed.

Tetley called the bunker comms room and Melanie answered. He asked her if Henderson was around, and if he was, could he please speak with him urgently. Henderson was in the bunker and it took a few minutes for him to get to the phone in the comms room.

"Tetley, why on earth are you calling me on the scrambler phone?" asked Henderson.

Tetley explained about their visit to Portland Prison that afternoon and then told him about the flicker of recognition Izzari had when he shouted out Connors' name. He also explained how he quickly regained his composure and resumed his silence. "I take it you have a plan to make him talk, Tetley, but are worried I'll not like it?" stated Henderson.

"Yes, sir, I'm afraid so. Let me explain.

"A number of years ago, we were on detachment in Norway and the Norwegians had picked up a spy on the NATO base at Bardufoss. They could not break him, but one of the interrogators had heard of an unorthodox interrogation technique used by the Russians on western spies during the Cold War. This involved taking a prisoner on a so-called transfer flight in a helicopter before first light, then making him sit on the cabin step of the aircraft and asking him questions, slowly ramping up the ferocity of the questions, and finally sticking a hood on him and threatening to throw him out from a great height. It supposedly worked every time," explained Tetley.

"I presume you wish for me to give you permission to use this technique on Izzari?" asked Henderson.

"Yes, sir," replied Tetley.

"I also assume you wish to use an aircraft from 845 Naval Air Commando Squadron?" asked Henderson.

"Yes, sir," replied Tetley.

165

"It is very unorthodox and could, in some circles, be seen as torture. However, considering the current situation and the fact we are very short on other avenues of investigation, I will consent with two provisos. One, you manage to get two aircraft assigned to us for the duration of this investigation along with the aircrews and ground crews as previously discussed and under our terms of entry into the Foundation. Two, the prisoner must come to no harm and will be returned to Portland on completion of your interrogation," finished Henderson.

"I understand, sir, and will comply with both provisos," answered Tetley, then hung up.

"So now all you need to do is persuade Smythe to join our merry band for the duration and convince him to play along with the prisoner interrogation," said Sam.

"That's my next chore, mate," replied Tetley as he headed for the door to the briefing room. Sam followed and changed the slide notice on the door to 'vacant' and then caught up with Tetley outside the CO's office door.

Tetley knocked and Smythe shouted, "Enter." Tetley entered, followed by Sam, who closed the door behind him.

"Everything OK with your scrambled call, Garside?" asked Smythe.

"Fine, sir," replied Tetley, "but now I have a proposition to put to you regarding a flight from the squadron and yourself. Firstly, let me explain what is involved, then you can make your choice. This has all been cleared with the joint chiefs and FONAC. We would like to invite a flight of two Merlins, along with flight crew and ground crew personnel, to join our outfit for the duration of the investigation into the attack at the FOB. They would be based at our HQ which is in a top-secret location, and for such access, you would all have to re-sign a more stringent

166

copy of the official secrets act that contains many more stipulations than the one you have currently signed. We will need a fuel bowser initially, but longer term, probably some fuel bladders and refuelling kit. I am to choose the personnel personally, and the security responsibility stops with me. Henderson is in charge of the unit, and you will be introduced to the others and the reporting line if all is signed and agreed.

"Before you make your decision, I must explain your first mission.

"If you disagree with the mission parameters, then feel free to say 'no' and we will walk away."

"When will you need the aircraft and personnel, Garside?" asked Smythe. "Tonight, for the aircraft and flight crews, but the ground crews and equipment can be picked up after our first mission tomorrow morning. It's better they all arrive at our HQ together, so the briefing and screening can be done in one hit," replied Tetley. "Sounds very cloak and dagger, Garside, can you explain this mission you feel I may not agree to?" asked Smythe.

"What I am about to say is top secret, and only those of us in this room and Henderson know the details; it must stay that way. Do you understand, sir?"

"I do, Garside," replied Smythe, more seriously now.

"We currently have a thin lead on the FOB attack. The mission for tomorrow, if you agree, will be as follows.

"Tomorrow, just before first light, two Merlins will be dispatched to the old Portland Naval Air Station, from which Sam and I will leave to pick up a prisoner from HMP 'The Verne' and return to the waiting aircraft. That is where we were today. We will board your Merlin with the prisoner, and the other will stay at the base along with your rear crewman.

"We will then head out over Portland Bill and the open sea,

then turn and head out over Exmoor. Sam and I will question the prisoner in the rear of the Merlin, and if, as we expect, he will not talk, I will give you a signal, and I would like you to fly as low as possible and bunt over the hedges and trees for about twenty minutes. If the prisoner still refuses to talk, I will put a hood on him and I will ask you again to fly around in an erratic fashion at speed for about ten minutes to disorient him, then take the aircraft up to about three thousand feet and hover. At that point, I will move the prisoner to the rear ramp and sit him on the edge, attach the safety sling and remove his hood. We will continue to question him and put him under duress by threatening to throw him out of the aircraft.

"If he still does not supply us with the information we need, I will hood him again and give you a code word to start flying erratically around again, throwing him off balance with only myself and Sam stopping his fall. You will then, after about ten minutes, hover at about eight feet off the ground. I will remove his safety harness and threaten to throw him out if he does not answer. Hopefully, the will to live will be greater than the fear of his cohorts, and he will give us the info, at which point we will return him scared but unharmed back to prison," finished Tetley.

This was also the first time Sam had heard the plan, as Tetley had only discussed it with Henderson. He looked at Tetley, aghast at the simplicity, yet illegality of his plan. Smythe was also in shock at the revelation of Garside's plan. "You do realise, of course, that this is illegal questioning and against the Geneva Convention, Garside? And you are asking us at the squadron to take part in this illegal act?"

"Firstly, sir, the Geneva Convention does not apply, as the prisoner is a UK citizen and not a member of a foreign nation's armed services. He is a homegrown terrorist that can lead us to those responsible for the deaths of our comrades. Yes! The

168

interrogation is unorthodox, but it is our best chance of getting the information we need at this moment in time. To be frank, this is our only solid lead," explained Tetley.

"If I agree to all of this, who is in command?" asked Smythe.

"I am in charge of this mission and will take full responsibility for all actions. However, if you agree to join us, you will report to Henderson and his chain of command at our unit.

"Are you in?" asked Tetley.

"Firstly, tell me what personnel you will select?" demanded Smythe uneasily. "Yourself and Lt Chalmers, along with Petty Officer Thomas in the *XRAY* Merlin.

You can choose the flight crew of the other aircraft; however, you have to trust these men implicitly," replied Tetley.

"I would choose Lt Peterson, Lt Poulter and PO Stafford for the *ZULU* Merlin Crew. I fully trust these men," answered Smythe.

"For ground crew Petty Officer Knocker White, Muddy Waters, Ginger Baker, Stinker Rankin, Hammy Hamilton and Nobby Clarke, sir," continued Tetley.

"Can I ask why you have chosen these men, Garside?" asked Smythe.

"Well, sir, at the moment, we don't know how the attackers of the FOB got the information on where and when the exercise would be, so we may have an internal leak. All the people I listed are the people I trust the most at the squadron; they are all survivors of the attack and are well motivated to find the culprits," explained Tetley.

Smythe was silent for a long while just thinking things through before he turned to Garside and Sam and said, "OK, we're in! I'll organise the men to be ready when we return tomorrow morning and the aircrews to leave this evening for this mysterious secret base of yours. We can airlift the bowser and tractor and take them with us in the morning when we pick up the men."

"Thank you, sir," replied Tetley. He took out a pen and pad from his chest pocket and wrote down a set of co-ordinates and handed it to Smythe.

"This is where we are going, sir," he said.

Smythe looked at a chart on the wall and matched the coordinates to a position on the chart, then turned to Sam and Tetley and said, "That's in the middle of nowhere, Garside; there's nothing there."

"All will be revealed," replied Sam.

They turned and started to leave the office when Tetley turned back and said to Smythe, "I have invited the lads for a beer at the Podymore at 21:00. You and the flight crews are welcome to join us. Can you get permission to leave the base for a couple of hours, sir?"

"I might take you up on that, Garside. Leave it with me, and I will have a chat with Captain Standen to get clearance to leave the base. I'll encourage the crews to attend; it may be our last for some time," he replied.

Tetley and Sam left the office, and Tetley said, "Let's go get some scran in the galley to line our stomachs for tonight."

"Now that's a good plan, Tetley! You're going to have to get Smythe to drop the Garside shit and call you Tetley, like everyone else, mate. He needs to chill out," replied Sam.

"I will see if I can convince him tonight in the bar after a few beers. On that note, we'd better not overdo it, or we will be very sorry tomorrow when the aircraft is pitching all over the place. Not too many beers tonight, or I might throw myself out of the aircraft to end the misery," said Tetley, laughing.

They headed over to the accommodation side of the base, with Tetley saying hello to lots of people on the way. When they got to the galley, they took their place in the queue and when they got to the front, they had steak and chips with onions, mushrooms and mushy peas. They filled mugs with tea from the urn and found an empty table to sit at. As they were eating, a few lads came over and spoke with Tetley.

"Is there anyone on this base you don't know?" asked Sam.

"I know most of the lads in the fleet air arm, Sam, I've been around the block a few times. The squadrons are like family while you are on them, so everyone knows each other's business and, on the whole, looks out for each other. Of course, you always get the odd dickhead who is just out to cause trouble and will fight with just about anyone who looks at him," answered Tetley.

"I think every service has their share of idiots like that, mate, met too many of them myself. I was gobsmacked when you laid out your plan to Smythe. I did not realise you were such a ruthless bastard," said Sam.

"I'm not really, mate. This is just the only lead we have, and if it takes a little persuasion to get Izzari to talk, then I'm happy to improvise. The only downside is, if he doesn't break, then we're fucked, mate! I knew it would be an issue for Smythe; he is a 'by the book' Rupert, plus he is taking orders from a rating. That must really piss him off. At the end of the day, everyone wants to find the bastards who did this, so he was left with very few options. Join our merry band and be involved in the investigation, or stay at arm's length and wait for news to reach him. Better to know something than to know nothing at all," replied Tetley.

"Now finish up and let me show you a lovely country pub; it's a short walk, but after eating that steak, I could do with the walk to ease it down," he continued. They both finished their food and headed for the main gate.

Chapter 13

It took about twenty minutes to walk to the Podymore down narrow country roads. Tetley pointed out to Sam the admiral's residence as they passed it, and then at the end of the road, the Podymore came into view, just across the junction.

It was a lovely building to look at, and Sam could imagine it being thatched at some time in its past. Tetley opened the red painted door and walked into a small area at the front of the building, he turned left to head towards the small wooden painted bar counter, pulled out a bar stool and sat down.

The barman came over and said, "Hi, Tetley, haven't seen you around for a while, mate, the usual?"

"Please, Brian," said Tetley, and Brian started pouring his pint and Tetley introduced him to Sam.

"Pleased to meet you, Sam, welcome to the Podymore. What would you like to drink?" he asked.

"Carlsberg for me, please, Brian."

Brian poured the Carlsberg for Sam, then set it down in front of him before going back to finish pouring Tetley's Guinness. He set it in front of Tetley and said, "There you go, mate, these are on the house as it's Sam's first visit."

"Cheers, Brian," they both replied, lifting their drinks in toast and taking a long sup. Before long, the others soon arrived and the bar was mobbed. The beer was flowing, but Sam and Tetley refused most of the offers of a pint from the lads.

Muddy came over and spoke with the two of them, "The lads

are grateful, mate, that you got them involved in the investigation and are looking forward to getting stuck in. Two cabs are fully fuelled and ready on the flight line. Is it right you're flying out tonight?" he asked.

"We are, mate! We need the cabs for a mission in the morning, but will be back before lunchtime to pick you all up. Tell the lads to pack some civvies as well, no point dossing around in combats all the time. There will be no booze or runs ashore for however long this takes, mate, so make the most of it tonight, but don't let me down, turning up pissed tomorrow. I have stuck my neck out to get you all involved, so pass the word. Best behaviour," explained Tetley.

"Will do, Tetley. I'll go and have words now before it gets out of hand," replied Muddy.

"I don't know how you do it, Tetley! All the officers and lads on the squadron seem to obey you when you dish out orders," said Sam.

"They are not orders, Sam, just pearls of wisdom. They want to be involved and I am their only way in, so they will play ball," explained Tetley before ordering more beer for them both.

There was a loud cheer as the door opened and Smythe, Chalmers and the other flight crews, along with Knocker White, came in, then approached the bar. Tetley's and Sam's beers were just being set on the counter, and Smythe told Brian he would pay for those and he continued to order for the others.

"I have already asked Muddy to tell the lads not to overdo it tonight. They need to be on their best behaviour tomorrow," Tetley told Smythe.

"Good idea, Garside! They'll probably listen to you more than me, anyway," replied Smythe.

Tetley toasted Smythe before taking a long pull of his

173

Guinness, then he turned to the small group of officers and said, "Can I just ask you all one favour, please? The unit we are joining is relatively casual names wise. They all call me Tetley, like the lads, so could you please call me Tetley instead of Garside? You will all be addressed as 'sir' regardless as befitting your rank, but please call me 'Tetley' or people will get confused with all the names."

"I think we can manage that, Tetley, for the duration of this secondment," replied Smythe.

"Thank you, sir," said Tetley, again raising his glass and toasting Smythe and the other officers. Tetley and Sam had one more pint before they made their excuses to the lads and left, followed by the aircrews.

On the way out, Tetley grabbed Knocker and asked him, "Can you make sure to call it a night in an hour's time? You'll all need to be on your 'A' game tomorrow, Knocker."

"No problem, Tetley. I'll make sure they leave the bar within the hour and get their heads down," replied Knocker.

"Cheers, mate!" said Tetley and walked out the door to catch up with the others. They all walked back to the flight line, and the aircrews went to the briefing room to get weather updates, etc. before coming back down in their flying kit and walking out to the flight line to start the Merlins up. When they were all spooled up and rotors turning, Sam and Tetley climbed aboard Smythe's Merlin and strapped themselves in. On the floor of the cab was all the kit the flight crews would need for their stay at the bunker, including sleeping bags and folding beds. They had also brought comfy pillows too, by the looks of it.

When Tetley had spoken with Henderson earlier that day, they agreed not to use the hangars until the following day, so transport would meet them all to drive them into the bunker complex. It took about forty minutes of flight before they landed and soon after, three Range Rovers and a trailer arrived to pick up the men and their kit. They split up as flight crews and jumped into the Range Rovers after loading their kit into the trailer. Sam took the free front seat, and Smythe, Chalmers, Thomas and Tetley squeezed in the rear for the short drive to the bunker. There was silence as they entered the tunnel leading to the entrance, and Henderson had already opened the large lift doors to allow them entry.

Henderson led the way and showed the crews to the briefing room, where he would explain where they were, their responsibilities as regards secrecy and get them all to fill in the lengthy Official Secrets Act, after reading it first, of course.

Sam and Tetley headed to the conference room to await their arrival. It took an hour and a half before the induction briefing was over and the flight crews came into the conference room accompanied by Henderson. All the Foundation staff had gathered, and Henderson introduced them and explained their backgrounds and their current responsibilities. Melanie brought up the 3D display of the FOB site and walked them through what happened that day, including Tetley's exploits. She then asked Tetley to go over the plan for the morning with the prisoner from Portland prison.

Tetley outlined his plan again; for the flight crews and for some of the others, this was the first time they had heard his intentions. Tetley explained that each part of the flight plan would be executed on his command, and each part had a code letter starting with Alpha.

Stephen spoke when Tetley had finished and exclaimed, "This is some trick to pick up on your travels, Tetley, and you've some balls to carry it out here in the UK."

"I have checked and double checked, this does not breach the Geneva Convention. We are not at war and the prisoner is not an enemy combatant. It is in the grey area for sure, but as long as no harm comes to him, we will be OK," he replied.

Henderson asked Tetley to show the flight crews to their quarters and to give them a tour of the facility on the way.

"Their passes do not give them access to most areas. However, you can show them each room so they have an understanding where things are. They have full access to the exterior doors, lifts, the galley, the restroom and their accommodation quarters. They will be allowed access to this conference room only when requested by myself or Melanie for specific task briefings pertinent to their role in this team," explained Henderson.

Tetley led the men into the galley and told them to grab a brew or something to eat if this was their wish before they started the tour. They all refilled their tea and coffee mugs to take with them. Tetley led them around the facility, starting on the first level, showing them the comms room, weapons store and then the TV and rest room. On the second level he showed them their accommodation, where they each dumped their kit and re-joined Tetley. He took them to the hangar and helipad lift, explaining that where they had landed the night before was directly above them and that there was room for both Merlins, and there was extra space below on level three for a possible third aircraft.

He then took them down to level three, which had the extra hangar space, the main power generation room and the firing ranges. Tetley explained that the lads would camp in the hangar space on this level when they arrived the following day.

"This is some facility, Tetley," said Chalmers. "We've had military exercises on Salisbury Plain so many times, and yet, we didn't know this was here."

"It was originally built during the Cold War in case the Russians sent nukes this way. This was designed as a command-and-control bunker, although Henderson and Melanie have upgraded a lot of the tech to bring it up to date. I'll take you back up to level two, and you can all get yourselves organised in your quarters and then get some kip ready for tomorrow morning's briefing at 04:30 in the conference room, and don't forget to swipe in and out wherever you go in here, as this helps to keep tabs on everyone's whereabouts," replied Tetley.

He led the way up to level two, bade the others goodnight and headed for his own bed. It was a big day for him in the morning and he needed to be as fresh as he could be.

Tetley was up, showered, dressed and in the galley getting a brew and a light breakfast before 03:30. Within fifteen minutes, the galley was packed with the flight crews, and soon after, Sam arrived with Melanie in tow.

"When you're done here, Tetley, can you come to the comms room as I have a prezzie for you?" asked Melanie.

"Sure," said Tetley. "Give me five minutes to finish up here and ask Sam to take the final briefing with the flight crews, and then they can plan their flights on the charts."

Tetley finished his small breakfast, made himself another Earl Grey tea and sat down next to Sam.

"Can you take the briefing, please, mate, and show the pilots where the charts are kept so they can plan their sortie? Melanie wants to give me a prezzie in the comms room," he asked.

"Lucky you," he said with a cheeky grin.

"Here only two minutes and Melanie is giving you presents already. No worries, mate, leave the pilots with me. They are in good hands," said Sam as he got up to leave. He was still

177

chuckling to himself. Tetley headed to the comms room and swiped himself in. Melanie came over and handed him a tiny box.

"This is an Earwig comms piece, and it works with this other small device that is built into your belt. We have added a transmitter and receiver between the layers of your belt. This allows you direct comms with us here in this room and between the other team members if they are on the same frequency. Comms are sent up to a satellite and relayed down to us and vice versa. You can hear very clearly in the earwig, which also houses a small mic. To power it on and off, there is a small pressel switch embedded in your belt buckle. Press once for 'on' and once again for 'off'. To send a distress signal, press and hold the switch for five seconds. We can then map your location and get help to you ASAP. When you are outside the bunker, turn it 'on' and do a comms check with us here. Your call sign is 'Tango' and the call sign for the bunker comms centre is Foxtrot. Each team member has their own call sign. Sam is 'Sierra'. Mine is 'Mike', Stephen is 'Papa', Bill is 'Bravo' and Henderson is 'Hotel'. We have kept the Merlin's calls' signs of '*XRAY*' and '*ZULU*' that you defined in your plan. The pilots have been given our frequency, which changes every week, or sooner if necessary, depending on the security situation."

"Nice bit of kit! Thanks Melanie. I will do a comms check when we are on the surface. How does it work in the noisy environment of an aircraft?" Tetley asked.

"It has noise-cancelling software built in, so there should be no problems, and the listening volume will rise dependent on the ambient noise around you. One last thing before you leave." Melanie turned and picked up what looked like a small remote control for a TV and handed it to Tetley. "This is the controller for the hangar lift system. Press the orange button as you hover

178

above the landing pad, and the camouflage foliage will slide out of the way, revealing the actual landing pad. When the Merlin lands and the rotors have been folded, press the green button and the lift will operate and take you to the first hangar level. If you need the second hangar level, press the green button again and the lift will continue descending. When you're all done, press the red button and hold it down and the lift will rise back to ground level. If you just press it once, it will stop at the second floor. Press the orange button again and the camouflage foliage will cover the pad again," replied Melanie.

"Thanks, Melanie. I'd better get moving, or they'll think I have bailed out," said Tetley, as he headed for the door and swiped out. He ran to the conference room.

Sam had completed his briefing, and the pilots were sorting their flight plans out on their charts.

"Are we set?" asked Tetley. Everyone replied in the affirmative. "Let's get a move on; we need to be at Portland before first light. The vehicles are waiting in the tunnel to take us to the Merlins. Melanie and Stephen will drive us out there and bring the vehicles back under cover when we are gone."

They all swiped out of the conference room and headed for the tunnel and the waiting vehicles. They split between the vehicles on a crew basis; *XRAY* crew in one and *ZULU* crew in the other. As soon as they were in the cars, they set off for the helipad and were dropped off at each aircraft. As planned, Sam and Tetley boarded *XRAY* with Smythe, Chalmers and Thomas, the flight crew. Tetley had earlier arranged for Thomas to bring enough safety harnesses for their needs on this mission before leaving Yeovilton and Thomas had stowed them near the ramp under one of the seats. As they strapped themselves in, the ramp rose to horizontal and as soon as the rotors were running, Smythe announced their departure. It took just under an hour to get to the old naval air station, where both Merlins landed on and shut down. As before, a car was waiting to drive Sam and Tetley to the prison. They were rushed through this time with none of the holdups from their last visit and were taken straight to the governor's office. Governor Wilson was waiting for them and was not in a very good mood.

"This is very inconvenient. I don't know who you gentlemen are, and I probably don't want to either, but interviewing a prisoner at this hour is inhumane. I made a protest to the justice minister and was told in no uncertain terms to give you exactly what you ask, or I could find myself unemployed.

"Exactly what do you want?"

"We want Izzari taken to the same interview room as before; we will ask him some questions politely and if he doesn't answer, we are taking him for a morning out in the fresh air. He will be returned unharmed, as soon as we have finished. Please get him moved to the interview room now and as quickly as you can. Get one of your guards to take us there too," demanded Tetley.

"You cannot remove a prisoner from this prison. This is a high-security facility, and I am responsible for all prisoners here," replied the governor, trying to stand up to the men before him.

"You have a choice. Do as we say, or leave, and we will promote the guard standing outside this room to governor and get him to do your job. You have had your orders from the ministry, so carry them out now," shouted Tetley angrily. The governor knew when he was beaten and picked up the phone to order Izzari taken to the interview room as fast as possible, then opened the door and told the guard to take Sam and Tetley there too, as quickly as he could. He also ordered him to obey the two men

180

with whatever they asked, including removing the prisoner from the prison.

The guard tried to protest, but the governor cut him off, "Do as they wish, they have full authority."

The guard took them by what seemed a much faster route to the interview room, and shortly after, a sleepy Izzari was brought into the room and sat down on one of the chairs at the desk. Sam told the guard to wait outside. When he was gone and the door closed, he nodded to Tetley to ask his questions. Tetley and Sam did not even sit down, which unnerved Izzari somewhat.

"How did you contact Connors, Izzari? Where did you meet to pick up the arms? How did you pay him and where?" Tetley asked in a quick-fire rate.

Izzari looked at them both and replied, "I have already explained I will not answer your questions."

"This is your last chance, Izzari, answer our questions, or you may not live to see this day out. I cannot control my friend here, he wants to kill you in revenge for his comrade's death. I cannot help you; he is in charge, and whatever happens to you is his responsibility," explained Sam.

Izzari just laughed. "We are in a prison in the UK. The UK does not kill prisoners or torture them. They are too soft to play by those kinds of rules. That is why we will win. Our cause is commitment enough for us Jihadis."

Tetley leaned in real close to his face so his nose was touching Izzari's.

"Last chance, Ibrahim, answer my questions or you're a dead man before this morning is over," whispered Tetley. Izzari sat back and said nothing. He just smiled up at the two men in front of him.

"Don't say I didn't warn you, Izzari," said Sam, as he took

some cable tie cuffs out of his pocket and went round behind Izzari and forced him face down across the desk. He then applied the cuffs and tightened them a bit too tight for comfort. Izzari started to shout and protest, but Tetley took a roll of masking tape out of his trouser pocket, ripped off a long strip and wrapped it over Izzari's mouth, shutting him up. He then took out a black hood, so black that when he put it over the now visibly shocked Izzari's head, he knew he would see nothing, not even a shadow. Between them, they each took an arm and lifted Izzari to his feet, then led him to the door. Sam opened the door, and the two guards outside were startled to see the prisoner hooded and cuffed.

"Show us to our car, please," ordered Tetley, and the two guards led off in the direction of the prison exit. Once outside, they shoved Izzari in the back of the vehicle and climbed in beside him, one each side, then ordered the driver to take them back to the aircraft.

When they arrived, they got out of the vehicle and manhandled Izzari out and onto the Merlin. Thomas passed them each a safety harness and a headset with a throat mike, then disembarked the aircraft and headed to the other Merlin to await their return. Tetley and Sam sat Izzari down on the webbing bench seats, then sat down themselves, one either side of Izzari. Tetley spoke into his comms system and said, "Point Alpha."

Smythe and Chalmers got the Merlin started and once the rotors were running it created a lot of noise and vibration that scared Izzari, who did not know where he was or what was going on. Once the cab was in the air, over the sea and away from the Prison Tetley removed the hood from Izzari.

"Welcome to our office, Ibrahim. If you do not answer our questions, this will be the last place you will see," explained Tetley over the comms system in the aircraft.

Izzari was looking around him at his unfamiliar surroundings and looked both scared and worried. Tetley slapped him hard on the back of his head to get him to concentrate on him rather than looking around. The aircraft had reached farmland surrounded by hedges and trees, and Smythe put the nose of the Merlin down and headed for the deck. He pulled up before they crashed into the ground and flew at speed, hugging the contours of the fields, popping up suddenly and down again to hop over hedges and trees that barred his way. Izzari was very uncomfortable with the movement of the Merlin, which was the whole idea, of course. So, Tetley started asking him the same questions again. "Where can we find Connors? Where did you meet him for the arms exchange? How did you contact him? How did you pay him? Did you pay him directly, or did you pay a middleman or bank? If you used a middleman, who is he and where is he? If you used a bank, which bank and where?

Izzari looked blankly at Tetley and Sam and said nothing. So Tetley asked him again and again, slapping his head hard after each question. Still, Izzari did not speak. Tetley looked Izzari straight in the eyes and said, "Time is running out, Ibrahim, if you don't answer our questions, you're a dead man."

Tetley pulled the hood back out of his pocket and put it on Izzari then spoke in the comms system, "Point Bravo."

Smythe and Chalmers took off at speed and flew very erratically, turning sharply one way, then another, climbing, then diving back to the ground. This went on for about ten to fifteen minutes before the Merlin climbed to the agreed altitude of three thousand feet and hovered in place. Tetley and Sam stood up and put on their safety harnesses, then unbuckled Izzari and stood him up.

"The clock is ticking faster now, Ibrahim, you need to start answering our questions," Tetley whispered in his ear over the comms. Sam attached a harness to Izzari, then they both moved him to the rear ramp and sat him down, with his feet dangling over the edge. Tetley slapped him again in the back of his head then spoke to him over the comms, "Can you feel the wind around you now, Ibrahim? There is nothing under your feet but sky."

"Where can we find Connors?" asked Sam from the other side.

"Where did you meet him?" asked Tetley. Izzari was shaking both with the cold and fear, but he still remained silent. Tetley and Sam both stood up and went behind Izzari. Tetley removed the hood and Izzari screamed when he realised where he was and how precarious his position was. He tried to shuffle back on his arse into the cabin, but Tetley and Sam stopped him, pushing him back to the edge again. "I am getting fed up asking now, Ibrahim. I have better things to be doing than wasting my time with you. Answer our questions, or we are going to see if you can fly," shouted Tetley into the comms.

"This is the UK. You will not kill a prisoner; you have to abide by the law," screamed Izzari.

"We answer to no one, Ibrahim. I think you have us confused with the police or prison guards. We can do what we want and there will be no questions asked. Look, I can do this and nobody will stop me."

Tetley moved forwards and pushed Izzari off the ramp.

"Oops, clumsy me," said Tetley, laughing over the comms. "Lucky you had that harness on Ibrahim. Try flapping your arms to see if you can fly. We can call this a practice run," he continued.

Izzari was dangling in the air, trying to get his feet back on the ramp, but the wind spinning him made it impossible. He urinated himself; he was so scared. "Thank God you're out there and not in here, Izzari! I would have had to clean that up," said Sam.

Sam looked at Tetley and nodded, then they pulled him back onto the ramp, sitting him on the edge again. Izzari was hysterical, screaming and crying between gasps for air.

"You have one more chance, Ibrahim. Either answer our questions, or you're for the high dive pal," said Tetley. Izzari was nearly on the edge of breaking so Tetley put the hood back on him and called 'Point Charlie' on the comms. Smythe put the Merlin back into motion, swooping and diving and generally throwing the aircraft in all directions, disorienting Izzari under the hood. Fifteen minutes later, the Merlin stopped abruptly and hovered again.

Tetley held Izzari while Sam removed the safety harness.

"Times up, Ibrahim, this is the last chance saloon." He pushed Izzari right to the point of losing his balance and held him on the aircraft by his sweatshirt collar. "Don't flap too much, mate, I might lose my grip and off you go," said Tetley. Izzari was crying uncontrollably and was doing his best to keep still.

"I bet that prison cell seems like a five-star hotel now, Ibrahim?

"Now we are going to ask you the questions one more time and once only. If you do not answer, off you go." Tetley pushed him in the back and he teetered over the edge, then he pulled him back again to the balance point.

"Where can we find Connors?" asked Tetley slowly and clearly. After a few seconds, Izzari said, "France."

"Where in France?" asked Sam.

"A rural village called Fenioux in the Deux Sevres. He has a factory there making campervans. He also stores his weapons there," answered Izzari.

"Where did you meet for the arms exchange?" asked Tetley.

"In the car park of a supermarket in St. Mere Eglise, close to Cherbourg ferry port. He had them hidden in a camper van built especially in his factory," answered Izzari.

"How did you get past customs at Cherbourg and Portsmouth?" asked Sam.

"He paid off the customs inspectors. He keeps them on his payroll," answered Izzari.

"How and where did you pay him for the arms?" asked Tetley.

"We used a halawadar broker in Rochdale. We paid him, and he contacted a halawadar broker in France, and he made the payment to Connors."

"We need you to provide us with the details of the halawadar in Rochdale," said Sam. Izzari gave him the address and name of the halawadar.

"See, that wasn't so hard, Ibrahim," said Tetley as he and Sam pulled him back into the Merlin and placed him on the seats again, putting the hood back on.

"Point Delta," said Tetley into the comms system. Smythe and Chalmers started the Merlin on its way back to Portland in order to return Izzari back to prison unharmed as promised. Sam looked over at Tetley and gave him the thumbs up on a job well done. When they landed at the old Portland Naval Air Station, they transferred Izzari to a vehicle and accompanied him back to the prison. Back at the interview room, they took off his hood, removed the cuffs and sat him down in a chair. Tetley asked one of the guards to stay with him while they went to the governor's office.

Sam knocked, and they walked straight in. "We have returned your prisoner to the interview room unharmed as promised, although he needs a shower and a change of clothes," explained Tetley.

"Thank you for your co-operation governor," said Sam, and they both turned and left the office, closing the door behind them. The guard on the door took them back to the transport, and they returned to the waiting aircraft. They boarded the Merlin again, and Thomas, the rear crewman, was back in his place in the rear of the helicopter. They strapped in and put on comms headsets.

"Back to Yeovilton, please, sir," asked Tetley over the comms system. The Merlin spun up and, when ready, took off in formation with the other helicopter and headed for Yeovilton.

It took about forty minutes of flight to get there and Tetley slept the whole way. When they parked on the apron in front of the squadron HQ building and the rotors and engines had been shut down, they disembarked and headed for the briefing room. It was empty, so Sam slid the door sign to 'engaged' and closed the door behind them. Tetley and Sam switched on their comms units on their belts and called the bunker comms room and asked the duty comms engineer for Melanie and Henderson.

They were on the line in less than three minutes and Henderson asked, "How did it go, Tetley? Over."

"It worked like a charm. I was a bit worried because he kept his mouth shut right until the end when we dangled him out of the helicopter, then he sang like a canary facing an alley cat! Over," he replied.

"What Intel was he able to provide you with? Over," asked Melanie excitedly.

"Connors is based in France, in a small rural village called Fenioux in the Deux Sevres. He runs a factory there, making camper vans as a cover for his arms dealing. Izzari met Connors in a supermarket car park in St. Mere Eglise for the arms pickup. They had been hidden in compartments in a specially purpose-built camper van. Izzari and friends drove it back to the UK via Cherbourg to Portsmouth. Apparently, Connors has the customs staff on the payroll at each end. Payment was made through a halawadar in Rochdale."

Tetley gave them the name and address of the halawadar.

"This halawadar took payment, and the halawadar in France paid Connors for the weapons. We don't have the name or address of the halawadar in France. Over."

"Great work, Tetley and Sam! When can you get back to the bunker? Over," asked Henderson.

"The squadron crews are getting loaded now, and as soon as they are set, we will be on our way. I imagine about two hours before we arrive. Over," replied Tetley.

"Excellent! We can sift through the Intel until you arrive and plot our next move when you get back. Over," said Henderson.

"Get the kettle on. We won't be long. Out," replied Tetley, signing out.

"Let's see how long the lads will be before we can leave," said Sam, opening the door to the briefing room and changing the sign back to 'vacant'. They headed down the stairs to the flight line office, and Smythe and Peterson were there signing the aircraft paperwork.

"How long before we can leave for our HQ, sir?" asked Tetley?

"About thirty minutes, Tetley, and we will be fully loaded and the lads ready to move. Once the Merlins are in the air, we will hitch on the bowser and a tractor, and off we go. You can go get a brew while the lads get the cabs loaded up. I will send Petty

Officer White to fetch you when we are set."

Tetley and Sam headed to the crew room to get a brew and relax for a few minutes. When they entered, it was empty. Smythe had everyone working to get the two Merlins sorted as fast as possible. Tetley pulled a small self-seal plastic bag from one of his many pockets and took out an Earl Grey tea bag and put it in a mug he took from the rack on the wall.

"Do you ever run out of those things?" asked Sam, laughing.

"Not if I can help it, mate. Always be prepared. That is my motto. What are you having, tea or coffee?" he replied.

"Coffee for me, please, Tetley, no milk or sugar," said Sam. Tetley made the brews, then handed Sam his coffee and they sat down in the comfortable chairs.

"I thought Izzari was going to hold out on us, mate," said Tetley.

"He held out long enough. I thought I was going to throw last week's dinner up a few times when the helicopter was flying low and hard, then popping up over the hedges and straight to the floor again. But when you dangled him out of the cab and let him hang by the harness, he was so terrified he pissed himself. I knew then he would break, but give him his due; he held on longer than I thought he would," replied Sam.

"We got some good intel in the end, though, Sam. Hopefully, we can now catch this bastard and see if he is involved in the planning of the attack," explained Tetley.

"It's complicated now, mate, as the fucker is in France. I doubt the Frenchies will let us play in their backyard. I hope Henderson has some pull over there with the DGSI or in the foreign office, mate," said Sam.

"He has the ear of the PM, so hopefully he can wangle something out so we can go get Connors," replied Tetley.

Chapter 14

The door to the crew room opened and Knocker White came in.

"We're ready, lads, if you want to come and board the Merlin," he said.

Tetley and Sam stood up and rinsed their mugs and put them on the draining board, then followed Knocker out to the waiting Merlins. They boarded *XRAY* as before and strapped in next to the other lads already on board. Air Crewman Thomas gave them comms headsets and they plugged in. The engines and rotors were already turning, so Thomas gave the all clear to Smythe and Chalmers, and they lifted off vertically and hovered about fifteen feet off the ground. Thomas leaned out the rear ramp and lowered the lifting gear from underneath the Merlin until it reached the lads on the ground. One of them used an earthing pole, basically a wooden broom handle with a metal hook on one end and a chain that ran from the hook to the ground. When the mechanic hooked the lifting gear, it earthed the aircraft with the ground so that any static buildup in the aircraft did not discharge itself through the mechanics waiting to hook on the bowser and tractor. Once the lifting gear was earthed, the mechanics hooked up the tractor to *XRAY* and the bowser to *ZULU*.

Thomas gave the 'OK' for Smythe and Chalmers to hover higher until the tractor was in the air. Once they were clear, the aircraft turned and started moving forwards in the direction of Salisbury Plain and the bunker gaining altitude as they flew until they were at the height they required for unimpeded flight.

It took about an hour and a half to get to the area of the bunker; Chalmers informed Tetley they were approaching the co-ordinates they had been give previously.

"Can you drop the tractor and bowser off to the side about fifty feet away from the co-ordinates, please, then hover until I get the lift revealed? When that is done, land the first cab, and the guys in the back can disembark and get the tractor and bowser ready to be moved," said Tetley.

Smythe flew the required distance from the co-ordinates and dropped down slowly under the guidance of Thomas in the rear, until the tractor was on the ground. Thomas then released the hook and the Merlin was free. Smythe flew back to the co-ordinates he had been given and hovered about twenty feet off the ground. Tetley stood up and went to the edge of the ramp where he could look down and took out the remote control he had in a pocket. He pressed the orange button on the controller and the foliage below started moving to reveal a painted letter H for the landing pad. When he was happy the foliage was out of the way, he told Chalmers they could land on the H.

Smythe brought the helicopter down, guided by Thomas, until they landed in the centre of the pad. The rotors and engines shut down, then all the lads disembarked. Tetley told Knocker the lads needed to fold the blades and tail before they could descend into the hangar. Knocker got the lads organised, and it took about fifteen minutes before the Merlin was ready for its descent.

ZULU had landed a short distance away but had not shut down. The lads in that cab were getting ready to fold the blades and tail when it was in the right position and shut down. Tetley pressed the green button on his controller and the lift started to descend to the first level. When it stopped, he pressed it again for the second-level hangar. Once it was stopped, the lads manually pushed the helicopter into the hangar space. When the ramp was clear, he pressed the red button and the lift returned to level one. He pressed red again and it rose to the surface. He went over to the other Merlin and plugged into the comms system, then asked if the lads could drive the bowser, then the tractor onto the lift first.

. Two lads headed over to the vehicles and drove them onto the helipad. Tetley operated the lift and it went down to the first level. Tetley directed the bowser to park on this level and for the driver to wait for his return. He pressed the green button again to reach level two, and he directed the tractor off the lift and asked him to prepare to move the second Merlin when it arrived. He then hit the red button and returned to the surface. This time, he asked the pilot to land on the pad and then the crew to fold the blades and tail. Once he was happy, he pressed the green button until he got to the level two hangar. Once there, he directed the lad on the tractor to move the cab off the lift and showed them where to park it. As soon as the cab was off the lift, Tetley pressed the red button until the lift was on the surface. He then pressed the orange button until the foliage covered the helipad again. He then went to the first level and brought the bowser driver down to level two to re-join his mates.

When he had them all gathered in the hangar, he explained to the lads, "Welcome to the bunker, lads. Level three below us is going to be your home for the foreseeable future, but first though, you have to go through induction and security protocols. So, if you bring your weapons with you, we can check them in with Stephen, who is responsible for all weapons on site. Don't give him any grief, as he is ex-SAS. From there, I will take you to the briefing room where Henderson will explain all to you and issue your security passes. Once completed, Henderson will give you a tour of the complex, then leave you on level three to settle in. Officers and flight crews can go back to your quarters, galley or rest room. OK, lads, follow me to the lift."

The men all gathered their weapons and followed Tetley, who took the first lot up and knocked on the weapons store door. Stephen opened it, and Tetley asked him to store the lads' weapons while he went back for the second lot. He returned a few minutes later with the second group and told them to sign their weapons in with Stephen. When they had all done this, he took them to the briefing room and asked them all to sit down and wait for Henderson to arrive. He then left and went to the conference room, where the others were waiting.

"Welcome back, Tetley. Sam has been telling us about your little adventure," said Henderson.

"Did he tell you how green he looked when the Merlin was flying at speed along the floor?" he replied, laughing and pointing at Sam.

"You bastard," said Sam, laughing.

"The lads are in the briefing room waiting for you, sir," said Tetley.

"Better not keep my audience waiting," he replied as he headed for the door. "Any updates yet?" Tetley asked Melanie.

"Not yet. Henderson and I have been asked to go to London for a meeting later this evening. Hopefully, we will have a possible action plan from there," she replied.

"Well, if there is no news and nobody needs me, I am going for a well-earned kip. If I am needed, you know where I am," said Tetley.

"Me too," said Sam. "A kip sounds just perfect at this moment."

Tetley and Sam swiped themselves out of the conference

room and headed for their quarters and some much-needed sleep.

A couple of hours later, Tetley woke, showered and dressed and headed for the hangar on level three to see how the lads were settling into their new home. The lads had started to get themselves organised, even running lines across the space so they could hang cammo nets for privacy between the bed spaces. Muddy saw Tetley arrive and came over to greet him.

"Some place you have here, mate, we have flown around the plain for many years and never even knew this was here," he said.

"It's some place all right. How did the induction briefing go with Henderson?" Tetley replied.

"Interesting, mate, a lot of paperwork to fill in and these passes we have to swipe for every door we enter or leave. A right pain in the arse, mate," said Muddy.

"It's necessary, Muddy, this is a top-secret gaff, mate. Only the righteous are allowed near the place. Even the helipad is camouflaged so it cannot be seen from the air. Great grub though, the chefs here are the dog's bollocks, mate, much better than navy chefs. Talking of which have any of you eaten yet?" asked Tetley.

"Not yet, mate; sounds like a plan though," replied Muddy.

"Go round up the lads, and we will head to the galley for some scran and a brew," said Tetley. Muddy went around and gathered the men, and they all headed to the lift.

"Don't forget to swipe your ID cards, lads, both here and at the galley entrance," shouted Tetley, and boarded a lift with the first lot. He led them to the galley on the first floor and swiped himself in, making sure the others did the same. They went up to the counter and asked the chef there what was for tea.

"We have rib eye steak, beef wellington, or a thai green curry. All the trimmings, of course, lads. Crème brule, sticky toffee pudding, or a selection of ice creams for dessert and there is plenty of hot water in the urn for tea or coffee. There is a fridge at the back for soft drinks, mineral water, sparkling and still."

"You're right, Tetley, mate, this is great food; what a choice," said Muddy enthusiastically. By the time most of them got their main course, the others arrived and swiped themselves in before heading to the counter. Knocker was in this group and asked the chef the same question and was pleasantly surprised by his answer. Everyone was very happy with the quality of the food and piled it on their plates as only servicemen can. Knocker joined Muddy and Tetley, and soon Hammy and Ginger arrived with full plates and cans of pop to wash it down.

Knocker asked Tetley, "How long do you think we'll be based here in the bunker, mate?"

"No idea, Knocker, I had to fight my corner to get you lads involved, and so far, it's paying off. Henderson is in charge, and I am sure he will keep you up-to-date in the investigation as we move along."

"Did he say anything to you all about it today in the briefing?" asked Tetley.

"He told us that you and Sam had made some progress today, and hopefully the pace will pick up very quickly from here on. He didn't go into details. I assume that is due to 'need to know' and, as usual, we don't need to know," Knocker replied.

"Its security protocol, mate. I'm sure he told you this base is top secret, apparently not even the PM knows this exists. This is Henderson's team and he runs a tight ship. I don't even have the full picture and that is how he plays it. Be thankful we are involved in finding the bastards who killed our mates and not locked down at Yeovilton, twiddling our thumbs. When we are done here, you can either go to the TV room or back to the hangar. I have to go to the conference room to do a bit of work," explained Tetley.

The lads finished their meal and grabbed something to drink before leaving for the TV room, or back to their quarters on level three. Tetley bade them goodnight and headed for the conference room. Sam, Stephen and Bill were there. Anita was in the comms room and Henderson and Melanie had not returned from London yet.

"Any word from London?" asked Tetley.

"Nothing yet, Tetley, and we have no idea when they will return either."

"Who are they meeting in London?" asked Sam.

"Again, no idea. They didn't say before they left," replied Stephen.

"Any other updates from the intel Sam and I got from Izzari?" asked Tetley.

"Not a peep, we assume it is all being hashed out in London now, so until they return, we will just have to be patient," said Stephen.

"Waiting is the worst part of this job, but it goes with the territory," said Sam.

"Tetley, how do you fancy a bit of shooting practice on the range?" asked Stephen.

"I'm up for that, mate, beats sitting here watching paint dry, lead on," replied Tetley. Stephen and Tetley headed for the weapons store and swiped themselves in.

"Now you've never used a pistol before, have you?" asked Stephen.

"No, mate, only the officers get those," replied Tetley.

"Well, we use the Sig Sauer P228 9mm with a thirteen-round magazine and one in the spout. It has no safety catch but requires a stronger pull on the first round. The first round is not always accurate because of that, but after the first round, the touch-sensitive trigger and little to-no-kick make it a very accurate weapon. We use pancake holsters that fit down the waist of your trousers or an underarm sling. The pancake is better for concealment and is what we mostly use," explained Stephen.

He took two weapons from a rack in the rear and a couple of boxes of 9mm ammunition. "Let's head to the range, mate, and try these," said Stephen.

They took the lift to the third level and swiped to enter one of the two indoor firing ranges in the bunker. This range was fifty metres long and had six automated target lanes. Stephen went to the first lane and set the weapons on the counter in front of him.

"Now watch and listen, Tetley, and see how the weapon is stripped and reassembled," said Stephen. He slid the slide back and locked it in place, then removed the magazine. He showed Tetley that the chamber was empty, then let the action slide forwards again. He pulled the slide back a second time, holding the unlocking lever down, and the slide came away from the weapon. He was then able to remove the barrel and then showed Tetley how to remove the firing pin. He set all the component parts in front of him and explained how best to clean and oil all the parts. He explained to Tetley that various grips were available for the weapon and everyone had their preference, and he could choose later after firing which one suited him best. This would then be permanently affixed to his weapon and kept in the store for his use only.

Stephen continued to show Tetley how to reassemble the weapon, then handed it to him and asked him to strip it down. Tetley took the weapon and followed the steps that Stephen had shown him, including presenting the open chamber to prove it was clear, then continuing to strip the weapon down. When

Stephen was happy, he reassembled the weapon fairly quickly.

"You catch on quick, Tetley, that was just about perfect, mate," said Stephen.

"Comes from being a mechanic, mate, anything mechanical we can strip down and rebuild," replied Tetley.

"Let's see how you fare firing the weapon, mate, something tells me this is going to be easy for you after seeing your handiwork at the FOB," said Stephen. He then used a remote on the counter to bring the target in to them and changed it for a fresh one, then pressed the remote to move it back to ten metres. Tetley and Stephen loaded six magazines, then Stephen asked, "OK, mate, load your weapon and fire five rounds at the target, and don't forget you need roughly ten pounds of force for the first round."

They both put on ear defenders and Stephen stood behind Tetley. Tetley loaded the weapon and pulled the slide back to stick a round in the chamber. He then used a two-handed grip, pointing down at the target while standing square to it. He fired the first round; it hit the target a little high. However, the next shot hit the target close to the centre. When he finished his five rounds, he put the weapon on the counter and took off his ear defenders, and turned to Stephen.

"Not bad, Tetley, for a first go, but I have a better stance to show you, it will help with your aim," said Stephen.

Tetley stepped out of the way, and Stephen picked up the weapon.

"If you turn to one side and grasp the weapon by laying your right hand in the palm of your left hand, then grip the weapon with your right and support your right hand with your left, then you'll find that a more stable and more accurate stance," explained Stephen. He stepped back and allowed Tetley to try the new style stance.

"That feels more natural and more stable. I also have a better view of where I am aiming to," said Tetley.

"Great, mate, now finish off the eight rounds in that mag and see how you go," said Stephen. They both put their ear defenders on, and Tetley took aim and fired the eight remaining rounds at the target. When he finished, he sat the weapon on the counter and took off the ear defenders.

"That was much better. I had more control over the weapon and I think I did much better," said Tetley.

"Let's find out, mate," said Stephen as he pressed the remote to bring in the target.

"Wow, Tetley, that was near as damn perfect. A great grouping of shots around the bullseye. Nice shooting, you're a natural," exclaimed Stephen.

"It's a nice weapon to shoot, little or no kickback and not too heavy in your hands. That stance you showed me works so much better," said Tetley.

"It's called the Weaver stance, and like most things, it came from the USA," explained Stephen.

"Now let's change the grips on the weapon and see which ones you prefer," he continued.

Stephen changed the standard grips to moulded soft synthetic ones, then handed it back to Tetley. They continued firing until all the rounds had been expended, then Stephen asked Tetley, "I think I already know, but which grips do you prefer, mate?"

"Definitely the soft-moulded ones, Stephen. So much more comfortable in your hands," replied Tetley.

"Yeah, it's most people's choice. The only downside is that they can perish over time and can become contaminated with cleaning oil and end up a bit brittle. So, you have to take care when cleaning your weapons and change them as soon as they start to degrade. This is now your personal weapon and I'll keep it in the store for your personal use only. If you want to use the range at any time, come and sign it out. Now as it's your personal weapon, let's return to the store and you can clean it before I rack it," he said, laughing.

They picked up all the spent cartridge cases and swiped out of the range and returned to the ammo store on level one. Tetley cleaned his new personal weapon, and then Stephen locked it on the rack with Tetley's name below it. They then swiped out of the ammo store and headed for the conference room. When they had swiped in, Stephen immediately asked Anita if there was any news from Henderson or Melanie in London.

"Nothing yet. It seems their meeting is turning into a marathon. We expected them to be back here before now, and it looks like they will be very late returning. I don't know if that is good or bad news," explained Anita.

"We might as well get our heads down now for the night and see what tomorrow brings," said Tetley, heading for the door and his accommodation.

"Might as well," agreed Stephen, joining him.

Chapter 15

The following morning at 07:00, Tetley was in the galley along with most of the other foundation staff members and some of the 845 Squadron crews when Melanie came in and announced,

"Listen up, everyone. There will be a meeting in the conference room for all foundation staff and Merlin aircrews at 07:30 sharp." She then turned and left the galley, presumably to go back to the conference room.

"Sounds like Henderson and Melanie have an idea what's going on at last, Tetley," said Sam.

"Hopefully it includes us getting our hands on Connors, mate," replied Tetley. "We'll find out soon enough lads," added Stephen. They all finished eating breakfast and then grabbed a fresh brew and headed for the conference room. When they all swiped in, Henderson and Melanie were stood around the large table conferring over something and stopped speaking when the men arrived. Soon after Smythe, Chalmers, Peterson and Poulter arrived and stood at the table opposite the foundation team.

"I am sure you are all wondering what happened during our meeting in London?" began Henderson. "We briefed the PM and then COBRA and the joint chiefs about the intel Tetley and Sam managed to prise out of Ibrahim Izzari. Needless to say, we did not brief them on your methods. At the end of the briefing, they asked me to recommend an action plan. I requested them to get the security services and police to raid the halawadar's premises in Rochdale and to look specifically for the details of the French halawadar's location so we can inform our French colleagues and round him up too. I also recommended going after Connors in France to bring him back to the United Kingdom for interrogation. I explained we could nip in, grab Connors and fly him home before the French even knew what happened.

"The joint chiefs were not happy with this plan, as they would prefer to have the French involved as we're NATO Allies. Sir Robert explained that we would not be happy if they mounted an operation in the UK without asking us first. He had a point. So, I asked them to give me a little time – about four hours – and I would revamp the plan. I called an old friend in Paris and arranged to meet him. Melanie and I flew to Paris last night and we met face-to-face with him in a hotel bar. You know what the French are like; they love to be wined and dined when talking business. When we returned from Paris, COBRA and the joint chiefs reconvened, and I put the revamped plan to them and, after satisfying their many queries, they authorised my plan. The plan is as follows:

"*HMS Ocean* is almost back to the UK from extended exercises with the US Navy. In fact, she is planned to dock in Portsmouth day after tomorrow. I have arranged to borrow *HMS Ocean* for the purposes of our mission, and the French have also agreed to lend their aircraft carrier, *FOCH*, to add authenticity to our cover.

"We will embark on *HMS Ocean* tonight and she will change course and sail for the Bay of Biscay to a position close to the French city of La Rochelle. We will join with the *FOCH*, and for a few days, the ships and crews will operate together while we do our work in the background. Stephen, you and Melanie will leave in roughly two hours to take up residence in a French holiday home on the edge of the target village of Fenioux. You will perform the necessary reconnaissance before we launch our snatch of Connors.

"Sam and Melanie, can you please go and pack the kit you need? The jet will fly you to Poitiers Airport, and a French naval officer will meet you there with a vehicle and allow you through without customs inspecting your baggage.

"Lt Commander Smythe, please ready your aircraft and men for departure to *HMS Ocean* at 17:00. Here are the rendezvous coordinates for the carrier. After we board *HMS Ocean*, the ship will sail at flank speed to get us to the operational area by 06:00 tomorrow morning. I will brief the flight crews once we are on board so that you may prepare the aircraft for the mission. The rest of you grab the kit you need and sign out weapons and ammo from Stephen before he leaves with Melanie. Please go and get ready for departure in the Merlins at 17:00 in the hangar."

They all swiped out of the conference room and left to organise the kit they would need for the mission.

"Henderson has some serious clout, Tetley, who else do you know could borrow two aircraft carriers and one of them not even ours?" asked Sam.

"No one, mate, but he has got us moving in the right direction, and hopefully in a day or so we will have Connors' balls in a vice and he will tell us who is behind the attack," he replied.

"Maybe it was Connors, mate. He is an ex-845 Squadron member and he has a beef with the navy for chucking him out," explained Sam.

"If he was, mate, he is about to be in a world of pain. The lads will tear him apart before we get him home to the UK. If we manage to snatch him, we'd better get him back on dry land as soon as possible, or he may go for a permanent swim in the channel before the ship docks in Portsmouth," said Tetley.

"You've a good point there, Tetley, one to mention to Henderson privately when you get the chance," replied Sam.

"Let's get to the ammo store and pick up our weapons, mate, before Stephen has to close up shop," said Tetley.

When they got to the ammo store, there was a queue of squadron lads picking up their SA80s and ammo. Muddy and Knocker had just picked up their weapons and came over to Tetley and Sam.

"More sea time, mate, and on ocean. It's a fine ship with great grub, plus we get our two cans per day," said Muddy.

"Not on this trip, mate, we are remaining dry until this is all over. You're not just Matelots anymore, mate, you signed on the dotted line to join this sneaky beaky outfit. Different rules apply here, Muddy. Make sure all the lads understand what is expected of them.

"Knocker, the bar is set very high and it's a long fall should anyone fuck up," replied Tetley.

"Will do, Tetley. I will keep the lads in line don't worry, mate," said Knocker. The squadron lads all left for the hangar to prep their kit and get the Merlins ready. That left Sam and Tetley to get their weapons from Stephen. Sam had his Sig Sauer, the same as Tetley, but he also had a Barratt M107 Sniper Rifle with a Barratt Optical Ranging System along with .50 ammo.

"Wow, that is some weapon, mate," exclaimed Tetley.

"Yeah, it is Tetley. It's my personal weapon. I'm trained as a sniper, so this may come in handy where we are going. Stephen has a similar rig and the scope is great for surveillance too," he explained.

Once they had sorted their weapons out, Stephen put his own weapons in a carry case, strapped on his Sig in a pancake holster, locked up the ammo store and went in search of Melanie. He found her in the comms room, talking with Anita and checking her personal comms.

"Are you ready, Melanie?" asked Stephen.

"I'm packed and ready to go. Let's find Henderson to see if there are any last-minute instructions. He was still in the conference room a few minutes ago," she answered.

They left the comms room and headed back to the conference room. When they swiped in, Henderson was still there, talking on the phone. They waited off to one side out of earshot until he finished his call and came over to them.

"OK, now you two are masquerading as a couple of tourists renting a holiday home for a week, so do some local tourist stuff too to add to your cover. There is a bar/restaurant called Café des Belles Fleurs, along with a hairdresser, CUT 46 and a bakery next to the church in the village square. Make yourselves known and eat and drink in the bar. You may get some local information there, and who knows, Connors may also use the bar. Do a complete recce of the factory inside and out if you can. If you spot Connors, follow him to note his movement pattern so we can pick the best location for a snatch. Keep your comms systems on at all times and any dramas, let me know ASAP. I will drive you out to the jet, then return and sort myself for a few days at sea with the navy," explained Henderson.

Stephen and Melanie grabbed their kit and swiped out of the conference room and headed for the tunnel and the vehicles. After Henderson swiped out, a minute or two later, he bumped into Tetley.

"I was just coming to see you," Tetley said. "I need to have a private word before we fly out to the ship."

"Can it wait for thirty minutes? I'm just about to drive

205

Stephen and Melanie out to the jet. I'll meet you back here on my return," replied Henderson, heading off to the tunnel.

Tetley returned to his accommodation and arranged the kit he would need for the mission. He would wear combats on the ship, and he packed a set of civvies just in case for when they got to France. Once he was sorted, he headed back to the conference room and was making himself a mug of Earl Grey tea when the door opened and in walked Henderson. "Coffee for me, please, Tetley, white with two sugars." Tetley made the coffee, then handed it to Henderson and sat down.

"What did you want to talk with me about, Tetley?"

"Well, sir, we have to be careful after we snatch Connors. If the lads on the squadron or the ship's crew think he is responsible for the FOB attack, they may be tempted to take matters into their own hands. I think once we have him on board, we should fly him off as soon as we can to isolate him," explained Tetley.

"I had already factored that into my plan, Tetley, but thank you for realising the risks involved and informing me of your concerns. After the capture, we will land on the *FOCH* and from there to a waiting aircraft that can fly us all directly back to the UK. We'll bring him straight back here, and the squadron Merlins and their crews will remain on *HMS Ocean* for a couple of days until they return to Portsmouth. We then have all the time we need with Connors to question him and get some answers. How does that sound to you?"

"Perfect, sir."

"Good! Now go get the aircraft and everyone organised and get them on the surface ready to leave. I have a couple more calls to make, then I'll join you in the hangar." Tetley got up and left the conference room, stopping at his accommodation to pick up his kit and weapons, then headed for the hangar. He found Lt

Commander Smythe and asked him if they were ready to load up and raise the first Merlin. Smythe told him the Merlins were ready, but to check in with Petty Officer White to see if the kit was stowed on board the helicopter and if the men were set. Knocker was organising the tractor to attach to the first Merlin, ready to drag it to the lift.

"Is everything ready, Knocker?" Tetley asked.

"Yes, mate, we're ready to move the cabs to the lift once it has been lowered to this level."

Tetley returned to the aircraft lift area and pressed the orange button on his controller. It flashed when the foliage was fully open. He then hit the green button and the lift started to descend; it paused on level one, and he pressed the green button again and it continued its journey down to the second hangar level. When the lift halted, Tetley turned and gave the thumbs-up to Knocker, and he got the Merlin moving towards the lift. Once it was on the lift, Tetley told him, "Get all the squadron lads on this Merlin Knocker except yourself and the tractor driver. When the cab is on the surface and the blades and tail have been unfolded, get Peterson to lift off and land out of the way, so we can bring the second cab up. Get Muddy to ready the lads to unfold the blades and tail of the second Merlin." He walked over to Muddy, who was waiting to go up on the lift with the Merlin, and handed him a walkie-talkie.

"Here is a walkie-talkie, mate. Call me when the pad is clear and I can lower the lift," explained Tetley.

The squadron lads got on the lift with the first cab, and Muddy gave Tetley a thumbs up. Tetley pressed the red button and the lift started to rise again, pausing slightly on level one. Pressing the red button again, he took the lift fully to the surface, and the sailors started unfolding the blades and the tail, getting the Merlin ready for flight. Peterson, Poulter and Stafford boarded the Merlin once they had completed their pre-flight inspection and fired it up. When the engines were running and the rotors turning, they lifted off the ground and moved the Merlin sideways about one hundred metres, then landed again, keeping the rotors turning. Muddy gave Tetley the OK on the walkie-talkie, and Tetley brought the lift back down to the second level. Knocker and the tractor driver moved the second Merlin onto the lift, then unhooked the towing arm and stowed the tractor and arm in the corner of the hangar. Henderson appeared with his kit just in time as the remaining crew – Sam, Tetley and Henderson – walked onto the lift. Tetley pressed the red button to take them via the first level to the surface, where the sailors got busy unfolding the blades and the tail of the second Merlin.

When all was done, Smythe, Chalmers and Thomas boarded the Merlin and started it up. Everyone boarded their assigned aircraft, and when Smythe's Merlin XRAY had lifted off, he hovered while Tetley pressed the orange button to close the foliage camouflage over the helipad. When this was done, both aircraft headed for the Atlantic and the rendezvous coordinates with HMS Ocean.

It took almost four hours of flying before Smythe came over the comms and announced he had HMS Ocean in sight. It took a further thirty minutes before they were landing on the deck of the big carrier. When they shut down, they disembarked and folded the blades and tail of each aircraft. The handlers moved the cabs to a lift and manoeuvred the Merlins into the hangar and chained them down so they would not move when the ship lurched in heavy seas. A sub-lieutenant came to meet them and requested Henderson to come and meet with the Captain in his ready room.

"Just let me get my men sorted first," requested Henderson.

He turned to Smythe and said, "I believe your squadron already has four Merlins deployed on this ship. However, I don't wish your men to mix with those crews. I've arranged a separate mess deck for our own use while on board, and that and the galley are where the men will remain when not servicing the aircraft. They must not fraternise with the other squadron members or ship's crew for the duration of this mission. Security on this is above Top Secret. Do you understand?"

"Yes, sir, I completely understand. Do you have the details of the mess deck we are to use, sir?" replied Smythe. Henderson turned to the sub-lieutenant and asked, "Can you show us to our quarters, please?

"Certainly, sir, if you would all follow me, the captain wishes to see you first in his ready room, sir, and afterwards, I will return and show your men to their quarters.

The captain's aide, Sub-Lt Morris, will show you to your quarters on completion of your meeting," replied the sub-lieutenant.

"Very good. Lt Commander Smythe, if you and your men could wait here, the sub-lieutenant will return and show you to your quarters," said Henderson.

"Very good, sir," replied Smythe and returned to his men.

"Tetley and Sam, can you accompany me to the captain's ready room, please?" requested Henderson, then turned to the sub-lieutenant and said, "Lead the way, young man."

The subby led the way through various passages and up ladders until he came to the captain's ready room. He knocked on the door and waited until the captain answered.

"Enter!" Then he opened the door and went in to announce the arrival of the three men. "That is all Sub-Lt Walker. Return to your duties."

"Yes, sir," replied Walker as he left the cabin, closing the door behind him. Henderson introduced himself, then introduced Sam and finally Tetley.

Tetley had been on board before but had never been even close to the skipper, never mind standing in front of him in his ready room. Captain Lewis shook everyone's hand and paused while shaking Tetley's.

"Heard some very spectacular things about you, Garside. Is it true you are to receive the Victoria Cross?" he asked.

Before he had the chance to answer, Henderson spoke, "It's all true, and more besides, captain. I asked Sam and Tetley to join me here, as they are the lynchpins of this whole plan. Sorry, forgive me, captain; we use first names on our unit, not rank," Henderson explained before continuing.

"Without these two men, we would not be standing here today. In effect, although I am the commanding officer of this unit, this is Tetley's mission." Tetley stared at Henderson's remarks, then looked at Sam, who just shrugged his shoulders. Henderson continued, "What time shall we rendezvous with the French Carrier, *FOCH*, captain?"

"Approximately 10:00 tomorrow morning," answered the captain.

"Perfect. We currently have two operatives in place, getting us up-to-date intelligence on the target's movements and location. I am also expecting a Royal Marine Quick Reaction Force to meet this ship very shortly. Have you been informed of their progress, captain?"

"Yes, sir, they are due to land on board within the hour," replied Captain Lewis.

"Tetley, I've arranged for backup should we need it in the form of a QRF commanded by your old friend Major Barnes.

When we insert into France tomorrow under the guise of a joint exercise with the French military, we will fly to a small private grass airfield on the edge of Fontenay le Comte. There is a small aero club there, and Major Barnes will use this as his FOB in the event we need assistance. We will all fly there tomorrow afternoon, and transport will be waiting to take us to the holiday home where Stephen and Melanie are based. From there, using the information they have gathered, we will formulate our final plan to snatch the target.

"The Merlins from 845 Squadron will be our way in and out, and we have purloined a Chinook helicopter for the use of the QRF. The French have kindly arranged transport for us and it will be waiting at the flying club. When we have snatched our target, we will return to the flying club and fly to the French Carrier. 845 Squadron aircraft will return to *HMS Ocean* and remain with the ship until it docks in Portsmouth. That will be in about one week's time, as we have to continue with the subterfuge of a joint exercise. We will return to the UK on a carrier-enabled fixed-wing aircraft launched from the *FOCH*. Captain, I know this is a large imposition we have placed on you after such a long deployment overseas, and we would like to thank you and your crew for your assistance," explained Henderson, outlining the plan.

With the pleasantries finished, Captain Lewis called his young aide to escort them to their mess deck. Rather than take them into the lower decks where the ratings had their quarters, he took them to the wardroom. He led Sam and Tetley to a double bunk officer's mess. Henderson had a room to himself. The subby then showed them where the heads (toilets and showers) were located, then led them to the wardroom galley. He explained they could eat at any hour of the day; the chefs would be happy to oblige. Tetley was stunned; never in his wildest dreams did he ever think he would end up in officer country. Both he and Sam went back to the hangar deck and retrieved their kit, then returned to their quarters in the wardroom and got comfortable.

Once they had stowed their kit, Tetley suggested they go and find the other lads from the squadron. So off they set to find out where they were billeted. They had to ask someone in the ratings galley and he pointed them down two decks to a smaller mess at the stern of the ship. When they arrived, the lads were mostly sitting in the mess square chatting about what was to come and how great it was to be back on board a carrier. Muddy and Hammy spotted them and called them over, "Where's your kit, lads? You need to bring it down here and get yourselves settled in."

"We are not being billeted here, Muddy, and have already moved our kit from the hangar. We just thought we would call by and see that you're all sorted, mate," replied Tetley, grinning.

"If you're not in this mess, where have they put you then? Even Knocker is in here, and he is like a bull at having to doss with the lads and not in the PO's mess," asked Muddy.

"Oh, they've put us in the wardroom, mate. Sam and I are sharing a cabin and Henderson has one to himself," said Tetley with as straight a face as he could manage.

"What the fuck! How have they put you two in the wardroom? Don't they know you're just a rating? The Ruperts in there will throw a hissy fit when they find out you're just a grubber like us, mate," said Muddy.

"No idea, mate, but I think Henderson has a lot to do with it; even the skipper deferred to him when we met a while ago," answered Tetley.

"You met the skipper? Where?" asked Knocker.

"In his ready room, Knocker," replied Tetley.

"Well, fuck me, I've been reduced to kipping with this bunch and you get upgraded to the wardroom. What have I ever done to deserve this?" whinged Knocker.

"Sorry, Knocker, not our doing. Henderson arranged it for security purposes. You will be joined by a load of Bootnecks soon too, lads, as Henderson arranged for Major Barnes and his QRF to back us up just in case," explained Tetley.

"That's all we need in the mess, a bunch of flaming Bootnecks cluttering up the place," remarked Ginger.

"Don't worry, Ginger," said Hammy. "They'll spend most of their time queuing outside the ice cream store, waiting for it to open." The mess erupted into howls of laughter as all the lads laughed at Hammy's joke. Marines on board ships were known to get lost and tended to queue behind any group of matelots standing in the gangways.

"We're off for some posh scran, so we'll catch up with you tomorrow in the hangar," said Tetley.

"Yeah, fuck off you Ruperts! Don't forget to stick your pinkie out when you're drinking that flowery tea of yours, or you'll be caught out as the imposters you are," replied Muddy, setting the lads off into hysterics again.

"Jesus!" said Tetley to Sam. "That's them without their beer ration. Can you imagine if they'd been drinking? I don't think we'd have got out of there in one piece."

They made their way back to the wardroom and found the galley. It was all laid with place settings and tablecloths. They didn't know where to sit. A steward appeared and asked them if they were eating or just having tea or coffee. "Eating, please," replied Sam.

The steward showed them to a table and passed them a

menu. "Take your time and let me know your choice, gentlemen. Can I get you something to drink while you choose?"

"Earl Grey tea, if you have it, please," replied Tetley.

"Coffee for me, please," replied Sam. The steward left to fetch their order, and they looked through the menu.

"How the other half live, mate!" said Tetley.

"I know it's criminal, mate! This is my first time in a wardroom too," replied Sam. The steward returned with their drinks, then he took their food order and disappeared again. A few minutes later, Henderson walked in and was about to join them when a steward appeared out of nowhere and asked him if he was eating or just having tea. He pointed to Tetley and Sam and explained he would join them to eat and could he have a pot of coffee first. The steward disappeared behind the scenes again, and Henderson came over and sat down.

"Believe it or not, this is my first time on a naval vessel; the closest to sea I have been before is on a cross-channel ferry. This ship is huge. I got lost twice just coming here. I fear you may have to show me back to my cabin after dinner," he said, laughing.

"How come we are billeted in the wardroom and not with the other lads?" asked Tetley.

"You can thank Captain Lewis for that. He arranged it all. I assume that as we managed to delay his ship's return to port and divert it down here for our own operation, he assumed we deserved the red carpet treatment. Don't argue, enjoy the experience," he replied.

The steward appeared and brought a pot of coffee for Henderson and poured it for him. He then took his food order and left them alone again. Just as they were being served, a number of officers arrived in the mess and were soon seated at a couple of tables, and a number of stewards hovered around them taking orders. It soon became obvious that Henderson, Sam and Tetley were the object of their conversations. Tetley looked at himself and Sam, who were still wearing combats, and Henderson, who was dressed in casual civvies.

"We stick out like sore thumbs. All the officers are in mess rig and we look like we have just climbed out of a trench on Dartmoor," remarked Tetley.

"We have no options, mate. We travel light in our line of work. Anyway, they will just be saying we are the bastards who stopped the ship returning to home port and wondering who the hell we are," replied Sam.

"Quite!" said Henderson.

When they had finished their meal, they left the wardroom and took Henderson with them back to their cabins. Tetley stripped, grabbed his washbag and towel and headed for the heads to freshen up before getting his head down for the night. When he returned to his cabin, Sam went off to do the same.

At 07:00 the following morning, they dressed in civvies and headed to the wardroom for breakfast, stopping along the way to pick up Henderson so he did not get lost again. When they entered the wardroom, it was almost full, and the conversation hushed to almost silence as a steward showed them to a table and took their orders. "This must be what it is like to be one of those Hollywood film stars when they walk into a restaurant." laughed Sam. This made Henderson and Tetley chuckle too. A moment later Major Barnes came in, and when he spotted them, he informed the steward what he wanted and headed their way.

"Good morning, gentlemen. How are you all faring?"

"Very well, thank you, Major Barnes. Please join us," replied Henderson.

Major Barnes sat down and explained they had flown in from Yeovilton with his men the previous evening.

"Thank you for joining us on this mission, Major Barnes. We will rendezvous with the *FOCH* at around 10:00 hours and we will get ourselves organised to fly off to the FOB at 14:30. Tetley will brief the flight crews in the squadron ready room at 12:00 hours if you would like to join us, Major. There will be a final briefing once we get established at the FOB, and I will explain your role in the operation then. Make sure all your men get a good lunch, as I am not completely sure of the exact timings of how long we will be away. A lot depends on our target's movements," explained Henderson.

"Happy to be part of it, Mr Henderson, and it will keep my men on their toes," replied Barnes.

The steward appeared and served the men their breakfast; all had chosen a full English. When they had finished, Tetley told Sam he was going to the hangar deck to catch up with his mates from the squadron. Sam headed back to his cabin and stripped down his weapons and set about cleaning and oiling them for whatever lay ahead. When Tetley got to the hangar, it was full of Merlins and a few Lynxes. He spotted Knocker over at one of the squadron's cabs, filling in some paperwork.

"How's it hanging, Knocker? Any issues with the cabs?" asked Tetley.

"Morning, Tetley. Nothing wrong with the cabs, mate, just catching up with some paperwork. How is life in the wardroom?"

"Honest to God, Knocker, those officers live like kings. They even get served in the wardroom galley by the stewards. How the other half lives. I prefer the ratings galley any day of the week, so you can shove all that ponsey shit up your arse," Tetley replied.

Knocker just laughed at him, "Do you know what's happening, mate, what's the plan?"

"All I can tell you, mate, is that we are flying off at 14:30 this afternoon for a destination I can't divulge at the moment. I'm sure Smythe will brief you all after he has been briefed by Henderson. Just make sure the cabs are in great shape before we fly off and the lads are ready. Keep them on their 'A-Game', mate, this is serious shit," explained Tetley.

"Thanks for the heads up, Tetley. Don't worry about the lads. I'll make sure they know the score before we fly off," replied Knocker.

Tetley slapped him on his back and headed for his cabin. When he got there, Sam was just rebuilding his Barratt Sniper Rifle. When he finished, he put it gently back in its carry case.

"Not long now until the briefing, Sam. Should we make our way to the squadron ready room?" asked Tetley.

"Yeah, and we'd better pick Henderson up on the way. He'll never find it and get back here without getting lost," he replied.

They knocked on Henderson's cabin door; he opened it and said, "Thanks for picking me up. This ship is too confusing to find your way around."

Tetley explained how it was done and that every deck and bulkhead had a number, and that was how you navigated around the ship. Sometimes you had to go up then down again to continue, and sometimes the other way around. Not many passages went from the front of the ship to the rear. This was for firefighting reasons and made dealing with battle damage easier, as you could seal off each bulkhead. This stopped fire from spreading and other areas of the ship flooding. It was all lost-on Henderson, who just followed them to the ready room.

Chapter 16

All the flight crews were there, along with Major Barnes, the flight deck officer, and the flying control officer from the ship's company.

Henderson had asked Tetley to take the briefing, as he knew more about flight operations on a carrier than he did. Tetley stood on the small raised section of the deck at the front of the room, facing the men.

"Good afternoon, gentlemen. We will be departing the ship this afternoon at 14:30 hours. The ship will be turned into the wind for flight operations at 13:30 hours. The Merlins will be spotted on spots five and six on the flight deck at 14:00, then loaded and pre-flighted, ready for departure. The Chinook for the QRF is already on deck at spot nine. Major Barnes and his team will be ready to board with their kit at 14:00."

Tetley pressed a button on a remote on the lectern and a chart of their operational area appeared on the screen. Using a laser pointer, he pointed out on the chart the position of the Flying Club.

"This Flying Club will be our FOB. We have permission to use the club building as our HQ. You will find the necessary coordinates in your flight packs after the briefing."

He used the laser pointer to point out the Village of Fenioux.

"This is our target's last known location. He runs a small campervan factory as cover for his arms-dealing business. He builds the vans to order, and this is how the weapons are shipped to his clients around Europe. We currently have two assets embedded in the village, gathering intelligence before we arrive. They are based out of a French holiday home in this small hamlet at the edge of the village. When we get to the Flying Club, all aircraft and their crews will remain at this location unless we hit problems and have to call in the QRF. If that happens, we have three possible rendezvous points notated as 'Alpha', 'Bravo' and 'Charlie'. The coordinates for these are also in your flight packs. The code word for the deployment of the QRF is 'FIREFLY' followed by the rendezvous point.

"If you are called in, your first role is to secure the landing zone to protect the aircraft, then evacuate assets on the ground. To make our arrival look more legitimate, three French Navy NH90 Caimans will accompany us on our journey to the FOB but land at the far end of the field. They will have no role to play in this operation. The Merlins' call signs are, as before, '*XRAY*' and '*ZULU*'. The Chinook's call sign is '*QUEBEC*'. Operational radio frequencies are in your flight packs. Once we have snatched our target at a time as yet unknown, we will return by vehicle to the FOB and board *XRAY*.

"Lt Commander Smythe will fly us to the *FOCH* where we will return to the UK ASAP in a carrier fixed-wing aircraft courtesy of the French Navy. *ZULU* and *QUEBEC* will return to HMS Ocean.

"After dropping us off on the *FOCH*, *XRAY* will also return to *HMS Ocean*, and both ships will continue joint flight operations for a week, and, on completion, both ships will return to their home ports. 845 Squadron Foundation aircraft and personnel will remain on board *HMS Ocean* until she is alongside, then will return to your new base. The same applies to the Chinook and the QRF detachment; only they will return to

RNAS Yeovilton. Any questions?"

Lt Commander Smythe asked, "Why are we to remain on board until the ship returns to port?"

"We have to continue with the subterfuge that this is a planned joint exercise with the French Navy. That is the only reason the squadron is staying on board," answered Tetley.

There were no further questions, so Henderson dismissed the crews and handed out the flight packs to the pilots, who then headed to the hangar and the flight deck to ready their aircraft and men. When they had left, Sam and Henderson approached Tetley.

"Excellent briefing, Tetley; you're a natural. They hung on your every word, and there was only one follow-up question from Smythe," said Henderson.

"He was suspicious that they were to remain on board; I hope my answer was sufficient," replied Tetley.

"You said it yourself, we can't take the risk the navy lads would turn on Connors. All our hard work would be down the drain if that happened, not to mention the scandal afterwards. Let's go get some lunch and then get ourselves ready to leave," said Sam.

"Lead the way, please," replied Henderson. They trooped off towards the Wardroom galley and a final feast before departure.

At 13:30, Henderson, Sam and Tetley returned to the hangar deck with the kit they would need for the mission. All three were dressed in civvies befitting tourists visiting that part of western France. They approached the Merlin call sign '*XRAY*', boarded and placed their kit in the rear of the cab, then went to check on the others. Tetley found Knocker organising the lads unchaining the aircraft from the deck, ready to be moved to the lift and up onto the flight deck.

"How are we doing, Knocker?" asked Tetley.

"We're just getting the cabs ready for moving to the lift, Tetley. The chock heads will spot the cabs on the flight deck, then we'll unfold the blades and tail and the pilots can do their pre-flight checks. We'll be set and ready for the 14:30 departure time," he replied.

"Excellent, mate, nice work," said Tetley, then he went off to find the pilots. They were all gathered together, going over their flight plans and routes to the FOB at the flying club. Chalmers spotted Tetley approaching and asked him,

"Do you think you are ready for this, Tetley? It's a big step up from being a mechanic and you're not exactly trained for this sort of thing."

"I'm as ready for this as just about anything else, sir, plus I have very experienced operators with me and they'll be taking the lead on this," he replied.

"Fair enough, Tetley, take good care of yourself and watch your back at all times," said Chalmers.

Just then, the alarm in the hangar sounded as both lifts descended from the flight deck. When they had lowered fully, the two Merlins, complete with flight crews, maintenance crews, along with Henderson, Sam and Tetley, were moved onto the lifts, then the lifts rose to the flight deck. As soon as the lifts reached the flight deck level, the tractors moved the two Merlins to the assigned spots, and the maintenance crews chained the cabs to the deck to stop them from moving around and then started to unfold the blades and tail. When that had been completed, the Badgers ran fuel lines out to the Merlins and re-fuelled them. On completion of the refuelling, all three helicopter flight crews started them up and got the blades turning. Once they were happy, they gave the sign to the handlers for the passengers to board. Each cab had its own share of the maintenance crew, which boarded first, then Henderson, Sam and Tetley boarded *XRAY*.

The Marines of the QRF boarded the Chinook with all their kit and weapons. The Chinook took off first and hovered at a safe distance until both Merlins left the deck and joined it. The Chinook then led the way, flying towards the French coast and the town of Fontenay le Comte and the Flying Club which would be their FOB. They were soon joined by the French Navy NH90 Caimans and it was an impressive site flying towards the coast. They flew over the holiday Island location of Ile de Re and to the north of the airport at La Rochelle, heading towards the French department of the Vendee, where Fontenay le Comte was located.

It took just thirty minutes of flight time to arrive at their destination, and the Chinook landed first and disembarked the QRF, who took up defensive positions around the perimeter, before the Merlins landed fairly close to the clubhouse and the Caimans landed at the other end of the airstrip. As soon as they hit the ground, everyone in the back of each Merlin disembarked and headed for the clubhouse, which was now their FOB. Two Frenchmen dressed in suits were there to greet them, and Henderson shook their hands and kissed them on both cheeks like they were long-lost friends, then led the way into the clubhouse itself.

Outside, all the aircraft shut down, and the flight crews followed them into the clubhouse that was now the FOB HQ. Henderson arranged some chairs and tables for his use, then pulled some maps out from his bag and laid them on the table.

He turned to Sam and Tetley and said, "Turn on your personal comms units and see if you can contact Stephen and Melanie and find out their current location."

Sam and Tetley powered up their comm belts, and Sam tried to contact Stephen and Melanie. Tetley was able to listen in, and soon Stephen came on and explained they were in a small town called Secondigny, following Connors and four men. Currently, they were in a wine cave in the middle of the town and had been there for around three hours. Sam relayed the information to Henderson, and he checked on the map for the town's location.

"They're only ten kilometres from Fenioux. If they've been in this cave for three hours, I doubt very much they are there just to buy wine. Inform Stephen and Melanie to continue following Connors and his men when they leave the Cave."

He turned to the two French suits. "Jacques, I think you and your associates may have to pick this up after we have snatched Connors. It may provide important intelligence into his network. I would be grateful if you could keep me in the loop in what you find," said Henderson.

Jacques nodded and made notes in a notepad he removed from his inside jacket pocket. Major Barnes arrived with two Marines and radio equipment. "Where do you want me to set the radio up, Mr Henderson?" he asked.

"Over at the far side of the room so they don't get in the way, please, Major," replied Henderson.

Barnes had the two Marines get the radios situated and told them, "These are, to me, manned 24/7. Any information must be passed to me, Mr Henderson, or a member of his team. No one else, understand?" Major Barnes explained to the radio operators.

"Yes, sir," they replied in unison and returned to listen in on the radios.

Henderson turned to Lt Commander Smythe and said, "Place your men in the next building and tell them to remain ready. I would prefer if only you had access to this building for security purposes, and anything you hear in here stays in here."

"Yes, sir," replied Smythe and left to organise his men.

"Jacques, do you have the keys to the vehicles we requested?" asked Henderson.

"*Oui*, of course, Mr Henderson," replied Jacques and handed over half a dozen sets of car keys.

"Tetley, go and find the vehicles that have been left for us and pick the best and drive it over here. We're leaving ASAP," ordered Henderson.

Tetley grabbed the bunch of keys and went looking for the cars they matched. It turned out all were Range Rovers, so Tetley unlocked one and fired it up, then drove it over to the entrance of the FOB HQ.

Henderson turned to Major Barnes. "I'm leaving you in charge of the FOB, Major. If you need anything, you can contact us on the radio, or if it's a problem with the locals, please speak with Jacques or his colleague, Thierry, and they'll sort it out. Any major issues, contact me ASAP at any time of day or night," instructed Henderson.

"Sam, let's go and join Tetley in the vehicle and get to Fenioux," he continued. Henderson and Sam grabbed their kit and headed outside to join Tetley in the Range Rover. Sam opened the boot and loaded his gear along with Henderson's. He carefully placed his rifle carry case on the back seat and climbed in beside it. Henderson climbed into the front passenger seat and strapped in.

"Let's go, Tetley.

"Next stop, the holiday home in Fenioux, please," he said. Tetley drove off; he had already put in the address on the vehicle's GPS and he followed its instructions. It took around thirty minutes to reach the village, then another ten to reach the holiday home.

The land around there was undulating with small fields and forests, unlike the coastal area where they had arrived around La Rochelle and Fontenay le Comte, which was flat as far as the eyes could see.

The holiday home was in a small hamlet called La Berlandiere, about three kilometres north of the village. It was a large former farm house from the looks of it, with a large barn just across from the small front garden, the perfect place to park the vehicle. The house itself looked to have recently been fully modernised. The paint on the exterior walls looked fresh, as did the paint on the woodwork of the windows. Henderson found the key under a plant pot on the raised porch and opened the door and walked in. Sam and Tetley followed. It had been modernised. Indeed, opening the front door led into a spacious living and dining room complete with a wood-burning stove at one end. Stairs on one wall led upstairs, presumably to bedrooms and bathrooms. A door to the right led into a charming country kitchen, complete with its own wood-burning stove. Opening a door on one wall of the living room led to a rear utility room complete with its own sink and a daybed. There were three other doors in there; one led to a downstairs bedroom, another to a shower room and the third to a large private rear garden, complete with an outdoor kitchen and barbecuing facilities.

Upstairs, there were two further bedrooms, one with an ensuite bathroom. There was a large, separate family bathroom too. This was a lovely place to base oneself for a holiday, or for snatching an arms dealer, for that matter. The two bedrooms upstairs had been taken by Melanie and Stephen. Henderson bagged the downstairs bedroom, leaving Sam and Tetley to rough it on the settees. Henderson got on the comms system and asked

225

Melanie for a sitrep. "We are now returning to Fenioux. It looks like they're heading back to the factory. If that's the case, I'll get Stephen to drop me off at the village bar in the square and I'll meet you there. Out," she responded.

Henderson looked at Sam and Tetley. "Let's go for some food, gentlemen, and get a feel for this location," he said.

They trooped outside and Tetley, last out, closed and locked the door, replacing the key under the potted plant. Henderson drove, Sam was in the front and Tetley in the rear. It only took a few minutes to reach the village square, and Henderson parked directly outside the bar/restaurant, Café des Belles Fleurs. They piled out and went in. There were a few people inside already eating and Henderson approached the bar.

"Good afternoon," said Henderson to the woman behind the bar.

"*Bonjour*, my name is Joy. Welcome to Café des Belles Fleurs. Are you all here on holiday?" she replied in perfect English.

"Yes, we are. In fact, we're hoping to meet with some friends who are staying at a holiday home nearby, and we're hoping they'll join us for lunch. Do you have a free table for possibly five people, please?"

"I do, of course, please follow me," Joy said, grabbing a menu from a holder on the bar and leading them into the rear of the restaurant, where tables were set for lunch. She showed them to a table big enough to seat them all.

"We just do a Menu de Jour; starter is salad from the self-service area over there, and you have a choice of cassoulet, escalope de pork, or quiche lorraine. A carafe of wine is included in the price; red, white, or rose. Would you like an aperitif while you make your choice?"

"An Orangina for me, please, and a bottle of Perrier with the meal. It's a little early for me to drink alcohol," replied Henderson.

Sam and Tetley took Henderson's lead and ordered soft drinks for themselves too, but asked for a beer with their meal.

"Nice little place this and the owner seems to be Welsh. Did you notice the rugby mural on the front of the bar counter?" asked Tetley.

"I did," replied Sam and Henderson nodded. A few minutes later, Melanie arrived, and they could hear Joy telling her that her friends had arrived and were seated in the back. Melanie came through and joined them at the table.

"Welcome to France," she said. "Connors and his merry band are back at the factory; it is just a short walk from here, and you probably saw the blue crane in its yard from the road when you came into the village. Stephen is keeping eyes on for now and will contact us via comms if he moves again. He seems to spend most of the day at the factory. We counted twenty workers in the factory and four burly bodyguards that go with him everywhere. He has a house at 9 Rue du Calvaire, an old modernised farm building by the looks of it with a swimming pool at the rear and a large field with trees separating him from a small estate of bungalows to the back. He does not venture too far from the village, and today was his first outing to Secondigny. He certainly wasn't tasting or buying any wine, as he came out empty-handed after nearly four hours," she reported.

"Are his bodyguards armed?" asked Sam.

"Most certainly," Melanie replied.

"I think we had better get some food before continuing this conversation back at the house," interrupted Henderson. They spent the next hour chatting about the area, just as tourists would

227

while eating their lunch. When they had finished the dessert of ice cream and fresh strawberries, they paid up at the counter, thanked Joy and climbed back in the Range Rover before heading back to the house.

Tetley went into the kitchen and made everyone a fresh brew before returning to the dining table and sitting down with the others. Melanie continued her sitrep.

"Snatching him at his home seems to be the best option, with the chances of civilian casualties' minimised. There are always two armed guards at the factory, plus his four bodyguards, but there are also civilian workers too, so that sort of discounts that option for the snatch. Connors returns to his home every evening around 20:00 hours; two guards stay outside, and two inside changing places every four hours. One of the exterior guards patrols the rear of the building and one patrols the front, never straying too far from the house. If we split our attack, we could take out the exterior guards simultaneously, then move to enter the house and take the guards down there too. This then leaves Connors open for snatching."

"I think we have a chance to think a little bigger here. We have the opportunity to take out the factory and possibly the wine cave at the same time. We don't have the numbers for this ourselves, but I think our French friends would love to get involved. If we let the French take down the factory and the cave then it leaves us free to concentrate on Connors. If we imbed one of our men with the French, then he could get an inventory of the weapons and photograph everything to see if we have a material link to the weapons in the UK FOB attack. That would be powerful evidence in any court of law. My thinking is to get Major Barnes to join the French, and we could offer the QRF Marines as a screen to cut off the village. We could drive the QRF in under cover of darkness tonight and get them in place and concealed before dawn, then we could do the OP tomorrow night after dark. The aircraft could pick us all up on the football pitch after the OP and fly us out to the waiting carriers. What do you all think?" explained Henderson.

"It has gone from a straightforward snatch to a complex operation with many moving parts that could go wrong very quickly. But I can see the logic of doing it that way," replied Sam.

"Do you think the French would really take down the factory and cave?" asked Tetley.

"Once I explain the situation to Jacques and Thierry, I am sure they would move heaven and earth to make it happen. This is their country, and bagging a terrorist arms dealing factory and staff would be a big win for them. If we snatch Connors and just leave the factory and cave, it could be sanitised before they get the chance to move against them after we leave," replied Henderson.

"Let's do it," said Melanie, and the other nodded their agreement.

"OK, Melanie you go relieve Stephen. I'll return to the FOB and speak with Jacques and Thierry and get things moving on their side. I'll also brief Major Barnes. I hope he understands French," said Henderson.

Melanie and Henderson left in the two vehicles, and Sam and Tetley made themselves comfortable while they waited for Stephen to appear. Henderson did not come back until just after midnight from the FOB. Tetley and Sam explained his plans to Stephen when he got back from watching Connors.

"Are the French coming to play?" he asked Henderson.

"They are indeed, Stephen. They have a Marine contingent on board the *FOCH* and were hoping we would invite them to the party. The QRF is currently making its way into position around the perimeter of the village as we speak, and the French Marines are landing at the FOB. Jacques is getting them briefed before they take up positions during the night. They are on our comms net, so we can communicate with them when we are ready to hit the house tomorrow night. Luckily enough, Major Barnes is fluent in French along with six other languages, so that was a bonus. Sam was going to relieve Melanie at 02:00, and then Stephen would relieve him at 08:00."

"Do you want me to stand my turn watching Connors?" asked Tetley.

"I would rather the others did that, Tetley, as they have the necessary training for surveillance operations, but thank you for offering," replied Henderson.

"Those of us who can, had better get our heads down and get some sleep, it will be a busy night tomorrow," said Stephen.

They all headed off to bed while Sam and Tetley stretched out on the settees. When Tetley awoke, Sam was gone. He looked at his watch; it was 06:50 hours. He got up, went and had a shower, then started on making breakfast in the kitchen for the others. There was a well-stocked fridge with everything needed to make a good Full English fry up, so he got started. Stephen was first down the stairs and he walked into the kitchen.

"Great smell that, Tetley! I could smell it upstairs," he said.

"There's a fresh pot of coffee made, mate, help yourself while I get this plated for you," replied Tetley. Stephen helped himself to coffee, and by the time he sat at the dining table, Tetley put the fry-up in front of him and sat opposite with a plate of his own. He had made himself the obligatory Earl Grey tea that he had become infamous for and took his first sip of his favourite brew.

"The first cup of the day is always the best," he said.

"Do you always travel with a bag of that stuff wherever you go?" asked Stephen.

"Indeed, mate, I am a grumpy bastard if I can't get it." Tetley laughed.

Stephen finished up eating, then washed up his plate, mug and cutlery before grabbing his daysack and heading out the door to relieve Sam.

"Cheers, Tetley, that was a great breakfast, mate," said Stephen, just before closing the door. Henderson was next down, closely followed by Melanie.

"The food is in the oven keeping warm, there is fresh coffee in the pot and the kettle is just boiled, if you would prefer tea," explained Tetley.

"Thanks, Tetley, this is great service. We must bring you on more ops in the future. I could get used to this," replied Melanie.

"You're very welcome, it's the least I can do if I'm not standing watch over Connors," answered Tetley. Henderson and Melanie sat down and tucked into their food. A few minutes later, Sam entered the house, and Tetley explained again where the food was.

"Cheers, mate," replied Sam, and went to the kitchen for some breakfast.

"What's on the agenda today while we wait for tonight's op?" Tetley asked Henderson.

"Well, we'll continue to monitor Connors, and I'm going to check in with Jacques and make sure the French are set for tonight. Other than that, I think we should stay here and wait until darkness falls," he replied. When they had all finished breakfast, Henderson headed off to check on Jacques and the French Marines. Melanie got on her personal comms system and

231

checked in with the FOB and asked who was now commanding the QRF in the absence of Major Barnes; the answer to that was Colour Sergeant Collins. Melanie checked in with Collins and asked if they were now in place and under cover. He explained that all the Marines were in their positions and well hidden from view so would not spoil the party. Happy all was in place, Melanie took out her personal weapons and started to clean them. Sam got his head down in the vacated back bedroom, and Tetley joined Melanie and cleaned his own weapons. When they finished, Tetley found some pool loungers outside, so he made himself comfortable on one and relaxed in the sunshine. Melanie relieved Stephen at 12:00 hours and Sam relieved her at 18:00.

Henderson arrived back to the house around 17:00 hours and announced everything was in place for the night's op.

Chapter 17

It got dark just after 22:30, and everyone left the house with all their kit as they would not be returning and drove to the rendezvous point. Melanie had replaced Sam by this point and was watching Connors. They all grabbed their weapons and slowly made their way to her concealed position. When they reached her, Tetley handed her a small flask of hot coffee, which she gratefully accepted.

"He's in his bedroom, which is located on the ground floor next to the garage doors. The guards are in place on the exterior, one at the front of the house and one at the rear. Two are inside, position unknown, but presumably one downstairs and one upstairs," she explained between sips of her hot coffee.

"Excellent. Melanie and Stephen, you take the rear and give us a call on the comms when you are in position. Sam, Tetley and I will take the front. It is imperative that we take out the two exterior guards without making any noise and alerting those inside. Once the exterior guards have been taken care of, we will make entry front and rear, quietly. Sam, you take the guard upstairs, Stephen will take the guard downstairs. If all goes well, we can snatch Connors without making a sound. Only then will I give the word to the others at the factory and cave to move in. If it goes noisy, then I will alert them sooner so the alarm is not raised before they breach. Right, move to first positions and let me know when the guards have been taken care of," instructed Henderson.

Melanie and Stephen crawled away to work their way round to the rear of the house.

Sam, Henderson and Tetley moved slowly towards the front.

Luckily, in France, the street lighting in small rural villages turns itself off on a timer at 22:30 every night to save money. Farming folk rise with the sun and go to bed when it sets, so there is little need for street lighting. Even the bar closes at 21:00, so the streets are deserted.

The small exterior wall at the front of the house was up to the edge of the road, but they could enter the property further along between some trees and hedging further down. It took nearly an hour for everyone to get silently into position. Stephen and Melanie were lying prone on a slope leading up to the swimming pool from the large field at the rear. Sam had moved forwards to a position behind a fruit tree in the front garden, while Tetley and Henderson remained in deeper cover further back. Everyone checked in with Henderson once they were in position.

"Go when you get the right opportunity to take your guard out," replied Henderson.

Tetley watched as the two guards met at the gable of the house, said a few words to each other then, turned their backs and resumed their patrols. As soon as they had turned their respective corners, returning to the front and rear of the house, Tetley saw Sam run forwards in a fast crouch, then grab the guard, clamping his hand over his mouth and stabbing him three times in the back. The guard fell at his feet, and he dragged him over and hid him behind the tree where he had started from. He reported in to Henderson that the guard was neutralised, and very soon after Stephen did the same.

Sam waved Henderson and Tetley forwards to the tree next to the fallen guard. Then they moved to the front of the house and

234

kept low under the windows. Sam used a mirror to locate the guard; he was sat on a chair near the rear French doors leading to the terrace.

"Stephen, the downstairs guard is sat by the rear doors leading to the terrace. If you knock on the door, he should open it thinking it's the exterior guard, and then you can take him out," explained Sam on the comms.

"Copy that, give me five," he replied.

Melanie remained hidden on the slope leading to the pool while Stephen crawled to the rear wall of the house, then stood up and approached the terrace doors. He knocked gently when he got there and saw the guard inside stand up, then reach to open the doors.

Stephen stepped back into the shadows, and the guard opened the door and stepped out. He was about to say something, but Stephen grabbed him in a vice like headlock, then twisted sharply, and the guard flopped in his arms. Stephen set him gently down, then waved for Melanie to join him before he entered the house, then moved to the front door and turned the key to unlock it and admit Sam, Henderson and Tetley.

"Cheers, mate," said Sam, passing him and heading slowly up the stairs to the left of the door in search of the final guard. The others moved further towards the hallway leading to Connors' bedroom and waited for Sam to return. When Sam had made it to the top of the stairs, he peered round the banister to see if he could spot the guard, but he was nowhere to be seen. There was a long corridor with rooms on either side, all with their doors opened. Sam listened for a minute or two and could hear nothing, then when he was about to move, he heard a loud ripping snort coming from the first room on the left. How lucky was this? The guard had gone to sleep in one of the rooms instead of standing guard. Sam moved slowly forwards on the wooden floor, being very careful where he placed his feet. He did not want a loose, squeaky board to announce his arrival. When he reached the door to the room, he turned his head slowly so he could look inside. The guard was fast asleep, stretched out on a big wooden bed. Sam crept in and, using his knife, first slit his throat so he could not scream, then stabbed him in the heart. The guard was dead before he could even register he was in danger.

Sloppy, very sloppy! thought Sam. Sleeping on sentry duty is a huge sin, and the guard had paid the ultimate price. He turned and checked the other rooms to make sure there was no one else, then slowly made his way back downstairs to the others. When Sam reached the others, he gave them a thumbs up sign to show all was now clear.

Stephen led the way along a small corridor that connected the main house with the garage and Connors' bedroom. The door to the room was closed, so Sam and Stephen stood to each side, then using his fingers, Stephen counted down from three, then pushed the door wide open. Sam rushed in and leapt on Connors in the bed, pinning him down with his legs so he could not move his arms and holding a hand over his mouth so he could not speak. Stephen joined him, pulling a roll of masking tape from a pocket and ripping off a strip to place over Connors' mouth. Sam then turned Connors over onto his stomach and gathered his hands behind his back. Stephen took plasticuffs from a pocket and pulled them tight on his wrists. Sam then rolled off Connors and lifted him out of the bed and onto his feet. Henderson took a small red lens, Maglite, from his pocket and shone it in Connors' face to make sure they had the right man.

"Bingo!" he said. He then got on the comms net to inform the others their part of the operation could start.

"Let's get out of here and head to the rendezvous point for pickup," said Henderson. Stephen and Sam grabbed Connors and forcibly marched him out of the bedroom and out of the house, heading back to their cars. They put him in the back of one, with Sam and Stephen on each side. Henderson drove, and Melanie and Tetley took the other vehicle.

The rendezvous point was the football field in the village; it was large enough for the Merlins to land in turn. When they arrived, they abandoned the cars, grabbed their kit and Connors, and headed for the edge of the pitch. Henderson, once again, got on the comms net, summoning the first Merlin to land. Almost as fast as he finished the request, a Merlin flared to land in front of them in the centre of the pitch. As soon as the wheels hit the ground, they ran to the rear ramp of the Merlin and boarded. They had hooded Connors in the car on the drive to the pitch, so they set him on a seat and strapped him in.

Sam and Stephen strapped in each side of him; the others sat facing them. The Merlin lifted off, turned and headed out towards the coast and the waiting French Carrier, *FOCH*, about an hour and a half flight time away. Nothing was spoken in the Merlin during the journey; everyone just watched the hooded Connors deep in their own thoughts. After a while, the *FOCH*'s lighted deck appeared, and the Merlin flew alongside the carrier, matching its speed before being directed to a landing spot on the deck by a sailor with lighted wands. As soon as the wheels hit the deck, they all disembarked and were directed by a French naval deck officer to follow him to a waiting fixed-wing aircraft that would fly them directly back to the UK.

They boarded the aircraft and were instructed to strap in tight, as the aircraft would be launched from the angled deck using the catapult.

When they were strapped firmly in, the engines revved to full throttle, then in the blink of an eye and a force of 8G, they were launched into the air. The aircraft then turned and headed in the direction of RAF Northolt in London. They had thought to use the airfield at Yeovilton but decided against it given the concerns for Connors' safety. It took an hour to get to London, and the French aircraft landed and taxied up to the parking apron. It did not shut down, as it was flying straight back to the *FOCH*. When the doors opened, the passengers grabbed their kit and directing the hooded Connors, disembarked the aircraft.

Vehicles were waiting for them on the tarmac, and they shoved Connors in the rear of one and headed for the terminal building about five hundred metres away.

When they arrived, Henderson got out and went inside, leaving the others to wait in the vehicles. After about ten minutes, he returned and reported that the other parts of the operation were all completed successfully and Major Barnes had a mountain of photographic evidence to show them on his return the following day. The French would fly him into Northolt, and he would hand over the camera to MI5. They would examine the evidence first. He directed Melanie and Tetley to follow him and the others back to the bunker on Salisbury Plain, where they would question Connors. Everyone was very quiet on the drive back to the bunker, left alone with their own thoughts.

It was early afternoon by the time they arrived and parked the vehicles in the tunnel. Sam and Stephen took Connors from the vehicle and led him into the bunker complex and deposited him in the induction room, tie-wrapped to a chair, and left him hooded.

They all then gathered in the conference room, and Tetley made everyone a fresh brew while the rest of the team dropped their kit against one wall.

When they all had a brew in their hands, Tetley asked,

"Who is going to question Connors?"

"We need to organise an interrogation area first and setup cameras and recording equipment. Everything has to be done by the book this time, as this will end up in a court of law. We currently have him in the induction room, which is perfect for the job. Melanie, can you ask Bill and his team to install the right equipment before we start? We'll move Connors into the briefing room while the work is done and return him when it's completed. I think Tetley would be as good as any person to start questioning him. If he hits a wall, I'll take over and then, if necessary, you can all have a turn. We go into the room in twos at all times. I will go in with Tetley, Melanie with Sam, Stephen and myself if we get that far. Keep your comms switched on so that those of us outside the room observing from the briefing room can throw in questions if need be and verify his answers. This is very important, so don't fuck it up. This will be shown in court as well as being viewed by the joint chiefs, the security services, and the PM. Regard this work as the most important work you have been asked to do so far in your careers; if we fuck this up, he may walk free. Sam, can you and Stephen move him to the briefing room now, then Melanie can get Bill and his team started?" explained Henderson.

The others left the conference room, and that left Tetley and Henderson. "Let's go and get some food while they get organised, and we can discuss the best way to question Connors," said Henderson. They set down their mugs and swiped out of the conference room and headed down the corridor to the galley. When they had got themselves some sandwiches and another brew, they sat at a table and began to eat.

"How would you approach questioning Connors, Tetley?" asked Henderson.

"I'm not trained to interrogate anyone, but I suppose I would start with the information Izzari provided us and use that a way in. It would be good to get confirmation from the intel that Major Barnes got in the raid on the factory. If we could match the weapons from the FOB attack to his cache at the factory, we could pressure him with that. He would then be facing all sorts of sedition charges along with terror and arms dealing charges. He could end up in prison for a full life term. If we can link him as being involved with the planning of the attack, then he's done for. Those photos from the raid are essential to getting him convicted," answered Tetley.

"Might I suggest you bait him with being an ex-squadron member and push him on loyalty to his navy comrades? I have a feeling that will push a button or two and maybe make him drop his guard," advised Henderson.

A few minutes later Bill and Melanie came in to the galley and reported that the cameras and recording equipment were installed and would run 24/7.

Anita and her team would monitor the equipment from the comms room, and the data would be stored on a secure, hard disc.

"Perfect! Thank you all for your excellent work. Melanie, can you get Sam and Stephen to move him back to the induction room? We will be along momentarily." instructed Henderson.

"OK, Tetley! We're on. I'll get us some writing pads and pens from the conference room and meet you back here in two minutes," he continued. Tetley made three fresh brews, one for himself, Henderson and Connors. He was just finishing up when Henderson popped his head in to say he was ready. They left the galley and walked round to the induction room and swiped in.

Tetley set his and Connors' brew on the table, then cut the cable tie cuffs to free his hands and sat down in front of the hooded Connors. Henderson nodded to Sam and Stephen and they left the room, closing the door behind them. Henderson placed his chair against the wall directly behind Connors and sat down, placing his writing pad on his lap. Tetley got himself set and placed his writing pad and pen in front of him. Then, after looking over at Henderson, who nodded and pulled the hood off Connors' head. Connors blinked his eyes at the bright overhead lights, then looked at Tetley in front of him. Tetley placed a brew in front of Connors and told him to take a drink. Tetley watched him closely as he blinked in the harsh lighting and took a few sips from the mug of tea. When he had set it down, he asked, "Where am I?"

"You're in the UK, Connors. Currently, based on information received from Ibrahim Izzari, we can charge you with terrorism, arms dealing and sedition offences, which hold a possible full life term," answered Tetley.

"How did you bring me to the UK without extradition proceedings in France, where I live?" Connors asked.

"It seems the French government wanted you out of their country. They don't like terrorists in France, apparently, so they deported you under emergency terrorism legislation setup after terror attacks on French soil some time ago," said Tetley.

"Tell me where you get your weapons from? By the way, the French authorities raided your factory in Fenioux and have seized all the weapons you had stored there and have arrested all the staff and the two bodyguards. They also raided a wine cave in Secondigny, and it seems they arrested a number of people there too. They are all cooperating with the authorities after the French threatened to take them to black sites in the Sahara unless they answered all their questions. All the computers and every bit of paperwork were seized, and experts are working through it all now. It seems if you do not co-operate with us, the French security services offered to help us by questioning you in a warm and sandy location far from prying eyes. So, you either help us, or we will pass you on to them. What's it to be?" asked Tetley.

"Those French bastards! Half of them are on the take. I even had some on my payroll. If you hand me back to them, I'll never be seen again," replied Connors. "It seems you have little choice but to help us then. So where do you purchase your weapons from, and how do you ship them to France?" asked Tetley again.

"OK! OK! OK! I used to buy weapons from the Balkans, but they were poor quality, and they couldn't supply me with enough, anyway. I did a robbery on a UK territorial army weapons store and got some kit there, but getting kit in the UK has too many risks.

"A contact in the Balkans put me onto a contact he had in Turkey, but warned that he worked for the Turkish military and the risk was all on me. He arranged a meet in Northern Cyprus and I flew out there to meet with him. He promised he could get me just about any weapon I wanted and in any quantity.

"A lot of the kit he offered was American, captured from across the border in Syria, but he also had Russian kit. He had one proviso for doing business with me; I was to provide weapons to extremist Islamic terrorist groups in the UK. They were planning a large attack against the British military in revenge for an attack on a Turkish arms convoy in Syria by UK and American aircraft. He had two groups infiltrated into the UK, and I was to supply weapons to both groups. I agreed, and I placed an order for a large quantity of small arms, grenades, ammunition, anti-tank missiles, mortars and even ground-to-air hand-launched missiles. The shipment was made buried deep in a grain cargo ship sailing from Turkey to Marseille. Customs at the French end were paid off, and the weapons were unloaded into a warehouse and then onto small lorries and driven to the factory in Fenioux. From there, we shipped some of them in specially built camper vans that were driven over the channel via Cherbourg, where I had customs on my payroll; the same in Portsmouth. We drove the camper vans to St. Mere Eglise and exchanged in a supermarket car park. The buyers drove the camper vans into the UK," explained Connors.

"How was payment made between you and the Turks and between you and the terror cells in the UK?" asked Tetley.

"It was all completed through halawadar's, so there would be no electronic trail," he answered.

"I know you, Connors! I'm surprised you don't recognise me," said Tetley, catching Connors off guard a little.

"How the fuck would I know you? I've never seen you before in my life," he answered.

"We were on 707 Squadron together. Then you went to 845 Squadron and I went to Clockwork.

"It was then that you started stealing rounds from the ranges and selling them on. They caught you, and you ended up in Colchester before being booted out of the mob," explained Tetley.

"Still don't know you. I hated the Navy! Bunch of righteous pricks! Most of the NCOs and officers did not know what day it was; always pissed out of their heads. There was one Chief Petty Officer McAlister. He was always pissed and he made my life a living hell. When he fucked up, he pointed the blame on me, so I was always in the shit," Connors spat out.

"Is that why you told the Turks about the exercise on

243

Dartmoor?" asked Tetley, disgustedly.

"Fuck yeah, I did! It was so easy to find out the details too. I just hung around the pubs in Yeovil, and soon enough, drunken sailors were talking about their deployments and upcoming exercises. I could have chosen any number of targets, but 845's exercise in Dartmoor was just too good a chance to miss. I told the Turks in a meeting in Paris, and they got one of their cells ready to do the attack. I even supplied the weapons free of charge for that one. I asked if I could take part, but the Turks wouldn't allow it." Connors roared.

"You hate the squadron and the Navy so much; you were happy to kill innocent sailors?" shouted Tetley in return.

"I just wish they had all been slaughtered, every last one of them fucking matelots!" Connors continued.

Tetley stood up and punched Connors so hard in the side of the head that both he and the chair he was sitting on toppled over onto the floor.

Tetley rounded on Connors and standing over, him leaning down into his face, he said, "I wish you had been there, you scumbag, then I could have blasted you to hell!"

Henderson intervened and pulled Tetley back and told him to leave the room; he then picked Connors back up and sat him on the chair again. He waved at the camera, and in a few minutes, Sam and Stephen came in. One stood in front and one behind Connors. Henderson nodded and then left the room to go and find Tetley. Tetley was back in the galley, getting another brew for himself. When Henderson walked in, Tetley asked him, "Do you want a brew while I am making one for myself?"

"Yes, please," answered Henderson. He sat down at a table and waited until Tetley brought the coffee over and handed it to him, then Tetley sat down.

"I wish you kept some booze around this place; I could do with a proper drink now," said Tetley.

"I think that might be arranged; wait here," replied Henderson, getting up and leaving the galley. Five minutes later he was back, and he took a hip flask out of his pocket, opened it and poured a generous measure into Tetley's tea and into his coffee. He raised his cup and toasted Tetley.

"I didn't think he would have opened up so soon and with so much detailed information. Well done, Tetley!" said Henderson.

"I think the idea of being whisked off to a French government black site in the middle of the Sahara Desert quickly concentrated his mind. He will end up in prison, but at least it's in the UK," replied Tetley, raising his mug of tea and tapping it against Henderson's, then he took a long drink.

"Brandy? Very nice, just hit the spot. I needed that! What about your rule of no alcohol in the bunker?" asked Tetley.

"Sometimes there are exceptional circumstances where rules may be broken, and this is one," he replied before continuing, "I think our work with Connors is done, we can pass him and our evidence onto the security services, and they can charge him or question him further," explained Henderson.

"What about the Turkish government? Are we going to go after them? After all, they are the masterminds behind the attack on the FOB, and God knows how many other attacks on the UK." asked Tetley.

"Those decisions are out of our hands and will be made at government level. We can but hope that if they do decide to go after the Turks, they may involve us in part of any planned operation. When it comes to nation states, our hands are tied," answered Henderson.

"So, what happens next?" asked Tetley.

"Well, there is the small matter of your medal presentation, which takes place next week. The day after your squadron returns with *HMS Ocean*, and then two days later, I believe they are holding a memorial service for your fallen colleagues at Yeovilton. Between now and then, I have a lot of paperwork to fill in, and you can get some range practice in with Sam and Stephen during that time. It never hurts to be prepared," answered Henderson.

"Will I be returning to the squadron now that the investigation is over?" asked Tetley.

"I have you until your squadron returns. That is the agreement I made with your CO. I'm not sure the Navy is finished with you yet," replied Henderson.

"I am not sure I will like what the Navy has planned for me. Once I get the VC, they will want to use me as their new poster boy, and that isn't me. Certainly not what I want for my future anyway, I suppose there is no full-time opening with you guys here at the bunker?" asked Tetley.

"Out of my hands really, Tetley. There's no doubt you have been a great asset in this investigation, but your contract is with the Royal Navy, not with us here at the foundation," Henderson explained.

"I understand. Oh well! Onwards and upwards," replied Tetley.

They finished their alcohol-infused drinks, then Henderson returned to the comms room to organise the transfer of Connors to the security services along with his recorded confession. Tetley went to his accommodation to shower and change and relax a little.

Chapter 18

One week later, *HMS Ocean* docked in the Portsmouth Navy yard, and the 845 Squadron aircraft and personnel flew back to Yeovilton.

Sam and Stephen drove Tetley back to Yeovilton along with his kit, in order that he could prepare his dress uniform ready for the award ceremony the next day. Along with the squadron lads getting their medals, their immediate families and the foundation team had been invited to the palace. Henderson and the rest of the team would make their own way to London, but Sam and Stephen insisted they drive Tetley to the palace. Tetley organised accommodation for them both at Yeovilton for the night, then he went to his own quarters to prepare for the following day.

When Tetley entered his room, the squadron lads he shared with were already there, getting their shoes polished and their uniforms cleaned.

"Hey, Tetley, how did it all go with Connors after the snatch?" Muddy asked.

"Hey guys. He sang like a canary after he found out the French Secret Service wanted to take him to a black site in the Sahara Desert to question him if he didn't co-operate with us," explained Tetley.

"Was he the one behind the attack on the FOB?" asked Hammy.

"He planned it and supplied the weaponry. However, it turns out the Turkish government was the mastermind behind it all," answered Tetley.

"Are we going after the Turks?" asked Ginger.

"Not at the minute, mate. Apparently, the PM and Parliament need to make that call. Turkey is part of NATO, so they should be allies, not enemies. Who knows? You know what politicians are like," replied Tetley.

"You back with us for good, mate, or is this just another pit stop?" asked Muddy.

"Looks like I'm back for good, Muddy. Sam and Stephen are going to drive me to the palace tomorrow. There's a spare seat going in the Range Rover if you want a ride, mate?" asked Tetley.

"Too fucking right, mate! Count me in," replied Muddy.

"How are the rest of you getting to London tomorrow?" asked Tetley.

"Smythe has laid on a coach to take the squadron personnel, so we are travelling in style, mate," replied Ginger.

"Nice one," replied Tetley.

"Best we get our kit in good order. The queen will be a bit miffed if we look like a bag of shite, and no doubt, Sir Robert would have something to say about it too," said Ginger.

They spent the whole evening getting their uniforms, medals and dress shoes gleaming before they got their heads down.

The following morning, they all went to the galley, had breakfast, then packed their uniforms in carriers and their shoes in bags wrapped in soft cloths to protect them, then headed for the squadron HQ.

Sam and Stephen were in the crew room having a brew when Tetley and the lads walked in. "You lads all set?" asked Sam.

"Ready as we'll ever be," replied Muddy.

Knocker White came in and told them the coach was ready, so they all grabbed their bags and trooped out to board the transport. Smythe was there at the bottom of the coach steps, making sure all the lads were present.

"Morning, Garside. It's a big day today for both you and the squadron. How are you feeling?" he asked.

"Pretty good, sir. However, I'll probably be a bag of nerves come the time," Tetley replied.

"You'll be great, Garside! I've no doubt at all about that. Do you have any family attending?" he asked.

"Yes, sir! My parents, my grandfather and my sister are attending. My grandfather is very excited as he is ex-navy; he was a gunner in WWII on *HMS Belfast*," replied Tetley.

"I'm sure you'll do them and the squadron proud! Meet you there," said Smythe as he boarded the coach to make sure everyone was on board.

They all set off in convoy out the gates of the naval air base and onto the A303 that would take them to London. The journey took about three hours, and when they arrived at the palace gates, a guide boarded the coach and showed them round to the rear to a parking area. Sam parked the Range Rover next to the coach and they all disembarked. Sam asked the guide where guests would gather and the guide showed them where to go. They wished Tetley the best of luck and told him they would see him after the ceremony.

All the recipients of awards were directed to a different area where they could change into their dress uniforms. When they were all sorted, a member of the palace staff spoke to each of them in turn, explaining what to do when their names were called, where to stand and how to greet Her Majesty. He explained when the presentation was over where they should go and wait.

Other than the squadron men who were injured and could

not be there that day, all the FOB survivors were in attendance.

In the anteroom, where they gathered, waiting for their names to be called out, they were arranged in the correct order. PO White would be first to receive the Military Cross, followed by the other ratings, with Muddy and Tetley bringing up the rear.

Each name was called, and each man marched crisply out into the presentation room and halted; they then left turned smartly and stood at attention. The queen spoke politely with each recipient for a moment, then pinned the award on each man. They then stepped back, saluted, did a right turn and marched into another anteroom to await the others.

When Muddy's name was called, he turned and shook Tetley's hand, then marched off to receive his medal. That just left Tetley standing with the organiser.

Suddenly someone in a morning suit came into the anteroom and spoke urgently with the organiser, who then came over to Tetley.

"AEM Garside, it seems there is a small change to the original plan. When you have received your Victoria Cross, please step back three paces and remain at attention. Some palace staff will place a kneeling chair in front of her majesty. When you are asked, please step forwards and kneel on the cushion with your left knee. There is a handrail there, if you need it to keep your balance. You may step back after the ceremony and continue as before," he explained, then returned to his position by the door.

Before Tetley could ask what the hell was going on, his name was called. He came to attention and marched smartly out to the medal presentation room and halted. He then turned left, saluted and remained ramrod straight at attention.

Her Majesty Queen Elizabeth II approached him and said, "Good morning, Andrew, welcome to Buckingham Palace. I have heard many good things about you from Prime Minister Barrington, Sir Robert Beaufort and, of course, Sir John Henderson at the foundation. It seems that if the UK is in a pickle, you are the man they would most recommend to get us back on top. That is high praise indeed!"

Tetley smiled and just said, "Thank you, your Majesty."

"Do you have any family guests here with you today?" the queen asked.

"My mother and father, along with my grandfather and my sister, are present, your Majesty," he replied.

"Ah yes! I believe your grandfather has been here before. He stood in the exact same spot you are standing on May 16th 1944, to receive the Navy Cross for gallantry from my father," the queen explained.

Tetley was gobsmacked and replied, "I didn't know that, your Majesty! My grandfather never discussed his war years with his family."

"Many people of that time have never spoken of the horrors they faced, but now that you have another thing in common, he may discuss it with you now," the queen replied.

She turned and picked the Victoria Cross up from its box on a small table behind her, then turned back to Tetley. Pinning it on his left breast above his other service medals, she said, "It gives me great pleasure to present this Victoria Cross to you from a very grateful nation."

"Thank you, your Majesty," replied Tetley, then promptly saluted and stepped back three paces as instructed.

While he remained at attention, two pale footmen came in and placed a kneeling chair in front of the queen, then promptly left.

A general standing behind the queen nodded towards Tetley,

and he stepped three paces forwards, bringing him up to the kneeling chair.

The queen approached and asked Tetley to kneel, which he did as instructed by the organiser in the ante-room. The queen turned, and the general presented her with a sword. She turned back to Tetley and promptly tapped him on each shoulder while saying,

"I proudly induct you into the Order of the Garter." She then draped a blue sash over his head from his left shoulder down to his right hip. A small gold badge hung from a gold link at the bottom of the sash. The queen then turned and took a large Silver Star from the small table and pinned that to his left breast below his medals. When she had completed this, she said, "Arise, Sir Andrew Garside!"

The queen then shook Tetley's hand before saying, "I believe you were not made aware of this award beforehand."

"No, Your Majesty, I was not!" replied Tetley.

The queen continued with a smile, "This award is only presented at my own discretion. I have had numerous conversations with the admiralty, the prime minister and Sir John Henderson over your future in the Royal Navy. They explained to me that while you are a very experienced naval airman, you do not feel the need to gain elevation in rank to command the men and women of your service. It would seem they feel your talents are wasted in the ranks and that you are a natural born leader. Sir John Henderson asked if it would be possible for you to work for the foundation, and we all agreed that your talents are best utilised in that form of work. However, they also informed me that you would be reluctant to completely leave your beloved squadron and colleagues with whom you have formed such a rare bond. This knighthood will allow you to work for Sir John and the foundation. While in periods of relative peace, you may return to 845 Squadron at any time and at any rank. Congratulations, Sir Andrew," the queen explained and held out her hand to shake Tetley's.

Still in a state of shock, Tetley shook the queen's hand and thanked her again. He then took a step back and saluted before turning right and marching off into the other anteroom.

All the lads were there, and they all congratulated Sir Tetley, laughing at the situation he had been thrust into. Muddy slapped him on the back and said, "If you think we're all going to call you 'Sir Andrew', you can fuck off. It's always going to be Tetley for us." The whole crowd burst out laughing.

The organiser appeared and explained that if they followed him, they could meet up with their invited guests in the banquet room, where a reception had been laid on. He also explained that there were official palace photographers who could take family photographs for personal use only.

They all followed him down a long corridor and into a large room with tables of food and drink and waiters standing behind them. All the lads headed off to meet their families, and Tetley was no exception. When his mother saw him, she rushed over and gave him a huge bear hug and a kiss on the cheek. His father hugged him too and took time to look at his medals. His grandfather shook his hand, and Tetley told him the queen spoke about him and about his medal presentation.

"She said it seems gallantry runs in our family, Granddad," said Tetley.

"More like we are good at finding trouble, Andrew," he said, smiling.

He spent a while with his family getting photographs done at the request of his mother, then he excused himself and went off to find the foundation team.

They were all gathered in one corner, chatting with Smythe and Chalmers from the squadron. When he approached, Smythe and Chalmers turned and saluted him.

"You can cut that nonsense out for starters! I am still the AEM I was when I walked in here," said Tetley.

"But now you are Knight of the Garter, Garside; that comes with some respect," explained Smythe.

"Ah yes! But the queen specifically told me I could be any rank I wished depending on my own preference. So, although I have all these nice new ribbons and medals, I am still the naval airman I always wanted to be," replied Tetley.

The whole crowd laughed, then stepped forwards to congratulate Sir Andrew. Henderson asked him if he could have a quick word before he continued to enjoy the reception with his family.

They moved away and found a quiet corner before Henderson said, "It looks like the PM and the cabinet are seriously considering a move against Turkish interests and, if so, he wants our involvement. It won't happen soon, and I want you to have some serious training beforehand. I have already arranged with your CO that you will re-join us after the memorial service at Yeovilton for your fallen comrades and after you have had three-weeks leave to rest and recuperate beforehand. So, enjoy the day with your family, and I will see you in a month's time at the bunker. Congratulations, by the way, Sir Andrew! Sorry to spring that on you. It was the only way we could think to keep you part of the squadron and work for us at the same time," explained Henderson.

"You're forgiven, Sir John, and thank you! I think." Tetley laughed.

With that, Henderson returned to his team and Tetley went back to his family and his squadron mates. The future seemed much clearer to him now, and he would be part of the foundation team that would be involved in hitting back at the Turkish aggressors.

Glossary of Terms

FOB	Forward Operating Base
Matelots	Sailors
Bootnecks	Royal Marine Commandos
Ruperts	Officers
FONAC	Flag Officer Naval Air Command
MOB	The Military
Head Shed	Senior Officers or Those in Charge
Reggies	Naval Regulators (Police)
DGSI	Direction Generale de la Securite Interieure (French Secret Service)
Halawadar	Informal System of moving money across borders
Pussers	Anything owned by the Royal Navy
Bowser	Refuelling Tanker
Heads	Bathrooms or Toilets
Scran	Food
MOD	Ministry of Defence
Sitrep	Situation Report
Stag	Sentry Duty
Slug	Sleeping Bag
Pit	Bed
DITS	Sea Stories
Gisits	Free Stuff